Our Home

A Windsor Peak Novel

Book 6

Denise Latham

ISBN: 979-8-9888952-8-2

Cover design by Book Designs by Shae.

www.deniselatham.com

Windsor Peak Series

Dedication

To Danielle.

The best gift my brother has ever given me was you as a sister. You are steady in your love for Jeff, for your kids, my kids, and our entire family. Your support, laughter, kindness, and love over the years has made you not only my sister-in-law, but also one of the friends I treasure most. What you do for everyone each day is not unnoticed. You are a wonder woman.

(And you gave me a nephew and two nieces who I adore, so bonus points for that!)

Part One

Chapter 1

The infant in his arms started crying, startling him a bit, but not enough to pull him out of his tunnel. Ben Burrows could see tears dripping down onto the baby's face and realized they must be coming from his cheeks, but he couldn't feel them. The doctor in front of him continued to talk despite him being unable to hear a word she said, and a gentle hand on his shoulder looked to be attached to the nurse next to him.

"Do you have any questions, Mr. Burrows?" The doctor waited expectantly, as if he had any thoughts running through his brain that would be helpful. He shook his head mutely, and she turned to leave.

"I'm very sorry for your loss," she said. Once she closed the door behind her, the nurse sat next to him on the bed.

"We did everything we could," she said softly. "I'm so sorry. What can I do for you right now?"

"I can't even think," he admitted.

She nodded. "Do you have a name for this little guy?" She reached over and rubbed the baby's cheek with one finger.

"My wife, uh," he cleared his throat. "Her father's name was Patrick, and she was trying to convince me to use it. It meant a lot to her. I would have given in. I was just giving her a hard time, you know?"

"I'm sure she knew that," the nurse said kindly.

"For a middle name, she wanted it to be Benjamin."

"Patrick Benjamin," the nurse said. "Beautiful. I know she will watch over him always. He's a baby with two souls. He will do great things in his life."

When another sob came out, she put her arm around him and let him cry. The sudden opening of the door caught him off guard, and his oldest son's face peeked through the opening. Ben quickly grabbed a tissue from the box next to him and swiped at his face, trying to compose himself. The nurse stood, and after a questioning look to Ben, opened the door fully. His two boys stood there, in their Sunday best, scrubbed clean of the wild look they normally wore. His best friend, Stella St. James, stood behind them.

Stella took in the scene and took a sharp breath, placing a hand on each of the boys' shoulders. "Benji?" she sounded timid, unlike anything he had heard from her since the day they met at four years old.

He shook his head, eyes brimming with tears once again, but forcing himself to focus on his boys. "Come meet your brother," he said.

Stella looked as though she was going to follow the nurse out of the room when Jake, his middle son, spoke. "Where's mama?"

Dan, the oldest, joined his brother, asking rapid-fire questions about their mother that Ben couldn't answer. He met Stella's eyes in desperation, and she immediately kicked into action. They had been friends for so long, she could read his thoughts and had gotten him out of many binds over the years. This was the biggest thing he had ever asked of her, even though he couldn't formulate the actual words to do so.

Instead, he counted on her ability to read him and know what it was that he needed.

"Boys, come here," Stella said. She sat on the chair in the room and gathered them close, Jake on one knee and Dan on the other. They were only four and two, and Ben's heart ached for their loss. "Your mama went to see the angels. She's in heaven now, but we can always talk to her, and she will be with you every day. You may not be able to see her, but she's there."

"But I want her here, where I can see her," Dan said. His lower lip jutted out, and his eyes were still searching the room as though his mom would appear. "Not there. Here."

"Me too," Jake said. He was clutching a small stuffed bear that he had named Bluey, and he held it even tighter against his chest.

"We all do, my darlings," she said softly, kissing one head and then the other. "But she left you a perfect new brother to watch over. I need you both to be the best big brothers in the whole world. Can you do that? We can all cry together now, because your mama was the best and we will miss her terribly. It's always okay to cry for her, and to smile when you think of her. As hard as that sounds, we can be happy that we had her and sad that we lost her at the same time."

"She comes home later, after she visits, right?" Dan asked, big tears rolling down his cheeks.

"No, son," Ben was finally able to say. "She's going to live there now. In heaven, watching over you."

The two boys cried quietly in Stella's arms, and Ben found his own tears flowing again. The baby in his arms remained sleeping peacefully, unaware of the anguish in the air.

Somehow, some way, he was going to raise three sons without his wife. Three babies, who Isobel had wanted so much, and now wouldn't see grow up. She would miss them going to kindergarten, which she was looking forward to since Dan was so smart and ready. She would miss first dates, and prom, and the first loves. But he needed to be there for the boys and get them through this first heartbreak before he could focus on anything more.

"Stella," he said, once the boys had quieted down. "Could you see about getting me out of here? I need to be home with them, not here."

"Let me go talk to the nurse," she said, wiping her eyes. "Boys, move over there with your dad and brother. We haven't even seen him yet, have we?" She stood and guided them to where Ben sat and helped them climb on to the bed with him. They snuggled in close to Ben, peeking at the baby as Stella stroked Patrick's cheek. She reached up and touched Ben's shoulder gently before heading to the nurse's station in search of someone who could help him escape the room where he had just lost his wife.

***

He lasted exactly two days alone before he realized exactly how over his head he was. Jake was still potty training, and had decided he didn't want to sleep any more. Dan was clinging to him every second of the day, and both boys were in bed with him at night. Dan because he couldn't be away from his father, and Jake, in a desperate effort to get him to sleep. If he wasn't in his father's bed, Jake was climbing out of his crib and wandering around the house, crying for his mama. Patrick was the easiest of the three, as he slept most of the time and only woke Ben up twice overnight for a diaper change and a bottle.

On top of his parenting duties, he was trying to plan a funeral for his wife, and the doctor continued to call to try to tell Ben what had happened. As if that would magically make him feel better about the sudden loss of the woman he had planned to spend his life with? He didn't see the point and dodged the calls constantly. The small town of Windsor Peak had descended on his house before he even got home from the hospital, filling his freezer with meals and stocking the nursery. Each day, a new set of women had arrived, helping him distract the boys for a few hours with playdates and activities, which he was eternally grateful for.

And Stella was a constant presence, one they all felt when she disappeared as dinner was served each night. Somehow, as her taillights disappeared down the mountain, chaos erupted. It was always the one time that little Patrick would get fussy, and the other two boys would start fighting or crying for their mother. It was all too much, he thought, as he poured himself a whiskey after putting all three to bed. The plans for the funeral were on his desk, to be held at the end of the week when Isobel's few family members could make it to town. He just had to make it through until then, and after that, he could find a way to survive. Making his way to the porch, he hoped for ten minutes of quiet to settle his brain.

He heard the car before he saw it and put the glass down next to him as he watched Stella climb out and walk towards him. "Did you forget something?"

"No," she said. "I just came to a realization."

"What's that?"

She sat in the rocker next to him and looked out at the stars before responding. "I've been caught up in my own grief over losing my friend," she said. "And I should have been here more. This is where Izzie would want me to be."

"You're here all the time," he said. "I couldn't ask for a better friend than you."

"You're exhausted, Benji," she said quietly. "I can see it in your eyes. This is a lot for one person to handle, and you're doing a great job. But I want to be here to help you."

"Stella, you have been."

"I know," she said. "But I was thinking I could stay for a few nights and help you more. I'll stay in the guest room, and we can take turns waking up with Patrick. You need some rest."

"Dan and Jake are in my bed," he said wearily. "It's hard to rest with all those elbows and knees poking me. It's amazing how much space a little boy can take up."

"Let's move them to their rooms," she said. "I'll be right there if they cry, and you can sleep."

"I can't ask you to do this," he objected.

"You didn't," she said. "I'm insisting. This is the least I can do for my two best friends."

They sat in a companionable silence until a cry from inside the house rang through the night. "I'll get that," she said, passing him her car keys. "Could you grab my bags from the car?"

He gathered the small suitcase and tote bag from the trunk and dropped them in the guest room for her, watching as she walked past carrying a crying Jake. "Want me to take him?" he offered in a whisper.

She shook her head. "Dan is asleep. Why don't you carry him into his room and then go to bed yourself? I've got this."

He did as she suggested, sinking into the bed, sure that sleep would never find him. Whether it was the whiskey, the soft pillow, the exhaustion, or the relief of having Stella in the house, he would never know, but he slept deeper than he had in years.

***

The next few weeks passed in a blur of grief and exhaustion. The funeral was brutal, seeing his little boys in their tiny suits stand solemnly in the church, not truly understanding what was happening. Stella had stood between Dan and Jake, offering them her support while also reaching over to touch Ben's arm when the sobs overtook him. Patrick remained quiet in his arms, seeming to pick up on the mood in the church.

They had all stood bravely at the gravesite and endured hugs and offers of condolences from friends and neighbors. When the next morning arrived, it was suddenly too quiet, and he found himself with little to do. Stella had pushed Ben to spend the morning on horseback exploring the mountain with the two older boys. Jake had shared the saddle with him, sitting close enough that Ben could feel his warmth through the front of his flannel shirt. Dan was confident enough on the tamest horse in the stable to be alone if they kept a slow pace. As they meandered along the trail, Ben found himself finally feeling normal. This was his life now, and he needed to figure out how to live it.

The night before he was expected to return to work from his paternity leave, he found Stella sitting in the kitchen surrounded by notebooks and papers. "Come sit," she said, patting the table next to her.

He grabbed a glass of water and took the chair next to her, picking up a calendar as he did. "What's all this?"

"I'm planning for you to go back to the office and trying to figure out how it will all work," she said. "I have the application for the nursery school in town for Jake, since he's old enough now to go. Dan settled back in nicely, and it will be an easier transition to get Jake started now before Dan moves to kindergarten."

"Good idea," he said. "I need to make sure he's done potty training."

"He is," she said, nodding. "Has been for about a week now."

"Really? I hadn't noticed. I'm sorry." He thought back over the last week and realized that Jake had been more independent, and he had missed it.

"It's fine," she assured him. "Patrick is the bigger question, as well as just managing the household, and I think I have a solution."

"Let's hear it," he said. The calendar in front of him was filled out with Jake's skating lessons, Dan's hockey games, a ski lesson for Dan, playdates, and upcoming birthday parties for friends. Everything was neat and color coded, well beyond what he would have been able to manage. Izzie would have even struggled to find this level of organization, he thought with a sad sigh.

"I'd like to move into the cottage out back," she said, shocking him.

"What?"

"You heard me," she said. "I'll manage the house, get the boys where they need to be, and take care of Patrick."

"But Stella…"

"There is no 'but', Ben. You need help and I'm here, and I already love these three boys," she said. "There is no one else I'd trust more than me to take care of them. Of you all."

"I can't ask you to give up your life for us," he said softly. He was filled with gratitude for the suggestion, but it was more than he could ask of her.

"We'll try it for a year," she said. "Then reevaluate."

"What about your job?" He remembered that she had told him and Isobel about her new job at the nearby city newspaper. She had been excited about the move to Burlington and what it would mean for her future.

"I'll do some occasional freelance stories for them," she said. "It will all work out, don't you worry. And my rental is month to month, so it's not a problem to leave that."

"I could pay you," he offered.

"Nonsense," she said. "I have a little nest egg my Grammy left for me. I'll be just fine. I may ask you to do some updates out on the cottage, but other than that, I don't need a thing."

"Stella," he tried again, only to be cut off by her hand patting his knee.

"Please, Ben. Don't ask a lot of questions," she said. Something in her quiet voice and averted gaze had him wanting to press further, but he held back and nodded at her. She had been his friend for as long as he could remember and had never kept a secret from him. He could wait until she was ready to share whatever it was, and he knew he needed the help. He wouldn't have made it through the last month of his life without her.

"Thank you." He choked the words out, overcome with grief again at their shared loss. She responded by resting her head on his shoulder, sitting quietly for a moment before getting back to the business of raising his boys without the woman he had planned to spend the rest of his life with.

Chapter 2

Before she knew what had happened, Stella was planning a first birthday party for little Patrick. Time had flown by as she, Ben and the boys had fallen into a rhythm. Jake had adapted well to preschool, falling into an immediate friendship with the girl who lived next door to them. Stella had lost count of the number of times she had stopped him from trying to walk to her house, not realizing that acres of land separated the two. Dan had moved on to kindergarten and appeared determined to be the best in the class, so focused on making his letters and numbers that she worried he was missing the fun. And the baby was the light of her life, bringing joy to the whole family. His happiness knew no bounds, and she was grateful every day for the doctors who had saved him when things had taken a turn with Isobel.

She was stirring a pot of spaghetti on the stove when Ben came in from work, the three boys running to greet him at the door. Despite the clear exhaustion he wore, he never hesitated to get down on the floor with them and hear about their days, as if it was the most exciting thing he had heard. Even Patrick's baby babbles got his full attention, and Stella loved witnessing it.

Once Dan and Jake moved on, he moved into the kitchen, carrying Patrick. "Has this guy eaten yet?"

"He did," she said, nodding. She watched as he set the baby down near his toys in the kitchen corner. "But I'm sure he'll have a little more when we all sit down. He is growing like a weed and eating constantly."

"I remember Izzie saying the same about the other two," he said with a soft laugh. "Seems like yesterday."

She poured him a glass of whiskey and slid it to him, which he accepted with a nod. Pouring herself a glass of wine, she moved to sit next to him. "His birthday is coming up," she said, nodding at Patrick. "Do you want a big party, or just us?"

"If I don't invite Izzie's family, I'll never hear the end of it," he said. He swirled the glass before throwing it all back. "Even if the thought of it makes my stomach hurt."

"It's been a year now," she said. "They must have realized that you can manage."

"I wouldn't have, without you," he said. "Sometimes I think her family is right. I should have just let them take the boys when they suggested that."

"No one would have benefited from that," she said adamantly. The thought of Isobel's parents taking the boys away from their grieving father had infuriated her months ago, and it still caused her blood to boil. "Least of all the boys. They lost their mother; they couldn't lose you too."

"I'm so tired, Stel. So very tired."

"I know," she said gently. "But it's getting better."

"I just can't sleep," he said. "No matter what I do, I feel like I'm failing someone."

"You aren't," she insisted. "The boys are doing great. You're doing well at work."

"You aren't living your life," he said. "You're stuck here with us, because I can't get it together."

"Ben, you have three young boys who are incredibly active," she said. "If I wasn't here, you would have to hire someone else or have them in daycare all day."

He ran a hand over his face and sighed. "I just feel like other people manage fine, and I'm drowning."

"There's no shame in needing help. Yes, other people don't have the same options as you, and it must be horrible. I can't imagine doing this completely alone," she said. "But you aren't. You have me, and the whole town. You need to give yourself some grace."

He nodded and then seemed to shut down. She knew better than to push him any further when he was like this. It was better to pretend all was well and let him come back to her on it. They had been friends since the day they sat next to each other on the first day of school; her terrified of being there, and him the self-confident boy everyone wanted to be friends with. If she needed to carry his confidence for a bit, she could do that for him.

***

The big party was to be held a week after Patrick's birthday, to avoid having a big celebration on what was also a day of loss. On his actual birthday, they had chosen to celebrate with a quiet dinner for the five of them. After dinner, they let the baby make an enormous mess out of a piece of cake. His brothers had delighted in the mess, making Patrick laugh even more, and Stella was glad to see smiles on all three of their faces. Ben looked drawn the entire day, and she knew that the weight of Isobel's death was heavy on him. After getting all three boys bathed and into bed, she found him settled on the porch. He had a bottle of red wine and two glasses next to him, as if he expected her to come look for him.

"Sorry to have left that to you," he said. "I thought dividing and conquering the mess would help, but apparently I got the better end of the deal cleaning the cake off the floor."

"You don't fool me for a minute, Ben Burrows," she said with a laugh. "You let the dog clean it up, didn't you?"

He laughed and met her eyes. "Guilty."

"It's okay," she said. "I thought you might need a minute to yourself. Are we having a drink to toast Izzie?"

"If you're up for it," he said. "I could really use the company."

He poured a glass and handed it to her before pouring one for himself. They sat in companionable silence, rocking in the chairs while sipping the wine and enjoying the sounds of the night. Stella waited him out, knowing he had something he wanted to say, and she knew he would get there, eventually. She was rewarded halfway through her glass when he cleared his throat.

"The doctor called me today," he said.

"What doctor? Are you alright? The boys?" She sat up straighter in her chair, turning to look at him.

"No, we're all fine," he assured her. "The obstetrician."

"Oh."

"I've been avoiding her for a year," he said. "She said we didn't have to talk about it, but she couldn't let the day pass without speaking to me, and getting an update on the baby."

"That was very kind of her," she said.

"I know she wants to tell me what happened," he said. "But what good will it do? Izzie is gone, there's no bringing her back."

"That's true," Stella said. "But it might help you come to grips with it. I know you, and I know somewhere deep down inside you're holding on to some blame."

His silence confirmed what she had been thinking all year. She poured a small amount into his empty glass before sipping her wine, considering her next words. This was the closest they had been to talking about Isobel's death, and she didn't want to blow it. "There was nothing you could have done. Even without knowing exactly what happened, I know there was nothing in your power that would have changed the outcome."

He sighed, pushing a hand through his hair before responding. "We don't know that."

"But you would, if you would just talk to the doctor," she said gently. "Who is it helping?"

"What?"

"You blaming yourself," she explained. "Who benefits from that? Because I know you aren't sleeping. I know the boys don't blame you, nor do I, or anyone else."

"Her parents do."

"And they are wrong," she said adamantly. "Grief comes in different ways. Right now, the best way they can cope is to blame you. They'll move past it and realize that celebrating what she left us would be healthier for everyone."

"What if there was something I should have seen?" his voice was so soft, she almost missed the words around the blaze of fury she felt toward Isobel's parents for making Ben feel this way.

"Benji, you aren't a doctor. Even they didn't see this coming," she said.

"But I lived with her. I saw her every day. I should have known if something was wrong," he said.

"This is why you need to talk to the doctor," she said. "Find out. Put it to rest one way or the other. It's not helping you, or the boys, or Izzie's parents even, to have this hanging over your head. Call in the morning and make an appointment to speak to her."

"Will you go with me?"

His words broke her heart all over again, showing how vulnerable he was, and had been, since Izzie died. "You know I will," she said. "I'll get one of the ladies at church to sit with Patrick when we go. You just make the appointment and I'll be there."

***

The phone was ringing as she came back into the house from dropping Jake at preschool. Dan took the bus now, a distinction he had held with great pleasure over his little brother's head. Stella had quickly intervened, whispering to Jake that not taking the bus meant they could stop for donuts anytime they wanted, which had ended any threat of fights. The two boys could be best friends or worst enemies, depending on the moment, and she did her best to keep the peace.

16

Hurrying to the kitchen, she answered the phone just before the answering machine would pick up. "Hello?"

"It's me," Ben's voice came through the line. "Can you meet me at the doctor's office at one?"

"Yes," she said. "I'll make some calls now and get someone over. Patrick will be napping, so that's perfect."

"Thanks," he said, his voice sounding shaky. "I'll see you there."

She busied herself with tasks around the house, and spent time playing with Patrick, seeming to check her watch every five minutes. By the time she fed the baby lunch and got him settled for his nap, she was exhausted. She took the baby monitor with her to the cottage out back, where she quickly changed into a skirt and blouse and brushed her hair. She ran back to the main house just as her friend was pulling into the driveway and managed to get the door open before the doorbell was rung.

"Hi," she said, briefly hugging Mary Knight. "Thank you so much for coming over."

"It's absolutely no problem," Mary assured her. "I miss the baby days, so I'm hoping he will wake up before I leave."

"We can have a cup of tea when I return and wait for him to get up if not," Stella promised. "How is Kendra doing in kindergarten?"

"Wonderful," Mary said, beaming at the mention of her daughter. "She loves it so much. I think she and Dan are running the show over there."

"That doesn't surprise me," Stella said with a laugh. "They are two strong personalities. It's better if they can combine their powers than work against each other."

"Very true," Mary said. "I brought something to read, so take your time. It's not often I get to sit and relax in a quiet house."

"Thank you again," Stella said, opening the door again. "I left the number on the refrigerator in case you have any emergencies."

"We'll be fine," Mary assured her, waving her hand. "Not a thing to worry about here."

Stella slowly drove through town to the medical building near the highway. Ben's car was already parked in the lot, and she could see him sitting in the driver's seat. She pulled on her coat as she walked toward him, surprised when he didn't get out of the car as she approached. She knocked softly on the window, causing him to jump. The door opened, and he climbed out, looking like a man about to face the gallows.

"This will be okay," she assured him. She linked her arm with his and steered him toward the entrance, afraid he would turn to run if she let go.

"If you say so," he grumbled.

They checked in at the desk and were quickly whisked into a private office. The nurse assured them the doctor would be right in, so they settled into seats across from the desk. Fortunately, she was correct, and the door opened before Stella could find a way to fill the heavy silence.

"Thank you for coming in," Dr. Bradshaw said, stopping to shake both of their hands. "I really appreciate your time."

"Thank you," Ben said stiffly.

"How is the baby?"

"Patrick is doing wonderfully," Stella said when Ben didn't respond. "A very happy, healthy baby."

"That's wonderful," the doctor said with a smile. "Mr. Burrows, I know you've refrained from hearing the details about what happened with your wife, but I would like to share if you're okay with it."

He nodded, seeming to get even paler, and Stella reached over to take his hand. His hand was clammy, and he held tightly to her in return.

"Isobel suffered cardiac arrest while we were performing the c-section," the doctor said. "As you know, an autopsy was performed to confirm. What we didn't know at the time was that she had an amniotic fluid embolism which put stress on her heart and lungs. There was no way to prevent this, and nothing would have alerted us in advance of the procedure. Would you like me to continue?"

Ben nodded, and the doctor folded her hands on the desk and leaned forward. "This is an extremely rare condition. The medical board thoroughly reviewed it, and was able to put my mind at ease that there was nothing we could have done. Myself, the anesthesiologist, the other physician in the room, and all the nurses were second guessing everything we had done. We were able to get some peace from the investigation, and I hoped it would do the same for you."

"I remember," Ben said. He stopped and stared at the floor for a moment before looking back at the doctor. "That you tried very hard to help her. I didn't know what was happening. I was moved aside by a nurse and heard a lot."

"We had to save the baby," the doctor said. "I had gotten to know Isobel enough to know that she would want that. It all happened so fast, and we did everything we could to get her back. But she was in very bad condition. My priority was to save the baby while the other doctors were trying to save her. I'm sorry that we were only successful on one of those."

"I'm incredibly grateful that you saved Patrick," he said gruffly. "I could never thank you enough for that."

They all sat in silence for a few moments, and Stella's heart ached as she watched Ben quickly wipe his eyes. "Dr. Bradshaw," Stella said before she could lose her nerve. "Are you positive there is nothing Ben could have seen before that day to know she was in danger?"

"Absolutely positive," the doctor said firmly. "Not only could you have not seen it, but I saw her each week. I examined her myself, and I'm a trained medical professional. Nothing was wrong during the pregnancy. She was in perfect health. This is a rare condition and happens suddenly. There was nothing you or I could have done that would have prevented this. It wouldn't have mattered where she was, or who the doctors were. That is something I questioned as well, and the confirmation that there was nothing that could be done allowed me to sleep at night. I hope the same is true for you."

Chapter 3

Stella had given him exactly what he needed after speaking with the doctor. She had hugged him for what felt like an hour and then left him alone to process what had been said. He hadn't realized how heavily he had been wearing the weight of his wife's death until it was lifted, and he didn't know what to do with the emotions that were untapped. He had spent hours sitting at Izzie's grave, telling her about their boys, and able to talk to her in a way he hadn't been able to since her death. By the time he returned home, the boys had eaten and were settled in with a movie. Stella had disappeared once he joined them on the couch, seeming to know that he needed their warmth and innocence to finish the day.

When all three boys had fallen asleep before the ending credits of the animated movie, he carried them to bed one at a time. Still not feeling tired, he had wandered around the house for a while, looking at all the little ways Isobel was still with them. Pictures hanging on the walls, her handwriting in the phonebook he kept on his desk, the decorative pillows on his bed that she loved so much. All the little touches of a woman who had loved them all deeply and done everything she could to take care of them, but had been stolen away too soon. By the time he climbed into his own bed, it was well after midnight, and he then spent a long time staring at the ceiling.

The boys were up early, dragging him out of his heavy dreams just as the sun came up. Ben felt as though he hadn't slept at all, yet the grit in the corner of his eyes suggested that he had gotten a few hours. He had expected to dream of Isobel, having spent so many hours thinking of her the day before, but she had eluded him.

"Daddy, today is the big party for Patty's birthday," Dan said. "How long until our friends come?"

"It's not even six in the morning," he said with a laugh. "It's going to be a long wait. The party isn't until noon."

He settled the boys in on either side of him, where they both promptly fell back to sleep. Just as he was about to drift off again, he heard Patrick's cry from down the hall. Not wanting the other two to wake up again, he quickly slid out of bed and made his way to the nursery, only to find Stella already changing the baby.

"Hey," he said softly. "You didn't have to get up this early."

She turned and seemed to be caught off guard, which was when he realized he was wearing only pajama bottoms. Her gaze swept his body quickly before she turned back to the task at hand, but he would swear that she started to blush. "I got up early to take care of a few things for the party," she said. "I thought I could get to him before he woke you. You need the rest."

"I'm up now," he said. "The other two were in my room before the sun came up, but I got them back to sleep."

"I'll bring him downstairs," Stella said, picking up Patrick from the crib. "Why don't you shower and meet us in the kitchen?"

She paused next to him so he could kiss his son, and she seemed stiffer than usual. "Stella, are you okay?"

"Fine," she said, sounding anything but. "I need to get some coffee started."

She hurried down the hallway, and he shook his head as he walked into the bathroom. He had enough to deal with today, with his in-laws descending on the house in a few hours. If Stella was still acting weird in a few days, he could push the issue.

***

Most of the town arrived at the same time, parking in the wide driveway or on the grass next to the large red barn they used as a garage. They all came bearing gifts for Patrick, as well as dishes to be served for the party. A local company had come early to set up a bounce house in the yard, as well as a few tents. It was still warm enough to enjoy the outdoors, especially with the sun high in the sky, and he planned a bonfire for anyone who was still there when the sun set. The house and yard were humming with voices and laughter, and Ben still couldn't relax.

"You look like you're waiting for bad news." Pete Hardy, a friend of Ben's since childhood, offered him a beer. "You probably need this more than me."

"Not yet," Ben said. "I'm waiting for Isobel's family to arrive."

"Oh, that's rough. Are things still strained between you all?"

"You could say that," Ben said. "We talk once a week, and they see the boys every couple of months. But every time, they make the statement that they would be better suited to raise them than a single man."

"They would be so over their heads," Pete said. "Let them think that, and I'll deal with it if the time comes."

Pete was a lawyer, and Ben trusted him implicitly, but the fear still nagged. "I can't lose my boys."

"And you won't," Pete said confidently. "You have my word on that. They have no basis to claim you're an unfit parent. They barely know the boys, and to take them away from where Izzie wanted them to grow up, and away from who she chose to parent with, is wrong. Try not to worry."

"I hope you're right," he said. "I just saw their car pull in now. I suppose I should go out and welcome them."

Pete clapped him on the back as he turned to leave, and Ben appreciated both the support and the free legal advice. The last thing he wanted was to fight with Izzie's parents, but they seemed determined not to get along with him. He stood in the doorway, watching as they climbed out of the car. Isobel's death had aged them both considerably, and he felt terrible about that. They were in their early sixties and had been enjoying the start of their retirement when their world had been rocked by the death of their only daughter.

Ben opened the door as they came up the walkway and mustered up a smile. "Joan, William, thanks for coming," he said, leaning down to kiss his mother-in-law on the cheek.

"Thank you for having us," Joan said. "It looks like you have quite the celebration going."

"A first birthday is a big deal," Ben said. "The whole town wanted to celebrate Patrick."

"I hope they didn't forget that it's also the day we lost our daughter," Joan said, wiping a tear away.

"No one forgot," Ben said patiently. "That's why the party is today, and not on his actual birthday. We had a nice mass to honor Isobel on that day, and everyone was there for that as well. I got a lot of cards and kind gestures. Everyone loved Izzie."

Joan nodded once and then proceeded into the house, glancing around with a judgmental look on her face. William was slower, shaking Ben's hand before following his wife. Of the two, his father-in-law seemed more sympathetic to his situation than Joan was, and he hoped that the older man would have a positive influence on his behalf.

The kitchen was full of women Ben knew from town, who were busy getting food out to the tables under the tents. Joan frowned as she looked around, then turned back to Ben. "Where are my grandsons?"

"Most likely in the bounce house," he said, pointing to the backyard. "Or running around with friends. I'll help you find them."

"Someone should be keeping an eye on them."

"Stella is out there," Anna Hardy, Pete's wife, called from the kitchen. "I just saw her."

Joan looked at Ben with a raised eyebrow, but then proceeded out into the yard, her husband trailing behind. Ben took a moment to contain himself before following. When they approached the bounce house, Stella was standing amid a pile of discarded sneakers, holding Patrick on one hip. Ben could see Jake laughing in one corner with his little friend Jenna from next door, while Dan bounced in the center with the older kids.

"Mr. and Mrs. Brickman, how nice to see you," Stella said as she smiled at the couple. "I bet you want to see this big guy first."

Stella tried to hand Patrick to his grandmother, but the baby clung to her shirt and a handful of her hair. Ben stepped forward quickly, disentangling his son's fingers and silently apologizing to his friend. "Come here, bud," he said. Patrick easily went to his arms, and he gestured to a table nearby. "Let's go sit. It just takes him a minute to warm up."

"Funny, he doesn't seem to have the same problem with that woman," Joan fumed.

"Take it easy, Joan," William said under his breath.

"Stella takes care of him while I work," Ben said. "Patrick is very comfortable with her."

Joan looked over to where Stella was helping Jake with his sneakers. Dan was sitting next to his brother, both boys listening intently to whatever Stella was telling them. "Seems she's comfortable around here, alright."

"Joan, I don't know what—"

"Nana, Grandpa," the boys called out as they ran toward them. Joan and William's faces lit up as the boys hugged them, and Jake easily settled onto his grandfather's knee as Dan took the chair next to Joan. Ben sat at the end of the table, so Patrick was between both grandparents, and listened as his boys filled them in on the excitement in their lives.

"I got a star on my writing test," Dan told them. "I got all the letters right and all the words."

"I's taking hockey lessons," Jake shared.

"It's just skating," Dan said, rolling his eyes. "I play hockey."

"Me too," Jake shouted at his brother.

"You're getting there, buddy," Ben said, shooting a warning look at Dan. "Three is when you start skating, and you can start playing hockey when you turn four."

"Baby," Dan said under his breath.

"Daniel," Ben said, but was cut off by Joan.

"Boys will be boys," she said, running a hand over Dan's hair. "Nothing to get excited about."

Dan looked smugly at Jake, who looked ready to tackle his brother in the dirt, so Ben knew he needed to separate them. "Dan, can you go to the food table and bring back a hamburger for Patrick?"

Once his son left the table, he turned to Jake. "Jakey, would you mind going to get me a fork and knife? And one of those juice boxes?"

"Sure, daddy," he said, heading in the opposite direction that Dan had taken.

"Joan," he said, once the boys were out of earshot. "I appreciate how much you care about the boys. But I need to discourage them from putting each other down or fighting. Those two are at each other's throats all the time, and I need to nip it in the bud."

"That's why we've been saying it's too much for you," Joan said. Her face was animated suddenly, looking too happy for his liking. "William and I, we were a team, and it was still a lot to raise two children. You have three, and you need more than one person. I think we would be much better suited to handle this than you."

Ben sat back in his chair, all the air gone from his lungs. No matter what he did, how he tried to manage the relationship, Joan would continue to throw these darts at him. The very thought of losing his children after having lost his wife made ice run through his veins, and he simply wouldn't allow it to happen.

"I need you to listen to me very carefully," he said, keeping his voice low deliberately. "These are my children. They will be raised here, with me. You are their grandparents, and I want nothing more than to keep you in their lives, so that they have another connection to Isobel. But I won't hesitate to cut you out of it if you continue to make threats against me."

"Let's all take a breath," William said. "Joan, we are here to enjoy Patrick's birthday and to spend time with the family. This is not the time or place."

"There is no time or place for this conversation," Ben said adamantly. "It's not happening. You will not take my sons from me."

Dan and Jake raced back to the table, the animosity between them put at rest for the time being. Ben carefully removed the burger from the bread before cutting it into small pieces for Patrick under Joan's watchful gaze and sent the other two back for plates of their own lunch. The boys chatted happily as they ate, keeping everyone entertained, but Ben couldn't focus on the words. Joan's threat kept circling around his heart, and the tension between the two of them was palpable. He excused himself to change Patrick's diaper and was happy to be caught up by friends for the duration of the afternoon. He wasn't going to spend his son's first birthday party being berated by his mothers-in-law, so any distraction was a good one.

***

Several hours passed before some neighbors started to collect their families and head home. Ben knew that his closest friends would stay to enjoy a fire and one last drink with him after the crowd thinned, giving him a chance to finally relax. Seeing Joan and William stand, he braced himself and headed in their direction.

"Are you heading out? I can find the boys to say goodbye," he said. "Patrick is napping, but I can wake him."

"No need," Joan said stiffly. "I'm sure we'll be seeing them soon enough."

"What does that mean?"

"Is that woman living with you? Did you really fill my daughter's place in your bed so easily?"

"What are you talking about?" Ben's jaw had dropped at her words, and he looked at William for an explanation.

"People were talking about how good you and Stella are together," he explained. "And how she moved in right after Izzie died."

"You both knew she was helping me," he said. "And that she was here helping me right after Izzie died. She was Isobel's

29

best friend. I've known her since we were Dan's age. There is nothing romantic about it."

"That's not what I've observed," Joan said. "And certainly not what your neighbors think. I will not have my grandsons raised to think this is appropriate behavior."

"Joan, you have this all wrong," Ben said. "Stella and I are friends. Nothing more."

"My daughter was a good girl," Joan said. "And we trusted you to take care of her. You failed at that, and I will not have something happen to her children because you can't keep it in your pants."

She turned on her heel and stormed away, leaving Ben staring at her back in shock. William hesitated, but eventually followed his wife into the house. Ben knew that Joan blamed him for Isobel dying, but she had never said it outright before now. Her anger was tangible, and he knew that she would stop at nothing to punish him. Even if that meant ripping three boys out of a loving home.

Chapter 4

Stella had just said goodbye to her sister and was returning to the backyard when Joan stormed through the kitchen door. The look on her face as she caught sight of Stella was murderous, and she followed it with a finger point.

"You," she seethed. "How dare you sully my daughter's memory this way?"

"What are you talking about? Mrs. Brickman, I never—"

"Don't you deny it," Joan continued. "It's all everyone has been talking about out there. How close you and Ben are, how you're living together. And how wonderful that you have each other now. It makes me wonder if there was something happening between you two before my beautiful Isobel died."

Stella gasped, placing a hand over her heart. "Never! I don't know what's happening, but I would never have done that to Izzie."

"But you took her place in his bed, didn't you?"

William stepped forward, placing an arm around his wife. "Joan. Let's go. This is not helping."

"I didn't," Stella said, sobs ripping at her throat. "She was my best friend. I miss her every day. I want to help her sons grow up the way she wanted them to."

"How convenient, then, that you were still single and childless?" Joan glared at her. "So that you could swoop right in and take her place, without a moment's thought."

"My only thought was of what she would want," Stella said. "Please, you have to believe me."

"I don't have to do anything," Joan said. "Other than taking these children out of this unfit home, which I will see to on Monday."

The bathroom door in the hallway opened, and Stella looked up to see Pete Hardy emerge. He met her eyes and shook his head slightly, indicating that she should remain quiet. Approaching Joan and William with his hand outstretched, he smiled. "I'm Pete Hardy," he said. "I went to school here with Isobel, Ben and Stella. I'm now an attorney, and I represent Ben in what I presume will be a custody case. I want to assure you that I'm the best there is, and you will not have any luck in taking the boys from him. I'd highly suggest you take some time to calm down and consider what this would do to your relationship with your son-in-law and grandsons before proceeding."

William took his wife's arm and nudged her toward the door. "We'll be going now," he said, avoiding Stella and Pete's eyes as he walked.

Joan made it to the door before she turned back, glaring at Stella once more. "I always knew you were trouble," she said. "I told Isobel to be careful, because you were always so jealous of her. I hope she sees now that I was right all along."

The door slammed behind them, and Stella collapsed into the chair behind her. She had never experienced such cruelty before, and certainly not at the hands of a woman she had known all her life. She had grown up as a regular guest at the Brickmans dinner table and had no idea she was so hated.

"Stella." Pete's voice brought her back to the present. "I can go get Ben for you."

"No," she said quickly. "I don't want to make this day any more difficult for him. I know she got her hooks into him earlier. He's already had enough."

"She won't win," Pete said. "You know that, right?"

"I should leave," she said. "This is going to make it harder for you, don't you think?"

"No," he said. "You live out back in the cottage, right? I believe you when you say there is nothing romantic between you two. She would have to prove it, so if what you're saying is true, we don't have a problem. And even if you were, that doesn't make Ben an unfit parent. He's a widower. He's allowed to date."

"Pete, I don't know what to do," she said.

"Exactly what you've been doing," he said firmly. "You sure you don't want me to get Ben? I'll have to fill him in on this at some point."

"Monday," she said. "Let him have the weekend with the kids without this hanging over his head."

Pete disappeared through the kitchen door, where she could see a bonfire being built. Children sat patiently with sticks holding marshmallows as the men worked on the flames, the sun setting behind the mountain. The party had been a success, and she had been looking forward to this quiet time with their closest friends, but suddenly, all she wanted was to be alone. But before she could sneak over to her cottage, she heard Patrick's cry from the floor above. Not wanting to disrupt Ben, she ran up the steps to get him from his crib. Rather than hiding in her home alone, she busied herself with the baby who had healed her heart after her friend had died. After changing him and getting some slobbery kisses, she felt calm enough to return to the party.

Dan and Jake grinned at her as she came out of the house with Patrick, both attempting to eat gooey marshmallows that were landing more on their shirts than in their mouths. "Ben, take Patrick," she said with a laugh. "These two are making a mess."

Ben took the baby and sat with him, and Stella saw that he had a small plate of food at his side for Patrick, along with a sippy cup of milk. The baby always woke up hungry, and Ben had prepared well. The thought that maybe he would manage without her tickled at the back of her brain, but she pushed it aside as she focused on Jake and Dan.

"You'll need baths before bed," she said.

"Shower," Dan said. "I'm too big to share a tub with my brothers."

"Shower it is," Stella agreed. "Whatever will get this layer of sugar and dirt off your body."

"I shower too," Jake said, not one to be outdone.

"Okay, go play with your friends for now," she said. "We'll deal with this at bedtime."

Ben waved to her, gesturing to an empty chair next to him. Pausing to pour a glass of wine before taking the seat, she noticed Pete watching them. He caught her eye and nodded, making Stella second guess whether sitting next to her friend was a bad idea. Ben's confused look got her moving again, and she settled in next to him, taking a hefty sip of her wine.

"Today went well," he said. "The boys will be exhausted."

"I'm glad you have the day off tomorrow to recover," she said. "I think everyone needs a lazy day."

"I was thinking of inviting people over to watch football, since we have so much food left over," he said quietly. "But you're right, I just want to sit and do nothing all day."

She laughed, and they sat listening to their friends chat for several minutes. Before she could stop herself, she leaned toward Ben again. "Did Joan upset you?"

"Why do you ask?"

"I saw the look on your face when you were talking," she said. "I thought it was best to stay far away."

"Yes," he said with a heavy sigh. "I don't know what to do about her."

"Time heals all wounds, right?" Stella said, smiling sadly at him. "Maybe this is part of her grief process."

"I would rather she throw herself into being here for the boys," he said. "Be a grandmother who is actively involved in their lives. But she doesn't want to leave her new retirement community, and it's hours away. What am I supposed to do?"

"Nothing," she said. "You're doing everything you can to be the best father possible. That's all Izzie would ask."

"You don't think she would be upset with me for fighting with her mom?"

Stella thought for a moment of her friend, who had never been quick to anger. "No, I don't think she would be. Izzie was many things, but she never really stood up for herself," she said. "She let you do that for her, or me. I think if she knew that her mom was trying to take them away, she would want you to fight back."

He reached over to squeeze her hand, holding it briefly before dropping it to help Patrick with his milk. Heart in her throat, she sat long enough to finish her wine before shepherding the older boys into the house for their showers. She waved to Ben to indicate he should stay where he was, and once the boys were in bed, she slipped out the front door to walk to her cottage without being noticed by the small group at the fire.

Once inside, she grabbed the phone and dialed her sister Heather's number, hoping she would answer. When it was picked up on the second ring, she sighed in relief. "Heather. I have a problem."

"Tell me," her sister demanded.

"Izzie's mom was here. I'm sure you saw her," Stella said.

"Looking sour as ever," Heather said with a laugh. "I don't know how Isobel was always so happy with that as her mom."

"She lashed out at me at the end of the night," Stella said. "I can't believe the things she said."

"Tell me." The sound of a blanket rustling came through the phone, and Stella could picture her sister settling onto the couch while they talked.

"She accused me of taking Isobel's spot in Ben's life," she said. "And the boys."

"What?" Heather's outrage came through the phone. "I didn't see her anywhere near to help him when he came home from the hospital alone with an infant. How dare she say anything but thank you to you? She should have been there, helping with her grandkids, but she stayed away. Even at the funeral, she acted like it was just her loss, and Ben was there with their three babies, acting more together than Joan."

"I know," Stella said with a sigh. "It was painful to watch. She went on and on to every mourner who stopped to talk to her, and it was just about her losing her only daughter. Which is horrible, and I hate that it happened. No one should lose a child. But Ben lost his wife, and these children lost their mom. It's just wrong all around. It wasn't just her tragedy."

"She made it about her," Heather said. "But she was always like that. Bitter and rude. She was terrible to our mom when you were little."

"Really? I don't remember that."

"Didn't you think it was odd that you were always at their house, but Isobel was never at ours?"

"Now that you said it, yes," Stella said. "But I never noticed before."

"Mom worked, and Joan looked down on her for that. Our house wasn't clean enough, mom wasn't around to monitor, I was a bad influence. The list goes on and on," Heather said. "I overheard mom and dad talking about it a lot."

"I'll have to talk to dad about it," Stella said. "But what do I do in the meantime? She's accusing me of sleeping with Ben and saying it gives her grounds to take the boys away from him."

A sharp gasp came through the phone line. "How dare she. Those boys love him, and you. No one in their right mind would take them away."

"I hope you're right."

"Stell, I have to ask…"

"What?"

"Is there anything going on with you and Ben?"

"Heather, you know there's not," she said. "There never has been."

"Not never," Heather corrected her in a gentle tone. "I know you had feelings for him once."

"That was a lifetime ago," she said. "And before he and Izzie started dating."

"He was your first kiss," Heather persisted. "I've been wondering if anything would happen, but you both seem so focused on the boys and grieving Izzie, I didn't think it had yet."

"Not yet, and not ever," Stella said. "Don't think like that. If the courts found out, it would give them a reason."

"That's just silly," Heather said. "It's not like when we were kids. No one would judge you if you and Ben were to have a relationship. I'd encourage it, as a matter of fact."

"It's not going to happen," Stella said stubbornly. "Do you think I should move out of here?"

"I can't answer that," Heather said. "I'm worried about you being too invested in a family that isn't yours. I want you to have your eyes wide open and make sure you're doing the best thing for Stella. You're always so giving to those around you. Make sure you don't get lost in this."

Stella gossiped with her sister about the party for a few more minutes before saying good night to her and hanging up the phone. It had been hard to focus on friendly neighborhood stories with the threat Joan had planted still taking up space in her brain. And the ideas that Heather had shared occupying her heart.

Yes, in an ideal world, maybe something romantic would have happened between her and Ben. They had been best friends since sitting next to each other on the bus the first day of kindergarten, and nothing had ever changed that. When they both turned thirteen, she had voiced her concerns about a first kiss. He had promptly offered to teach her, promising it was easy. While Stella had felt the first swirl of a crush forming after that, they had remained just friends. Then Stella noticed that Ben's focus was more on Isobel, who was developing into a beautiful young woman. Suddenly, she was the third wheel, and the excuse Isobel needed to get out of her house to see Ben.

She had never felt any ill will toward her friend for stealing Ben's heart. Or for Ben, for not feeling the same way about her that she did him. The one time she did open up to Ben about her feelings, she sensed that it wasn't reciprocated and backed off quickly. Fortunately, Ben had also pretended it didn't happen, so she let it go. She was by their side through their entire relationship and stood at the altar with them as they exchanged vows. Never once did she wish she was in Isobel's place, and she had never thought of Ben in a romantic way through all those years of their marriage. But now that the idea had been put out into the universe, her heart was whispering to her, asking why it was such a bad idea.

Chapter 5

"Ben, do you have a minute?" Pete was standing in the doorway to Ben's office at the bank, holding two cups of coffee in his hands that he held up as he spoke. "I brought sustenance."

"Come in," Ben said. "Shut the door behind you. I have a feeling I know what this is about."

"I'm sorry for dropping by your work like this," Pete said. "But I knew you would be here early on a Monday, and I wanted to catch you before you got too busy."

"I appreciate that," Ben said. He accepted a cup of coffee from his friend and gestured to the chair across from his desk.

Pete sat and opened the top of his coffee, taking a long sip before setting it on the edge of Ben's desk. He crossed his legs and leaned back, meeting Ben's eyes. "I think we may need to do something about Isobel's parents."

"They were pretty emotional on Saturday," Ben said. "Joan especially. I'm hoping that as time moves on, they'll start to feel better about everything."

"I'd prefer to handle it before something gets filed in court," Pete responded. "I don't want the kids to be put through any kind of investigation or have you or Stella feel like you're walking on eggshells."

"What does Stella have to do with this?"

"Didn't she tell you?" At Ben's headshake, Pete frowned. "I hope I'm not overstepping, but you should know. I was in the bathroom when the Brickmans were leaving. They cornered Stella in the kitchen, and Joan said some awful things to Stella. I went out and interrupted. I talked to Stella after the fact, but she was pretty rattled."

"What did they say to her?"

"It was Joan. William stayed quiet. She accused Stella of having an affair with you when Isobel was alive, and of being glad Izzie was gone so she could take her spot," Pete shared. "I came out an introduced myself as your attorney and assured them that they would have no luck beating me in court to gain custody. I suggested they take some time and think about what would happen to their relationship with you if they proceeded. Not to mention what the boys would think of them if they were to find out."

Ben saw red, he was so angry. "For her to even suggest that I would have been unfaithful to my wife is bad enough," he fumed. "But to claim that I've moved on so quickly, or that I'm not a good father, just makes it so much worse."

"For what it's worth," Pete said. "There is no timeline for moving on. You could have started dating the month after Izzie passed, and it still wouldn't make you a bad father. And I presume this is all just a figment of Joan's imagination?"

"Of course it is," Ben snapped. "I wouldn't do that to Isobel."

"Ben, she's gone," Pete said gently. "Nothing you do now is an insult to her or her memory. She wouldn't expect you to take a vow of chastity because you lost her."

"That's beside the point," Ben said. "I'm not, and have not been, involved with Stella romantically."

"I suspect that Joan is looking for a target for her anger over losing her daughter," Pete said. "And Stella is an easy one for her. I would anticipate more animosity aimed at her, so it might be best to keep her out of sight if Joan and William come to visit. What I'd like to do today is send them a formal letter, alerting them that I am retained as your counsel and that we would like to reach an agreement with them rather than put the children through a trial. Does that sound alright to you?"

"You don't think we should just give them time to move past this? I hate to make it seem like I'm threatening them with anything," Ben replied.

"This one won't have any threats. I'll simply tell them that as a witness to the anger over the weekend, and their statements made in my presence, I would like to work toward a solution that is least disruptive to the boys," Pete said. "I think it's better to be proactive in this type of situation than to be waiting for the other shoe to drop."

"That makes sense," Ben said. "You don't think I should try to talk to them first?"

"I'll offer that in my letter," Pete said. "That we can all sit down with a mediator or family counselor if they like, and see what can be worked out. I don't think you should talk to them without me present."

Ben sighed, knowing his friend was right. Joan had always been tough to handle, and he could get himself into a heap of trouble if he said the wrong thing now. "Okay, let's try it."

"I should have asked you first," Pete said with a soft laugh. "Do you want me to represent you in this?"

"Of course, I do. There's no one I trust more."

Pete stood and gathered his belongings before turning back to Ben. "One last thing," he said. "I know it's probably early for this kind of warning, but better safe than sorry. Be aware of how you act when you're in public. I don't know if they would hire someone to follow you or Stella, but that's the first thing I would do if I were retained on their side."

"But you said the relationship between Stella and I doesn't matter," Ben argued. "Now I have to be careful not to be seen with her in public?"

"No, not like that," Pete said, shaking his head. "You can carry on as normal. But don't be arguing with her, or anyone else, for that matter. Make sure you're as present as possible at the kid's activities. Just always be aware that someone may be watching, and if they catch you on a bad day, or a bad minute, it could come back to hurt us later."

Ben thanked Pete and watched as he left the office, closing the door behind him, likely to give Ben a private moment to process what was happening. He wanted to rage, to throw things through the glass window behind him, or to call Joan and give her a piece of his mind. But that wouldn't help, and more than ever, he had to control himself. He wasn't a man with a temper normally, unless you came after him or his family. And of all people, Joan knew how to push his buttons, so he had to keep himself under control. There was too much at risk to lash out now.

***

Days passed with no word, and Ben felt himself relaxing. If Joan and William were going to act on the threats, surely, he would have heard something by now. Pete had confirmed that the certified letter had been signed for, and that he had not received a response. Ben let himself feel hope that the matter would be a distant memory soon enough.

The hope faded on Friday afternoon when he saw Pete walking towards his office door. His friend had a serious look on his face, and Ben knew in his gut that it had to do with the Brickmans.

"Sorry to keep barging in on you like this," Pete said as he entered Ben's office. "I needed the walk over here to gather my thoughts, and I'd rather talk to you face to face than over the phone."

"You heard from Joan?"

"From her attorney," Pete confirmed. "Who claims that they are ready to proceed in suing you for custody of the boys."

"What?" Ben nearly shot out of his chair. "I thought we were going to try to talk?"

"That's what I plan to respond with," Pete said, raising a hand to keep Ben in his seat. "I'd like to be able to show the court, if we get to that point, that we were trying to maintain a peaceful relationship with them prior to this. And then I'll destroy them."

Pete looked angry, which helped Ben calm down. He had the right person in charge of this; there was no doubt that Pete could handle Joan and her lawyer. "What do we do now?"

"I can almost guarantee they'll have someone following you," Pete said. "Again, it's the first thing I would do to start looking for a reason to give the court that you're unfit. I'd avoid drinking in public or even buying liquor right now. If you need something, have a friend buy it for you, or use cash only. Nothing on credit cards that can be used against you. You need to be with the boys whenever you aren't here at work, to make it clear you are handling single parenthood just fine."

"Does that mean Stella can't be with us? She wanted to be at Dan's game tomorrow," Ben said.

"She can be," Pete said. "But make sure you're the one doing the parenting."

"She's not going to handle this well," Ben said. "She loves them so much."

"Which will be obvious to anyone watching," Pete said. "I just want to make sure that you are also there, and that you look to be the person doing the bulk of the work. What happens behind closed doors doesn't need to change."

"Do you think she needs to move out?"

"Absolutely not," Pete said. "I want to prove that the boys have a stable, secure home life with you. Stella is a big part of that. I have to ask this, so forgive me. But do you pay her?"

"Stella? No. I offered, but she refused," Ben said. "Her grandmother left her a chunk of money, and without needing to pay a mortgage or rent, she insists she doesn't need more."

"You might need to start," Pete said. "Write her a check every week. Even if she just uses it to buy groceries, I want to be able to make it clear that she is there as hired help, not as a domestic partner."

"She's going to hate this," Ben said.

"It's temporary," Pete said. "Just until we get this over with."

"I'll talk to her tonight," Ben said. "This is going to be hard."

"I'm sorry," Pete said. "I wish I could make it easier. Want me to come over later and we can all talk?"

"No, it's better if she and I are alone," Ben said. "But if she has questions, I'll give you a call."

"Sounds good," Pete said. "And I'm sure I'll see you around this weekend."

***

Their Friday night tradition since Isobel's death had become Ben bringing home pizza, which they followed with a movie. Ben had stopped at the rental store before getting the food, picking up a movie about a dog that played basketball, which he knew would entertain the boys. It would also have a happy ending, which he hoped would put Stella in a good mood for the conversation they would need to have once the boys were sleeping.

Patrick only made it for the first half hour of the movie before he was rubbing his eyes, so Ben took him upstairs to bed, waving for Stella to stay. Dan and Jake were mesmerized by the dog on TV, and even he found himself laughing a few times. There was no doubt in his mind that the older boys would be trying to train their dogs in the morning, or that their old dogs would ignore any such efforts.

"Dada," Patrick said, patting his cheek and planting a wet kiss where his hands had been.

"Love you, buddy," he said in return. They sat in the rocking chair after Patrick had been cleaned up and helped into clean pajamas, and Ben read him two books before placing him half asleep into his crib. Ben stood and watched him for a moment, still in awe that this sweet boy was a product of him and Isobel. Every day, he felt lucky that Patrick had survived his traumatic birth, and it helped his resolve to fight to keep the boys where they belonged. Here, with him.

As soon as the movie ended, he scooped Jake up off the couch and gestured to Dan. "Let's go. Time for bed," he said.

"Want me to help?" Stella offered from her spot on the couch.

"No, you relax. I've got this," he said. "But don't disappear. I want to talk to you once they're settled."

She looked at him with a question in her eyes, but he avoided them and headed up the stairs. His plan to have her in a good mood for the conversation had worked, but suddenly he hated that he was about to take that away from her. He made quick work of getting the boys into clean pajamas, helping them brush their teeth, and getting them into bed. Dan had declared himself too old for a bedtime story, and now read to himself out of the early reader books that Ben had found at the local store. Jake still enjoyed the quiet time, and Ben took his time reading two books before the little boy was sleeping.

He dragged his feet going back downstairs, first checking on Patrick and then sticking his head into Dan's room. Dan had fallen asleep with his book on his chest, so he closed it and placed it on the bedside table before switching off the lamp. Both Dan and Jake now slept with nightlights in their rooms, which the pediatrician had assured Ben was normal. They had lost their mother at such a young age, so developing a common fear, like of the dark, wasn't unheard of.

Once all was quiet, he took a deep breath and headed back down the stairs to break his best friend's heart.

Chapter 6

Ben went to the kitchen when he came back downstairs, returning to the family room with a bottle of red wine and two glasses. He settled next to her on the couch, pouring the wine and handing her one before leaning back with his own glass. Stella took a fortifying sip before turning to face him.

"Do you need me to move out?"

"What? No," he said. "Why would you say that?"

"You've been acting weird all week," she said. "And especially tonight. You didn't pay any attention to the movie, and I think you only half heard what the boys were saying at dinner."

"I was distracted, yes," he said. "I'm sorry for that."

"Will you tell me what's going on?" Her heart was thumping so hard against her ribs, she wondered if he could hear it. Whatever he was gearing himself up to say was clearly not good news.

"I talked to Pete just before I left the office," Ben said. "He came over to see me. Joan and William have hired a lawyer and state they are going to try to get custody of the boys."

"They can't do that," she cried, jumping to her feet. "How can they be so cruel? The boys are happy and healthy. They've finally adjusted and stopped looking for Isobel everywhere we go."

"Sit down, please," Ben said, his tone gentle. He waited until she sat back down before continuing. "They're grieving and not acting rationally. You and I can see that, Pete can, but they can't."

"Why won't their lawyer tell them this is a bad idea?"

"Good question," he said. "My guess is that he'll make money off them before he shares that. Or maybe it's because he only has their side of the story and doesn't know me from a hole in the wall? I don't know."

"Once he sees what's happening, he'll have to put a stop to it," Stella said. "Taking them away from you would be criminal."

"I agree with you," he said. "But I need to prepare for a lawyer and then a judge to examine all aspects of my life."

"Starting with me, I'm guessing." The nerves in her stomach were causing her to feel nauseous suddenly. The idea of walking away from Ben and the boys she had grown to love so much was horrifying to her, but she would do it if it meant they would get to stay together. "I think I should go."

"Absolutely not," he said vehemently. "That is not happening. The boys adore you, and you make it possible for me to work and provide for them. I couldn't have gotten through this last year without you, and the last thing I'm going to let Joan do is hurt you as well as us."

"Then what do we do?" She wiped a tear from her cheek and was surprised when Ben reached over to take her hand.

"We're a team, Stel," he said. "Me and you. Us and the boys. We're all in this together. We're going to fight and win, I promise. We just might need to do things a little different for a bit, but I'm willing to do anything to make it work."

"Different, how?"

"I need to start writing you a check every week," he said. "I know that makes you uncomfortable, because we've been over this a million times. You can cash them and use them for grocery money if you'd like or keep the money for yourself. Whatever you want to do with it is fine."

"Is this to use in court?"

"Yes," he said. "It will take away Joan's accusation that you and I are romantically involved and that you've just taken Isobel's spot."

Her stomach sank further as she met his eyes, seeing the awareness of what his mother-in-law had said to her. "Pete told you?"

"He did," Ben said with a nod. "I hate that she did that to you, that she said those things. You know how much I appreciate all you've done, right?"

"Yes," she said. "And I love being here with you all. But if you need me to leave, at any point, you just need to tell me."

"I will," he said. "All we can do right now is have pure honesty between us, and fight this together. Pete gave me some more advice, if you're okay with hearing about it."

She nodded, preparing herself by taking a healthy sip of the wine. Ben did the same, then set his glass down and leaned back onto the couch. He ran a hand through his thick brown hair, and she could see the weariness on his face. Worry for him helped her to focus on the issue rather than react emotionally, and told herself to hold it together now, and break down later if needed.

"Pete thinks that Joan or her lawyer will have me, or us, followed," he said. "He said that when we're in public, I should do as much of the parenting as possible."

"Does that mean I shouldn't be seen with you and the boys?"

"No. I asked him that, and he said as long as it appears that I'm the one making decisions and parenting them, it's not a problem for you to be there as well," he said. "For example, tomorrow at the rink, I'll help Dan get ready for his game, and that means I need help with Patrick and Jake. But once he's on the ice, I should manage the other two. Does that make sense?"

"Sure, until you get so into the hockey game that you forget Jake's tendency to wander," she said. Hearing the bite in her voice, she shook her head. "I'm sorry. That came out cruelly, and I didn't mean it to. I just think that it does take more than one person with three young children, especially when one of them is a runner."

"You're right," he said. "I'll have to be more observant, and maybe we can brainstorm some ways to keep Jake entertained. I was thinking about it on the drive home, and I do tend to let you manage them when we're out, and I realize how selfish that is of me. You'd also enjoy watching Dan play, and I haven't been fair in how we've done things. This will help us find a balance."

"You've always been fair, Ben," she said. "You're too hard on yourself."

"No, I don't think I'm quite hard enough. I've been going through the motions for a year now, and letting you hold it all together for me," he said. "I don't know that I've told you how grateful I am. I honestly don't think we would be doing as well as we are without you. I could never repay you for what you've done for me and the boys."

"I get to love them, and be loved in return," she said. "That's all I need."

They sat in silence for a few minutes, sipping at their wine, before Ben let out a big yawn. She laughed and picked up both empty glasses to bring to the kitchen on her way out. "Goodnight, Benji," she said. "I hope you're able to get some sleep tonight."

"You too," he said. "Thanks for not freaking out about this. I promise that Pete will handle it all as discreetly as possible. I don't want this to disrupt our lives."

"I think Joan has other ideas," she said with a rueful smile. "Oh, and I think you've opened up another can of worms with the boys."

"What's that?"

"They are conspiring on how to get the dogs to play hockey," she said. "They're sure they have the next famous dog right here with us. And when Dan and Jake want to work together on something, I'm on board. Even though it means a few days of chaos and dogs barking, most likely."

"I knew I should have rented Aladdin again," he said with a groan.

She laughed and left, placing the glasses in the dishwasher and the half-full bottle of wine on the counter. Turning off the lights, she slipped out the back door to walk the short distance to her cozy little cottage. Once behind the closed door, she finally fell apart and realized that her worst fears could come true. This could all be ripped away from her in an instant, and she was not in any way prepared to lose Ben and the boys.

***

"Stella, the oddest thing just happened." Nancy Keegan, who lived near Ben's house and had a granddaughter in Jake's class, grabbed Stella's arm as they were passing in the grocery store. The older woman tickled Patrick's chin, and he grinned up at her from his perch in the front of the carriage.

"Hi, Nancy," Stella said. "Are you okay?"

"I am, but I'm worried about you," Nancy said, glancing over her shoulder. "I parked just after you and had to make sure I had put my checkbook in my purse, so I was a little slower getting out of the car. When I did, I noticed something odd."

"What?"

"There was a man parked in a car across the street, and he took your picture," Nancy said. "I was going to go confront him, but I was afraid he would get violent."

"Are you sure he took a picture of me, and not the store? Or something else?" Stella glanced around the store, only seeing familiar faces.

"Well, I can't be positive, of course," Nancy said. "But he had one of those long lenses and it was pointed right at you.

He's in a maroon sedan, parked across the way. Look for it when you leave. He might still be there."

"I'll do that. Thanks for letting me know," Stella said. "How is Jenna doing at preschool?"

"Oh, she's loving it," Nancy said with a smile. "She and Jake are just inseparable. It's adorable."

"I'll let you get back to shopping. We have to pick the kids up in just a little while," Stella said.

She continued her trek up and down the aisles, smiling and talking to Patrick as she normally would, with a sense of dread running down her spine. Was this what Ben had warned her about? Did Joan already have someone following her? She wished she could duck into the bank and talk to him, but that wasn't a good idea if there were pictures being taken. Better to continue with her day as if nothing were happening. She wasn't doing anything wrong, and she needed to remember that.

After paying for her groceries, she wheeled out of the store slowly, putting on her sunglasses first to keep her eyes covered. Her gaze swept the cars parked across the street, and sure enough, there was a maroon sedan with the window rolled halfway down. She could see the end of a lens jutting out, pointed in her direction. Loading the groceries in the trunk and then buckling Patrick into his car seat seemed to take an eternity, during which all she could think of was the pictures being taken.

She pulled out of the parking lot and started the short drive for the preschool, noticing that the car pulled out behind her. The school was on the same property as the local golf course, and it had a large parking lot. Rather than pull up close to the school entrance, where she would normally park, she stopped in the first spot in the lower lot, forcing the car following her to have to make a decision. He either had to drive past her and be conspicuous in his car as golfers and parents were milling around, or he would have to turn around. She stood outside the car before unbuckling Patrick, watching as the car hesitated in the driveway. When another car pulled in behind him, the photographer made a wide U-turn to leave the parking lot. Stella allowed herself a moment of pride before turning to get Patrick out of the car to walk in and get Jake from school. One victory, however small, was enough to help her deal with the anger that came from knowing Joan was proceeding with her threats.

Jake was covered in dirt when she entered the school, so they took several minutes to scrub his hands and face before trying to leave. She loved that the school had the kids outside learning most of the day, but Jake was a rough and tumble kid and always came home filthy. She laughed with the teachers that it was a sign of a good day and certainly meant he would conk out for a nap at the same time Patrick did, so she considered it a win. Jake was hungry and anxious to go home, so they gathered his belongings and headed out just as Nancy was coming in to get her granddaughter.

"Did you see him?" she whispered to Stella near the children's cubbies.

"I did," she said. "Although I can't be certain of what he was doing."

"I'll be keeping my eye out," Nancy promised. "I'm not letting any stranger harass you or Ben. Or the boys. They've been through enough."

"I appreciate that, Nancy," she said. "But please be safe. I don't want to cause you any trouble."

"This town takes care of their own," Nancy said. "Don't you worry a bit."

Jake waved goodbye to his friends as they walked out the door. Stella didn't spot the maroon car in the parking lot but still forced herself to walk slowly and not be worried about being visible. She needed to act as she did every day, not like she had done something wrong. Jake was chatting away next to her, so she forced herself to focus on his recitation of his day at school and pushed the photographer to the back of her mind.

Ben arrived home as she was putting the finishing touches on dinner. The boys were all enjoying the last few minutes of daylight, playing on the swing set that had been installed just outside the kitchen window. She could see them the entire time, yet today she had struggled to allow them to play, knowing she would need to go inside before they were ready. Despite sitting out with them for almost two hours, if someone was patient, they would be able to get a picture of the three boys appearing unsupervised.

"Ben, can you bring the boys in?" she asked as soon as he walked in the door.

He paused, hand on his tie, and looked at her. "Everything okay?"

"I'm a nervous wreck," she admitted. "Bring them in, and I'll tell you about my day once they're settled for the night."

He went out the back door and returned, Patrick in one arm and a crying Jake in the other. Dan trailed behind, looking guilty, and went straight to the sink to wash his hands.

"What happened?" she asked, taking Jake from Ben. "Are you hurt?"

"He didn't want to come inside," Dan said, a stubborn tone in his voice.

"And that's why he's crying?" Ben asked, staring at his oldest son.

"Maybe I pinched him. But only because he wasn't listening," Dan said.

"What did I tell you about disciplining your brothers?"

"That it's not my job," Dan said, hanging his head.

"Thank you. I'd like you to remember that. And please say you're sorry to your brother," Ben insisted.

Dan muttered his apology under his breath, but when Ben went to speak again, Stella shook her head. He sighed, then placed Patrick in his highchair while Stella calmed Jake down. They all enjoyed a quiet meal, mainly spent with the boys back on the same team, talking about how they were training the dogs to be their hockey goalies. Ben relaxed as the evening went on, and Stella hated knowing that she would ruin his mood as soon as she shared the details of the photographer. Would keeping it to herself be helpful, or cause more harm?

Chapter 7

Ben found Stella sitting on the front porch, wrapped in a blanket. The nights were starting to get cooler as fall headed towards winter, but it was still their favorite place to unwind at the end of a busy day. The fresh air and sounds of the night always helped quiet his always racing mind, but he could tell Stella was not having the same luck tonight.

"Something is on your mind," he said, settling into the rocking chair next to her.

"You always could read me like a book," she said with a soft laugh.

"Remember the time Bucky Johnson stole your lunch, and you didn't want to tell me?"

"Bucky should have been named Bully," she replied. "Always picking on me, and I never wanted you to get in trouble for defending me."

"I knew with just one look," he said. "I think it took about five seconds for you to tell me, and I had your lunch back in under a minute."

"That boy never did learn," Stella said.

"He had a crazy crush on you," Ben said. "He just didn't know how to get your attention the right way."

"He most certainly did not. He was cruel and picked on me all the time."

"You made him nervous," Ben countered. "He didn't know how to act around you. But the point is, I could always tell when he did something, because I could read it on your face. And you have that same look right now. Did someone steal your lunch?"

She sighed, making him realize this wasn't a lighthearted moment. Something really was upsetting her, and from the look on her face, he wasn't going to like it. She glanced over at him and then fiddled with her blanket as she started to speak. "I went grocery shopping before picking Jake up," she said. "Apparently, a man was following me and taking pictures as Patrick and I went into the store."

"What?" He sat straight up in his chair and peered into the darkness around them, wondering if someone was watching them right now. "Are you sure?"

"Nancy saw him," she said. "She told me inside the store. When I left, I saw him myself. And to make matters worse, he followed me to the preschool."

Ben stood and paced on the porch. "This is ridiculous. They can't do this."

"They can and they are," she said. "We need to be prepared, because I have a feeling this will only get worse."

"Maybe if I talk to them," he said. His stomach was churning, both over what his in-laws were doing and the thought of sitting down with them. But he couldn't allow them to rip his family apart.

"You need to talk to Pete," she said. "Maybe he can set up a meeting with them or find a way out of this."

"I can't lose them, Stel."

"You won't," she said. "If you need me to leave, I will. But I won't let you lose the boys."

He sat back down, wanting the comfort of hugging her or grabbing her hand, but knowing that a picture like that would be used against him in a custody case. It didn't matter that Stella had been a friend for as long as he could remember, or that nothing was happening. Reality didn't matter anymore, just the perception of his grieving mother-in-law and how things might look in a court of law.

***

The meeting was set up for noon on a Monday, a week after Stella had seen the photographer. Pete had spoken to the Brickmans lawyer several times before finally getting them to agree to a face-to-face meeting. Pete was driving, Ben in the passenger seat, nervously bouncing his knee.

"I'm going to go at them pretty hard," Pete said. "I have no problem being their enemy. I know it's going to make you uncomfortable, but we need to make sure they know what it would be like to be in trial with me."

"They are still grieving," Ben said. "Isobel would hate this."

"I know, but she'd also hate your sons being taken away from their home, and the man she chose to have them with," Pete said. "Just try to say as little as possible and let me do the dirty work."

By the time they parked behind the small law office near where the Brickmans lived, Ben was nauseous and fighting the urge to run far away from this meeting. Pete climbed out of the car and grabbed his briefcase from the back seat before meeting Ben by the trunk. "You ready?"

"Not even a little," Ben answered honestly. "But I'm ready for this to be over."

They were greeted by a well-dressed receptionist, who showed them into a small conference room. A coffee station was set against one wall, along with a water bubbler and some pastries. The long table would seat twelve, and Pete indicated for Ben to sit at the center with his back to the window. He poured them each coffee before sitting next to Ben, pulling some papers out of his briefcase. After an agonizing ten minutes, the second attorney entered, followed by the Brickmans. The two lawyers shook hands while Joan and William avoided Ben's eyes.

"Thanks for setting this up," Pete said. "I hope we can have a healthy conversation here that is in the best interest of the children and avoid spending a lot of time in court."

"If that means your client is here to agree to let the loving grandparents raise the children of their deceased daughter," the other lawyer said. "We're all ears."

"Mr. Preston—"

The other lawyer cut Pete off. "Dustin is fine."

"That simply isn't happening," Pete continued as if the other man hadn't spoken. "The boys are well cared for and loved by their father. No one will support them being yanked out of their home."

"You mean by a woman named Stella St. Claire," Dustin inserted.

"Yes, as most single parents do, Mr. Burrows has employed someone to assist in caring for the home and the children," Pete said. "It shows his dedication to both that he was not afraid to ask for help."

"Yet he didn't ask the grandparents for help," Dustin said.

"Nor did they offer support," Pete countered. "As a matter of fact, Mr. Burrows didn't hear from the Brickmans for three months after Isobel tragically passed away. Not only did they not offer to help, but they also weren't there to support their son-in-law and grandsons at the most difficult period of their lives."

"They were grieving the loss of their child," Dustin said.

"Which would make most people move closer to those left behind," Pete said. "They did not. They have seen the boys five times in the year since Isobel passed. I have some questions to ask them now, if you don't mind."

The other lawyer made a gesture that he should proceed, so Pete turned to Joan. "What is the name of the pre-school that Jake attends?"

She stammered and looked at William, who shrugged his shoulders. Pete turned to Ben and raised an eyebrow, so he responded. "Woodside."

"What is the name of their pediatrician?"

Again and again, he grilled them on the names of teachers, favorite foods, bedtime habits, favorite activities, best friends, and more, and the Brickmans were unable to answer. Ben, on the other hand, was able to provide the information without fail.

"You live in an age restricted community, correct?" Pete switched gears suddenly, throwing Joan off balance.

"Yes," William said.

"Is your house on the market?"

William looked confused and looked at Joan before shaking his head. "No, it's not."

Pete consulted his paperwork for a minute, the room heavy with the silence before he looked up again and met William's eyes. "Is this something you want, Mr. Brickman? To return to changing diapers, packing school lunches, doing homework, spending your weekends at youth sporting events? Is this how you want your retirement to go?"

William froze as Joan turned a steely gaze on her husband. "We want to have the boys with us," she responded.

"I apologize, but I asked your husband," Pete said, his gaze unrelenting.

"My wife, uh…" William's voice trailed off, and they all sat waiting for him to compose himself. "She's having a hard time. Losing Isobel has been extremely difficult."

"I assume you recognize how hard it would be if you were a small child, and your mother was gone suddenly? Or if you were to lose your spouse with three young children also depending on you? Do you have any sympathy as to what my client has been going through over the last year?"

"I do," William said, his voice sounding gruff. "I would like to do more to help."

Ben leaned forward, meeting William's eyes. "I'd love for you both to be a part of the boys' lives, and to help as much as you can. But I won't let you take them from me. You have to see that being with me is the best thing for them."

William turned to look at his wife, who sat with her back straight and her arms crossed. Ben started to speak to her but stopped when Pete put a hand on his arm. Pete leaned back in his chair and crossed his own arms, waiting for Joan to look up at him. "Here's where we stand, Mrs. Brickman," he said. "You're a loving mother and grandmother. My heart breaks for your loss, no one should lose a child. That includes my client, who has three you are threatening to take from him. I knew Isobel well, and I know how much she loved Ben and her children. I know with absolute confidence that she would want them to be at home with him. I also know that she would want you to be a part of their lives. How can we resolve this?"

She took a shaky breath and looked as though she wasn't going to answer at first. Pete waited her out, and she shook her head slightly. "I saw what was happening," she said. "At the birthday party."

"What do you mean by that?" Dustin asked.

"That woman is taking my Isobel's spot," she responded.

"No one is taking Isobel's spot," Ben said. "My boys know who their mother is. They miss her and we talk about her every day. Her pictures are on the walls and in their bedrooms. No one could replace her, she created them. But I need help. And Stella was Izzie's friend, and mine, for a long time."

"We should be doing that," Joan said, her chin raised. Everything about her body language suggested that she would still fight him tooth and nail, and he didn't know what she needed to hear to end this.

"But you live hours away," Ben said. "And you have your own lives to live. Izzie was so happy for you both when you retired. She kept saying how you would have a chance to travel and try new things. She wouldn't want you to be going backwards in life, held here for the next eighteen years while the boys grow up. You should be there are grandparents that the boys love, who can show up and spoil them rotten for a day or a weekend."

"What is it that you really want, Mrs. Brickman? Because I don't believe it's being a full-time guardian to three boys under the age of six," Pete said. "What will make this all go away, so you and Ben can go back to having a relationship where you respect each other?"

She stared at the table before looking at William. He shrugged his shoulders and indicated she should talk, making it even more clear to Ben that Joan was the leading force behind this. When Joan finally cleared her throat and spoke again, she was staring right at Ben.

"I want that woman out of your house," she said.

"Not going to happen," he replied before Pete stopped him.

"Ms. St. Claire is acting as a housekeeper and nanny. Mr. Burrows works full time in an executive role at the bank, and is expected to be named president of the bank when the current one retires. He needs help, and this is someone he trusts implicitly," Pete said. "There is no room for negotiation about that. I can guarantee that if Ms. St. Claire was sitting at this table, she would be able to answer every question about the boys that you weren't able to."

"And she'll know even more, since she's sleeping with him," Joan said, pointing at Ben. "In my daughter's marital bed."

"That's never happened," Ben said.

Pete shot him a look before he spoke again. "Mr. Burrows romantic life is none of your business, quite frankly. But if he says that's not happening, I don't know what else would put your mind at ease."

"Promise me," Joan said. "On Isobel's memory. Promise that you'll never get involved with her."

"Why do you hate her so much?" Ben couldn't stop himself from asking. "She's a good person. She was a good friend to Izzie, and she's gotten me and the boys through the hardest year of our lives."

"Because she's alive and Izzie isn't," Joan spit out.

"Mr. Burrows is a young widower," Pete said. "There is a high chance he will remarry. He could even have more children. Do you expect him to live a life of solitude to ease your concerns?"

"No," Joan said with a sniff. "Just not with her."

Ben and Pete exchanged a look, and when Pete stood, Ben did the same. "I think we're done here," Pete said. "If I were you, Attorney Preston, I would give your clients some good advice against wasting money on a trial. We're happy to work out a visiting agreement, and Mr. Burrows has always made it clear that Mr. and Mrs. Brickman are welcome in his home. If they continue to make threats about custody, that welcome will wear out. I would think very carefully before proceeding any further."

Ben followed Pete out of the conference room, looking back one time at his in-laws. William met his gaze, looking ashamed, while Joan cried at his side. Although they didn't speak, Ben took comfort in the small nod William offered him, as if indicating that he would make sure things were resolved. All Ben could do was hope the message was enough to keep anyone from threatening to take his sons away.

Chapter 8

Stella had spent the day anxiously cleaning every inch of the house. She had wanted to take the two younger boys to the playground after school, but the worry about being followed had her bringing them home instead. After feeding them both lunch, they had settled into the playroom before needing naps, leaving her with nothing to do but wait. Knowing that Ben was facing the Brickmans and making a decision that would impact all of their lives was making her frantic, and scrubbing seemed to help.

When the phone rang, she jumped on it, hoping it was Ben back in his office. Instead, her sister's voice came through the line. "How are you holding up?"

"Not well," she admitted. "I'm about going out of my mind."

"No word from Ben yet?" Heather asked.

"Nothing," she said. "I have no idea how long they'll spend at that lawyer's office, or if he will go back to work after. I wish I had a way of knowing what was happening."

"I'm sure Pete will take care of it," Heather said. "He's very good at what he does. I know he seems like a nice guy, but he has a reputation as a shark as a lawyer."

"I just hope he can make this all go away," Stella said. "He's been so anxious. I know he hates thinking that I'm being followed, or that anyone is taking pictures of the kids. This has been a tough week."

"How are you doing otherwise?" Heather asked.

Stella sighed, sitting down at the kitchen table. "Most days are great. I love being with the boys, and I stay busy."

"You aren't regretting this decision? Because this is a good time to make a change if you are," Heather said.

"No, I don't regret it! Why would you think that?"

"I don't know," Heather said. "I've just been thinking of all you're giving up. What about your chance at your own family?"

"We both know why that's never going to happen," Stella said. "Let's not revisit it, please."

"Stella, there is more than one way to have a family," Heather said. "And you deserve love."

"I have so much love in my life right now, more than ever before," Stella said stubbornly. "I've dated plenty and had my share of bad relationships. Ben and I are best friends, and I enjoy his company. The boys bring me so much joy. This is all I could ever ask for."

"Being a nanny? I'm not trying to be cruel," Heather said when Stella gasped. "But it's true. You're there as their caretaker, not their mom."

"I don't know what's come over you," Stella said, feeling hurt and angry. "But this is out of line. I need your support, especially on a day like this. Not to make me feel worse."

"I'm not trying to," Heather said. "I just want to make sure you've thought this through all the way. What happens when Patrick goes off to college? Where does that leave you?"

"He just turned one," Stella argued. "That's a long way off."

"But it goes by so fast," Heather said. "And I don't want you to look back on your life and have regrets."

"The only regret I would have would be walking away from these boys," Stella said. "They need me, and I need them. I would leave if it meant Ben wouldn't have to fight Izzie's parents for custody, and I offered to do so. But he and I both agree that I should stay."

"Just make sure this is fair to you," Heather said. "And at the risk of really putting my foot into it, I have to ask one more question."

"The answer is still no," Stella said.

"I wasn't going to ask if anything has happened between you two," Heather said, laughing softly. "But is that something you're hoping for?"

"No," Stella said firmly. She heard sounds from upstairs and knew at least one of the boys was waking up, so she hurried her sister off the phone. It had absolutely nothing to do with not wanting to admit to herself, never mind Heather, that some days she did have to fight an attraction to Ben. The further they got from Isobel's death, the harder it was to think of him as her best friend's husband.

***

She heard a car door in the driveway a short time before Dan's bus would come up the hill. Peeking out the window, she was relieved to see that it was Ben walking towards the house. There was no way to tell from his body language how the meeting had gone, so she rushed to the door to let him in.

"How was it?" she asked, then kicked herself for bombarding him as soon as he came in the door. "Sorry, I've been a mess all day."

"Same," he said. He pulled off his jacket and hung it in the closet above where he had placed his briefcase and loosened the tie around his neck. "Do you mind if I change quickly, and then I can fill you in?"

"Of course not," she said, waving toward the stairs. "Take your time. The boys are coloring in the kitchen. I'll just check on them."

He came back a few minutes later, just as the bus pulled in and beeped the horn. She rushed to wave to the driver so he would let Dan off, then met the little boy halfway across the driveway. After getting him settled at the table with his brothers, she followed Ben across the large room to stand by the stove where they wouldn't be overheard.

"Sorry, I had to take a minute to process everything," he said. "It was pretty brutal."

"Don't be sorry," she said. "I feel terrible that you're going through this."

"Pete really laid into Joan," he told her. "Asked her a million questions about the kids that she couldn't answer. Then established that they don't even live in a house that the boys could move into, and the logistics of caring for three young kids. William stayed quiet most of the time, but it became clear that this was Joan's thing, and he was an unwilling accomplice."

"Which you had suspected all along," she said.

He nodded and continued. "We really didn't resolve anything. Pete suggested to their lawyer that he give them good advice and share that this was going to cost them a lot of money and not have the outcome they want. I got the sense that William was going to put a stop to it, but only time will tell."

"Did she say why she's doing this?"

Ben hesitated, and she knew instantly. "Well…"

"It's because of me?"

"Partly," he said, nodding. "But that's not all of it, Stel. They're grieving and are a little lost. I wish they had just come to me and asked to see the boys more, or to be more involved in our lives. I don't think I gave them the impression that they weren't welcome, but maybe I did somehow. I think we can fix this without anything drastic happening."

"Why does she hate me so much?" Stella asked, fighting back tears. "I was a good friend to Isobel."

"I can't answer that," Ben said. "It isn't rational. But grief isn't, is it?"

"What happens now?"

"Now we wait," he said. "Pete will follow up with the lawyer in a few days, and if they have agreed to drop it, I'll try to work out a healthy line of communication with them. I don't know how well it will go, but I'll do my best."

"What should I do in the meantime? I don't want to keep the boys cooped up in the house because I'm afraid of being followed," she said. "But I also don't like the idea of a stranger taking pictures of us."

"We're going to assume that has been shut down," he said. "Starting right now, as a matter of fact. Let's take the boys out for pizza and ice cream. We could all use a treat."

She watched as he went to talk to the boys, who all cheered at the idea. She conjured up a small smile when Jake looked her way and nodded when he asked if she would go with them. If Ben was able to put this out of his head and carry on, she would force herself to do the same.

***

Days passed with no word from Isobel's parents or their lawyer. Stella had to stop herself from asking Ben every night as he walked through the door, not wanting to drag him into her anxiety. Thursday night he attended his monthly poker night, and came home after the boys were in bed. She had just settled herself on the couch with a movie and a glass of wine when he came in with a smile.

"They agreed to drop it," he told her. "Pete talked to their lawyer this afternoon, and they said they weren't going to proceed."

"That's great news," she said, hugging him quickly. "Have you heard from them at all?"

"Nothing yet," he said. "I'll give it a few days and then reach out to William. I need to tread lightly, but we need to find a path to being a family again. Whatever that looks like."

He disappeared into the kitchen and returned with a second wineglass, as well as the bottle she had left on the counter. "Do you want to go sit outside? It's not too cold."

She nodded and followed him, frowning when she realized his car wasn't in the driveway. "How did you get home?"

"Pete dropped me off," he said. "After he gave me the news, I may have relaxed a bit too much and was a little heavy-handed with the whiskey."

"You deserve to relax once in a while, Benji," she said. "This has been so stressful for you."

"And for you," he said, holding up his wineglass to toast hers. "I'm so grateful to you for all you've done for us. And for being here, by my side, no matter what."

"I can't think of anywhere I would rather be," she admitted.

"The boys are lucky to have you," he said, slurring slightly. "I'm lucky to have you."

"I feel the same way," she said. "I love them all so much."

"And me?"

"What?" She stared at him, shocked at the question. He was gazing out at the night, squinting as if he was trying to see something in the distance.

"Do you remember when we were thirteen? And you wanted to learn how to kiss?"

"I do," she said slowly, not sure of what direction his mind was going.

"I had never kissed anyone before," he told her, finally meeting her eyes. "I lied to you."

"Why did you do that?"

"Because if I told you I didn't know what I was doing, you would have found someone else to kiss," he said. "And I wanted to be the one."

"But then you and Izzie—"

He laughed, placing his glass down on the table. "Yes, me and Izzie. You were dating that guy," he said, waving his hand. "The baseball player. What's his name?"

"Seth," she said. Ben had never liked him, which had made their shared prom experience tense. She and Isobel had planned the whole night out, expecting the best nights of their lives. Their dates had sat sullenly in the rented limousine, refusing to talk to each other and making it tense for everyone. As soon as they arrived at the venue, her date had insisted they go sit with his baseball team, tearing her away from Ben and Isobel.

"Seth, that's it," he said. "I hated that guy."

"Why?"

"Because of the way you looked at him," Ben said. "You never looked at me like that."

"Ben, you're drunk," she said. "Let's get you upstairs to bed."

She stood and pulled on his hand, stumbling backwards when he stood up quicker than she expected. He caught her, one big hand splayed across her back, the other on her shoulder. He pushed the hair back behind her ear and smiled down at her, pulling her even closer. When he leaned down and kissed her, softly at first and then with more urgency, she could have pushed him away. She should have pushed him away. But what her heart screamed and what her mind whispered were very different things, and it was too easy to listen to her heart.

Chapter 9

Patrick's first day of kindergarten was an emotional day for Ben. His boys had gone five years now without their mother, and they were thriving. Dan and Jake were active around the clock, doing well in school and at hockey. Patrick had completed his first year of learn to play hockey and considered himself ready for the NHL. Surprisingly, both of his brothers were willing to take him out to the driveway and practice, although they refused to help each other. All three were happy, healthy young boys and he couldn't be prouder.

Ben had been promoted at work, and with the additional responsibilities came longer hours. He felt guilty when he was at work that he wasn't with the boys more, and when he was home, he worried about what he should be doing at work. Through it all, Stella had managed the house and the boys, making it seem effortless. He would be lost without her, and seeing her help Patrick with his backpack reinforced that thought.

"You ready, big guy?" Ben kneeled down to ask Patrick, who had a grin on his face.

"Ready, daddy," he said. "I get to go on the bus!"

"Yes, you do," he said. "And your brothers will make sure you get to school okay. When you come home, it's just you and the other kindergarten kids."

"Where are Dan and Jake?" Patrick looked at his older brothers with worry.

"They stay for the whole day, but you get to come home and have lunch with me," Stella said. "Then we can go to the playground to celebrate."

"And get ice cream?"

"Yes, just don't tell your brothers," Stella replied with a wink.

Both older boys let out a yell, unified for once in their complaint that they wouldn't get ice cream. Stella herded them all towards the door, making a deal that if one of them sat with Patrick on the bus, she would take them all after school. They all posed for pictures on the front porch, and then again getting on the bus, before disappearing down the hill.

"It's crazy that he's already off to school," Ben said. Stella was wiping her eyes with a tissue, and he moved closer to check on her. "Why are you crying? He's going to be fine."

"It gets me every year, seeing how fast they are growing up," she said. "But seeing little Patrick climb onto that bus, it took all of me not to drag him off. I wasn't ready."

He hugged her, a rare moment of physical contact between them. For years now, he had made an effort to keep some distance between them, and she did the same. They had settled into an easy rhythm; one he tried hard not to think too much about. After the first night of passion between them, they had decided it was to be forgotten. Unfortunately, or fortunately, it was something they had agreed to forget about several times now. Although a big part of Ben wanted to pursue the feelings between them, the drama his mother-in-law caused gave him pause. And Stella wasn't pushing him to be more, so he left his own feelings on it unexamined.

"I thought the Brickmans were coming this morning?" Stella asked as she pulled away from him.

The reminder of his in-laws was like a bucket of ice water to the face, and he took a deep breath. "They decided against it," he said. "Said they would come to visit over a weekend when they can see the boys more."

"They haven't made much of an effort in the last few years," Stella said. "It's like they forgot they wanted to take them away from you."

"Almost," he said quietly, before pointing at his car. "I've got to run. I'll see you later."

Driving the short distance to work, his thoughts were stuck on Joan and William. Although they had agreed not to pursue custody four years ago, Joan had wanted him to sign a series of agreements. The fight had gone on for two years, with her making ridiculous demands and Pete refusing to let him agree. She started with wanting the boys for two weekends a month, and the entire summer. Then she wanted them for holidays, and was adamant they spend Mother's Day with her, rather than honoring their own mom. When she had demanded he sign an agreement that he wouldn't ever enter a relationship with Stella, he had put his foot down. Refusing to agree to any of her demands didn't make it less suspicious to her that he wouldn't sign that one, and she continued to make his life difficult over it.

When the topic of Patrick's first day at school had come up, Ben had first agreed to them being a part of the occasion. But the more he thought of it, the less he wanted to, because it would have taken away from the moment for him and Stella. It wasn't fair to Stella especially, that she would be expected to miss the milestone of Patrick's because his grandmother would be uncomfortable with her there. It was well past the time for Ben to do something about Joan, and yet he had no idea what his next move should be.

Pete arrived in Ben's office shortly after lunchtime, as if he knew there was something brewing. "Got a minute?" he asked as he walked in, closing the door behind him.

"I guess I do now," Ben said. "Do I even want to know the latest?"

"Fortunately, this isn't about the Brickmans," Pete said. "I wanted to ask you for a favor."

"Anything," Ben said. "I owe you."

"Don't ever agree to something blindly," Pete said with a laugh. "Your lawyer will not be happy."

"In that case, what can I do for you?"

"Erica and I are going to get married," Pete said. "I wondered if you would consider being my best man."

"Of course I will," Ben said, standing to hug his friend. "I'm so happy for you."

"Are you sure it won't cause you any painful memories?"

"It's been five years," Ben said. "And I can be sad when remembering my wedding day while also being happy for you on yours. I didn't think you would ever get married, so this is not something I would miss."

"You and me both," Pete said with a laugh. "But Erica is the first woman who has made me want to settle down. She's pretty incredible."

"And you're getting up there in years," Ben said teasingly.

"I'm younger than you," Pete said with a laugh. "But you're right, it's time for me to settle down. Erica is hoping to do it in the next few months. I hope that's not too fast for you."

"All I have to do is rent a tux and plan a bachelor party," Ben said. "That shouldn't be a problem."

"And bring Stella," Pete said. "Erica is just having her sister, and I'll just have you. We figured most of our friends wouldn't want to be in the wedding party. But she obviously needs to be there."

"Of course," Ben said. Although the words came out easily, he couldn't pinpoint his feelings on the matter. The thought of getting dressed up and going to an event together felt very much like putting themselves on display, and he didn't know how to feel about that. A small-town rumor could easily get back to the wrong ears, and he needed to be very careful.

"You've got a weird look on your face," Pete said. "In-laws causing more problems?"

"No, they've been oddly quiet. I'm bringing the boys to New Hampshire in a few weeks for a hockey tournament, and I feel awful, but I had to ask Stella to stay home," he said. "I rented a three-bedroom condo, thinking she would come, but I know Joan would blow it out of proportion."

"Which we both know she would," Pete said. "But could she just be somewhere else when Joan and William are visiting?"

"That would seem weird for the boys," he explained. "And I don't want to teach them to lie to their grandparents."

"True," Pete said. "But at the same time, I do think that you're letting them dictate your life."

"What do you mean? I barely see them," Ben argued.

"But you would be doing things differently if it weren't for them, wouldn't you?"

"I don't know what you're talking about," Ben said, suddenly wishing his phone would ring or the computer would make a noise he needed to deal with.

"Keep telling yourself that," Pete said. "But you and I both know that if they weren't in the picture, you and Stella would have a much different relationship."

"Why do you say that?"

"Because I've seen you together," Pete replied. "And more importantly, Erica has. And she senses a connection between you two."

"She's a romantic," Ben said lightly.

"Well, she's usually right about these things," Pete responded. "Maybe it's something to consider. You've been widowed for more than five years now. That's a long time for anyone to be alone."

***

"Pete and Erica are getting married." Ben and Stella were in their usual seats on the porch, the house quiet once the boys had gone to sleep. Patrick had been full of stories from his first day at school and had conked out early. The other two were trying to be more grown-up and hide their excitement, but he was happy that all three had a good first day at school.

"That's exciting," Stella said.

"It has me thinking," Ben said. He stood and started pacing along the porch, unable to keep still any longer.

"About what?"

"Us." Ben stopped and looked at her, seeing the surprise on her face.

"Is there an '*us*'?"

"Yes," he said. "Or at least, I want there to be."

"Not just a drunken night once in a while?" Her voice was teasing, but he could feel the hurt that was behind it. The back and forth between them had been going on for so many years. He needed to take a stance.

"No," he said. "Screw Joan. And everyone who might think badly of us. I want to be with you. I was listening to Pete go on about this wedding and wondering why it can't be us? Why isn't it? We could have more children. Give you the daughter you've always dreamed of, to go with these three."

"Benji," Stella said, standing to meet him at the porch rail. "You're not thinking straight. Joan has your head spinning, and now Pete's news. Don't jump to something you don't mean."

"What if I do mean it?" His eyes searched hers, but she was either better at hiding her feelings than he was, or she didn't want him the way he did her.

"Let's take some time, think it over," she said. "See if you really have those feelings towards me because of me, or because I'm here."

"That's not—"

She put a finger over his lips. "I know you would never do that on purpose," she said gently. "But it would worry me just the same. Be sure. You have this weekend away with the boys, it will give you a chance to think things through."

***

"We're going to be late," Dan's voice cried from the backseat. He was sitting directly behind Ben, who was trying to drive as fast and safely as possible to their destination in New Hampshire, where they were due for a hockey tournament. A storm had escalated well beyond what was forecasted, and Ben was stuck between continuing to drive to keep Dan happy or stopping for safety. The wind was pushing the car as rain thrashed the roof, and he could barely see through the storm.

"We still have two hours," Ben said, gritting his teeth. "I can't go any faster and still be safe. I can stop at a hotel, and we can go the rest of the way tomorrow if you want to get out of the car."

"No," Dan yelled. "I have to be there. Who else will score the goals? I told you we should have left yesterday."

"You're ten, Daniel. I don't take advice or that tone from a ten-year-old."

Jake snickered and then cried out when Dan probably hit him. They were separated by Patrick, who had fallen asleep despite being squished in the middle of his two bickering brothers. When they had set out, the trip was going to be an easy two-hour ride, and Ben had hoped the boys could hold it together for that time. He had been wrong.

"Dan, we left very early for this game," Ben said. "If you hit your brother again, I will turn around and we will miss the entire tournament."

Dan sunk down in the seat and pouted, but stayed quiet for the remainder of the drive. When Ben pulled into the ski resort that hosted the hockey tournament, he sighed in relief. They still had plenty of time for Dan to make his game, and they had arrived safely. This was his first time taking the boys away for the weekend without Stella, and he wanted to prove he was capable. Especially because his in-laws lived in the neighboring town and promised to come by each day, no doubt wanting to see how unsuccessful he was at parenting these days.

He needed this weekend to prove Joan wrong. And to prove to himself that he could do this. Not to mention, he had promised Stella to do some hard thinking about the future. It was no wonder the biggest storm of the year had hit this day, when it felt like all corners of his life were coming together to cause turmoil.

Chapter 10

"He said what?" Heather sat frozen, a bite of her salad on the fork inches from her mouth. The sisters were out to dinner at the local pizza place, where Stella had hoped to be able to get some quiet advice. Her sister's loud voice was slightly muffled by the gang of kids playing video games nearby, and it didn't appear that anyone around them had heard.

"Shhh," Stella whispered. "I'm not trying to be the talk of the town."

"Sorry," Heather said, looking around. "I didn't mean to yell. You just caught me off guard."

"Trust me, I know the feeling," Stella said dryly. "You're supposed to be helping me, not making it worse."

"I can't tell you how to feel," Heather countered. "What did you say?"

"That he should take the weekend to think it over," she said. "He's away with the boys. And his in-laws. It should be interesting."

"He won't have time to think," Heather said with an eye roll. "But what I want to know is, what do you think? Or feel?"

"You know how I feel about him," Stella said. "I confessed all my inner thoughts to you months ago."

"Tell me again."

"I've loved him since I was a little girl," Stella admitted. "Foolishly and selfishly."

"Selfishly? I don't think so. I'd say you're the opposite. You never once got in the way of his relationship with Isobel."

"But now, am I holding him back? I feel like I've blocked him from pursuing any romantic life outside of me," she said.

"I thought it just happened that one time?" Heather narrowed her eyes and stared at her. "What exactly is going on between you two?"

"I love him," she responded. "Don't judge me."

"I would never," Heather said with a sigh. "But we need to figure this out. If you love him, why won't you just agree to marry him?"

"First, because Joan strictly forbids him from being involved with me. I'm afraid if we did publicly have a relationship, or certainly if we got married, that she would sue him for custody," Stella said.

"Well, that's absurd," Heather said. "It's been over five years since Izzie died. If she really thought he was unfit, or this was an inappropriate home for the boys, she would have already done something. She can't sue because she doesn't care for his new wife. Although that's odd too, you were always at their house when we were growing up. Why did she let you be there all the time if she didn't like you?"

"That was as Izzie's friend, not as the woman who got involved with her dead daughter's husband."

"Okay, point taken. What else?"

"What would the town say?"

Heather stared at her. "You can't be serious. Who cares?"

"I do," she said simply. "And Ben should. He holds a respectable position at the bank. Gossip isn't good for him."

"Again, it's been five years. He's allowed to have a love life."

"Right, but I've been living with him the whole time," Stella argued.

"In the guest cottage," Heather fired back. "Not the same thing. Everyone who knows you both would know you didn't jump into his bed the minute Isobel died."

Stella gasped. "Do you think people would jump to that conclusion?"

"No," Heather said, laughing. "You're being crazy. You're both grown adults. You were all close friends, and you've been there for him. The only thought anyone should have about it is that they are happy for you both."

Stella pushed the lettuce around on her plate and wrestled with her thoughts. Heather was right, she knew that. But she hadn't voiced her biggest fear, and that was the one holding her back.

"There's something else," Heather said. "Tell me."

"I feel like if I say it out loud, it will be true."

"That's not at all how things work," Heather said. "What is it?"

"What if I'm just convenient?" Stella whispered, fighting back tears. "If this has nothing to do with me at all, but I'm just there and he's lonely."

"You can't possibly think that," Heather said. "Tell me you're not serious."

"Why wouldn't I?"

"Because you're beautiful, both inside and out. You're caring, and kind, and everything good," Heather said. "He should make you feel that way every single day. And if he doesn't, then no, you shouldn't marry him."

The words sat heavy in Stella's stomach, and she wanted to pretend she hadn't heard them. "It's just that we're so busy with the boys," she said. "And I think he's still a little uncomfortable with the whole idea."

"The idea of you and him together?"

"I think so."

"It sounds like you have a lot to talk about," Heather said. "Because I've been married for a while, and we are busy with our kids. But Andy still makes me feel like a desirable woman. Like he's lucky to have me. And I want the same for you."

They finished their meals and headed out into the cool fall evening. "Want to come spend the night with us?" Heather offered as she pulled on her coat.

"No, we have the dogs at home," Stella said. "I'll be fine."

Heather gave her a fierce hug. "Call me, no matter what time, if you need me. Okay?"

Stella nodded and turned to head to her car, trying to hide her tears. Knowing Heather, the phone would be ringing as soon as she walked in the door to check on her. That gave her approximately five minutes to compose herself and find a way to believe that her world wasn't falling apart around her.

***

"We're home!" The excited cry came at the same time the front door opened, and the sound of feet pounding in the hallway woke the sleeping dogs. All three boys came careening into the kitchen, each jostling to be the first to say hello to Stella.

"We won," Dan boasted. "Champions of the whole tournament."

"Grandpa gave me five dollars for my lost tooth," Patrick told her.

"I tried to mountain bike and hurt my knee," Jake told her, pulling up his pant leg to show her a large bandage.

"Well, this sounds like quite the weekend," she said, smiling at all of them. "I can't wait to hear all about it. But first, do you think you should help your dad empty the car?"

They ran out as fast as they had come in, returning minutes later, dragging bags up the stairs. She heard Ben's heavy footsteps following the boys up and felt the butterflies start flapping in her stomach. She wondered if he had made any decisions over the weekend and was anxious either way. Heather had made her promise to be honest with him about her feelings, and it was not a conversation she was excited about.

For so many years, she had been happy to be a little unseen. The second daughter, the best friend. Not someone in the spotlight, or a person who needed praise. But suddenly, she longed to hear that Ben desired her, that he felt the same way about her as she did him. Anything less would be devastating, yet she struggled to tell him that. Speaking up for others was easy, but when it came to matters of her heart, she was too nervous to fight for what she wanted.

By the time he stepped into the kitchen and smiled at her, she was ready to fall apart. Their eyes met, and she was trying to read him when Patrick came crashing through the door. "I have another loose tooth," he declared. "See?"

He opened his mouth wide and showed Stella the tooth that was barely starting to wiggle. "I think it has a few days left, Patty."

"I think I'll eat an apple," he said, choosing one from the basket of fruit on the counter. "If this one comes out, I'll have ten dollars!"

"I don't know that the tooth fairy is going to match what your grandfather gave you," Ben warned him. "What did you get under your pillow?"

"A dollar coin," Patrick said.

"A special dollar coin," Ben corrected him. "If you save that, it will be worth more than the five dollars. I promise."

"But can't I go spend it at the candy store?"

"No," Ben said, laughing. "You can spend the five dollars if you want. As long as you don't eat it all at once. Or rub it in your brother's faces."

"I'll get them something too," Patrick promised.

"The coin can go in a special case," Ben said. "I'll show you. Come with me to my office. And you can see Jake and Dan's too, so you can see what it will look like in a few years."

Patrick raced down the hall, Ben slower to leave. He looked over at Stella and smiled again. "What I wouldn't give for his energy."

"Same," she said lightly. "How was the weekend?"

"I'll tell you all about it later," he promised. "How was yours?"

"Quieter, I assume."

Patrick bellowed down the hall for his father, causing Ben to roll his eyes and Stella to laugh. "My commander awaits," he said. "We can talk later, when the boys are in bed, if you're okay with it?"

She nodded, and he turned to leave. He disappeared, then stuck his head back in the doorway. "I'm very glad to be home with you," he said. He left again before she could respond, which was a good thing, because talking around the lump in her throat would be difficult.

***

Dinner was rowdy, with all three boys trying to talk over each other and share the excitement from the weekend. Stella resorted to passing the saltshaker around the table, indicating whose turn it was to talk.

"And dad said an assist is just as good as scoring," Dan said as he concluded his run through of the championship game. He was the last to share his news and had been as patient as possible while waiting.

97

"It absolutely is," Stella said.

"We talked a lot about how important it is to be a team player," Ben told her. "Not just focus on scoring yourself, but making sure your teammates look good as well. So, I was very proud that he took that to heart and passed rather than taking the shot for that winning goal."

"It was hard," Dan admitted. "But also not. I wanted Sean to get a goal too. He's been working really hard so far this season."

Dan stood to start clearing the plates and kicked Jake's chair to indicate he should help. Jake, who was still eating, turned to glare at his brother. "Knock that off," he said.

"You need to help too," Dan said. "And Patrick should have to. He's not a baby anymore."

"They will," Ben said. "Let them finish eating."

The two younger boys seemed to slow down in their movements, likely to drive their older brother crazy. Dan was someone who liked to go full throttle at something the moment he decided he wanted it, and waiting on them was painful. When they finally finished, he jumped back to his feet and cleared the table in record time.

"All three of you need showers before bed," Ben said. "Plan ahead. I'm not listening to excuses at eight o'clock about why you couldn't shower before I say lights out."

They all raced to the stairs after thanking Stella for dinner, and the room was suddenly too still. Ben sat calmly across the table from her, both hands wrapped around his coffee mug.

"One hour," he said. "Then they'll all be in bed, and we can talk. Okay?"

She took a sip of her tea to occupy her mouth. The questions were burning the tip of her tongue and waiting to hear what he had to say was torture. Nodding at Ben as the boys began fighting upstairs, she forced herself to smile. "Sounds like we need to go on a peacekeeping mission."

"I'll go," he said with a sigh. "You relax."

***

A little over an hour later, she was on the porch, wrapped in a blanket, when he came out. He was carrying a bottle of red wine and two glasses, which he put on the table next to her. "I've been thinking about something all weekend," he said, still standing in front of her.

"What?"

He offered her a hand and pulled her to her feet, kissing her soundly once she was in his arms. "That."

"Oh." She felt breathless and unbalanced and reluctant to let him go.

"You look beautiful tonight," he said, pushing a piece of her hair behind her ear. "But you always do."

"Thank you," she said, ducking her head to avoid showing him how much his words meant to her. They both took their seats and picked up a glass of wine before she asked what had been on her mind all day. "Did you think about things? How did it go with Joan?"

"Those are two broad questions," he said with a quiet laugh. "Let me deal with the Joan situation first. They did come over and visit with us all weekend, and watched Dan's games, which I appreciate. We all had dinner together one night, and I encouraged them to spend time with the boys alone, which they didn't want to do. It was a rough thing to watch, if I'm being honest."

"Why is that?"

"The boys were so excited to see them, and it didn't seem reciprocal. I know it's still hard on them, seeing Izzie's boys growing up without her," he said. "But instead of focusing on the kids, they hid behind their grief."

"That's sad," Stella murmured. "I was hoping they were doing better."

"They're thinking of moving south," Ben said. "Izzie's brother lives in Florida with his wife and kids and has been pushing them to move down. I told them I thought it was a good idea."

"How did they take that?"

"A little suspicion at first," he said. "But then I told them it would be fun for us to visit, and that I was sure they could use the sunshine. They seemed to come around."

"Do you talk to Izzie's brother often?"

"A couple times a month," Ben said. "We usually check in with each other, see what the kids are up to. I know it's hard for him too, but he has been a good friend over the years. He has actually encouraged me to date, unlike his mom."

"Oh, has he?" Her heart picked up pace, wondering where this would go.

"He doesn't know anything about us, so don't worry about that," Ben said. "Although I think that should change. I did spend the weekend thinking about it."

"And?"

"Did you?" he fired back at her without answering.

"I did."

"But you want me to go first?"

She nodded. "Yes, please."

"I want to be with you, Stella. In every way possible. I want you to be by my side as I raise these boys," he said. "I would love to have another baby so you could have your own. I want it all."

Heather's words were bouncing around in her head, making her think of all he hadn't said. Her own insecurities were begging to be spoken, but she couldn't quite form the words. Ben sat, patiently, as she struggled to think of how to respond. Her own inadequacies were at the front of her mind, as she knew she couldn't give him at least a part of what he wanted.

"I guess I'm still not sure," she said finally. "Yes, I want to be with you. But I don't know if that's enough. And I don't think I want the boys to know, or the town. Or your in-laws."

"But it's been five years," he said.

"I know," she said, nodding. "I'm not saying we can't be involved. I just think we need to wade in slowly."

"What can I say that will convince you otherwise?"

She studied her wineglass and took a long sip before shrugging. "I just think we need to be careful."

"And I feel like I'm missing something," he said. "Let me back up. I've fallen in love with you. I rely on you in so many ways, but the biggest is emotionally. You're there for me as a best friend, and so much more. There is no other woman who could ever take your place."

"Can we just keep it between us for now? I promise it won't' be forever," she said.

"We'll officially be together, but no one knows but us? How will that work?"

"Same as it has been, I guess," she said, shrugging. "But without the constant question over our heads about whether we are pursuing a romantic relationship or not."

"I'd rather do it my way," he said, a stubborn look in his eye.

"I know," she said softly. "But if you could take the slower path with me, I would appreciate it. There are some things I need to work through before I can be completely comfortable."

"Do you want to talk about them?"

She shook her head, knowing she could never put her own self-doubts into words. It would devastate him and possibly make him question his own feelings. He was offering her everything she had ever dreamed of, and a part of her wanted to jump fully into it. The other half knew she needed to protect her heart at all costs, even if he didn't understand.

Chapter 11

"Dad, the most amazing thing happened today," Patrick yelled out as he slammed the front door closed. He ran into the kitchen, leaving a trail of snow behind him, eyes alight with whatever news he was anxious to share.

"What happened? Can you take your boots off, please? You're making a huge mess," Ben said. He was sitting at the kitchen table reading the newspaper and sipping a cup of coffee while Stella made dinner, which had become their usual routine. He got home from work and changed, then settled in to keep her company. It was a chance to catch up on the day's events and what was happening with the boys before the true chaos began. Which was happening earlier than usual, based on Patrick's entrance.

"I met a talent agent," Patrick said, toeing off his boots and leaving them in the hallway. "I was working the ski lift, and she stopped and talked to me for a long time. She works in Hollywood, and she wants me to come out to do a screen test! I told her I had to talk to you, but she really, really wants me to come. They'll even buy our plane tickets. Isn't that amazing?"

"Patty," Ben said slowly. "Calm down. This is probably some kind of scam."

"It isn't! She gave me her card. Here," he said, thrusting it at Ben. "She works for the top agency in California. We looked her up. She's legit."

"We can't just drop everything and go to California based on what a random woman said to you," Ben said.

"Dad! You can't say no," Patrick said with a moan. "Please, at least talk to her. I told her where you worked, and she said she was going to come in tomorrow first thing to meet you."

"You what?"

Stella approached the table and picked up the card, studying it. "What did she have in mind for you, Patrick?"

"She said I had the perfect face for a show she was helping cast," Patrick said. "She asked if I had any acting experience, and I was worried about telling her no. But she said it was fine. They would do a screen test and get me into classes if I needed them. But she said the most important part of the role is the look of the actor, and that I was perfect for it. Everything else I can learn."

"They probably tell a hundred people that," Ben pointed out.

"But he'll meet her and hear her out," Stella said, shooting a warning look at Ben. Patrick jumped out of his chair and hugged her, then ran to the stairs.

At fifteen, he was always in motion, a jumble of long arms and legs. Ben had no idea how time had passed so quickly that he now had three teenage boys. He hadn't thought he would survive the first years alone, and now they were all getting ready to leave the nest. Dan was already settled into college in New York, and Jake was going to graduate in a year and head off to school himself. Patrick was the easy-going one, always ready with a smile and to share a laugh, rarely asked for anything. Ben knew that if this was a serious offer, he couldn't possibly say no, when the boy had barely caused him a moment's worry in all these years.

"Ben, I think this might be real," Stella said. "I've heard of this agency before."

"That doesn't mean she's actually affiliated with it," he argued. "I can't imagine some random woman saw Patrick and decided he had to be famous. That seems really crazy."

"Crazier things have happened," she said. "And he is unfairly handsome. Borderline beautiful, you might say, but I'm impartial."

Ben sighed, running a hand through his own thinning hair. "As am I," he said. "I just don't want to get his hopes up for something that won't even work out. I'm sure they play the odds, and tell more kids they have what it takes, expecting more than half of them to not follow through."

"If that was the case, she won't come to see you tomorrow," Stella pointed out. "Let's keep an open mind about it and see what happens."

***

The next morning, Ben arrived in his office early, expecting to get some work done before his usual slate of meetings took place. The last thing he expected was a woman sitting in the reception area of the bank, looking every bit the Hollywood executive that Patrick claimed she was.

"Mr. Burrows?" She jumped out of the chair as he entered the bank, walking towards him with a hand outstretched to shake. "I'm Allison Blake. I met your son Patrick at the ski resort yesterday and told him that I would be in to see you."

"Yes, Ms. Blake, nice to meet you."

"Allison, please." She shook his hand firmly and matched his stride as he continued into the bank. "Do you have a few moments so that we can chat?"

"Yes," he said. Getting this over with was the best way to move past it, and then he could break the news to Patrick that this was not a real thing.

She followed him into his office, waiting for him to place his bag down before taking the seat across from his desk. "Patrick was right about me being able to recognize you," she said. "He told me to look for an older version of himself."

"That's very nice to say," he said with a laugh. "But my son is far more handsome than I've ever been. What can I do for you?"

"I want Patrick to come to Los Angeles for some screen testing," she said. "I know this is unusual, but I believe that he could be the next big star in Hollywood. I've been casting this role and striking out for weeks now, and here I am on vacation, finding the perfect face."

"What exactly would this entail? He is in school right now, and has a lot of commitments," he said.

"A few days to a week to start," she said. "We can try to get him back home as quickly as possible, but I should warn you. The project has already started filming, and we would want him to join as soon as next week if the screen test went well."

"What does that mean?"

"He would join the filming," she said. "The rest of the cast is in place and doing rehearsals now. His character doesn't join until the third episode, so we have a little time, but not much."

"Wait," he said, holding up a hand. "You want him to move to California? And do what?"

"Join a tv show cast," she said. "It's going to be next season's biggest hit. I can already promise you that. We have some of the biggest names in place already, but this one role needs to be an unknown, and no one has fit the bill. Until now."

"Patrick has zero acting experience," he said.

"That doesn't matter," she said. "In an ideal world, yes, he would know the basics. But he has natural charisma, and that comes through on the screen. Or at least, I think it will. The rest we can teach him. A few weeks with an acting coach and he'll be ready to go."

"This seems crazy," Ben said, running a hand through his hair. "Stuff like this doesn't happen in Vermont."

"I know, it was just a great coincidence that I ran into him," Allison said, leaning across the desk to meet Ben's eyes. "I've been doing this for a long time, and I've never felt as strongly about someone's potential as I do Patrick. I'm telling you; he could be the next big star."

"And what if he just wants to be a high school kid?"

"That's fine," she said. "There's no obligation or contract to do the screen test. We would pay to fly you both out, put you up in a hotel, and just ask that he come in for the test. Meet the rest of the cast and see what it would be like. If he decides he doesn't want to pursue it, that's fine. We will part as friends, although I may keep trying to convince him when new roles come up."

"We looked you up last night," Ben admitted. "I was hesitant to believe any of it when Patrick came home. What do we need to do if we decide to let him try this?"

"I'll take care of all the details," Allison said. "I'll have your travel plans made and meet you in California. Would you be able to fly out tomorrow?"

"Tomorrow?" he asked, shocked. He thought he would have a few weeks to think this through.

"Yes," she said with a nod. "As I mentioned, every other part is already cast. We need to get this last role filled, and time is of the essence."

He sighed, glancing down at the calendar on his desk. The rest of the week was light, so he could take a few days off. Dan was away at college for his second year, and Jake was a high school junior craving independence, so neither of his older sons needed him around. "I suppose I could make it work," he said.

"Great," she said. She stood, as if knowing he could change his mind at any moment. "I'll get the travel details sent to you in the next few hours. Do you have a card with your contact details?"

He passed her one, watching as she slipped it into her purse. "I'm going to make some phone calls and then head back to California today," she said. "My assistant or I will send you all the details. I'll have a car pick you up at your hotel the day after tomorrow to bring you to the studio."

"Thanks," he said. He watched her leave and hoped that he hadn't made a huge mistake. This would make Patrick happy, and maybe a few days in Hollywood would make him realize that life as a TV star living far away from home wasn't a great idea. Hopefully, they would be on a plane back to Vermont by the weekend, with Patrick content to continue life as a normal high school student.

***

Four days later, and Ben was so far over his head, he didn't know which way was up. Patrick had been met by several people when they had arrived at the studio the previous day and had been swooped away. The next time Ben saw him was almost two hours later, when he was allowed to take a chair in the shadows of the film set, watching as his son interacted with another actor on camera. Patrick had looked so at ease; Ben immediately knew his life was about to change. They had dressed him and styled his hair, probably had applied makeup to his flawless skin, making his looks stand out even more than usual. Normally the most handsome kid in the room, now he looked like a movie star, and less like a kid from Vermont. Ben watched transfixed as Patrick went through different motions, directed by a man just behind the camera. In between takes, the other actor would talk quietly to Patrick, making him laugh.

After an hour, the actor was replaced by an actress, who Ben recognized from a show the boys had watched as kids. She greeted Patrick with a smile before taking her place and running through the scene. When they were told to kiss, Patrick's hesitation had the actress step closer to him, speaking into his ear quietly and apparently having success in helping him relax.

At the end of the day, Allison approached Ben, along with the man who had been behind the camera. "Mr. Burrows, this is Stan Williams. He's the director of the first season of the series, as well as one of the creators."

"It's a pleasure to meet you," Stan said, shaking Ben's hand. "Your kid is incredible."

"Thank you," Ben said. "Will he be out soon?"

"He's just changing and meeting the rest of the cast," Allison said. "We wanted to talk to you before officially offering him the role."

"He's perfect for the part," Stan said. "A natural on camera, and the other actors loved him. He's exactly what we've been looking for."

"I have to admit, I'm a little lost here," Ben said. "This is so outside my wheelhouse, I don't know how this all works."

Allison nodded and patted him on the arm. "We know," she said. "I already made a call to the most reputable agency in the city, who most of the cast works with. They agreed to have an agent and lawyer meet with you both tonight if you're in agreement. They can guide you through the contract process."

"But he can't live here alone," Ben said. "How does that work?"

"He would need a guardian, or to claim independence," Allison said. "We could have someone help him with the process of emancipation, which would allow him to live alone."

"Absolutely not," Ben said. "He's not moving across the country and living alone at fifteen."

"Understood," Allison said with a nod. "We can work that out. There are several people that I've worked with in the past who could act as his guardian. Or if you have a family member or friend who could live with him, that would work as well. But let's get through the first steps first and see if he wants to move ahead with this before we get lost in the finer details."

They were driven back to the hotel in the back of a Town Car, Patrick gushing about who he had met and what he had done the entire way. Ben listened to his son, feeling numb as the realization hit that no matter what, his life was about to change. There was no way he could say no to Patrick's obvious joy, and no chance he could leave his son alone thousands of miles away.

Chapter 12

The phone was ringing in the kitchen as Stella came in the back door, carrying a pizza box. She rushed to put it down on the counter and answered the phone before the machine could pick up. "Hello?"

"It's me," Ben's voice came through the line, though he was so quiet she struggled to hear him.

"Is everything okay? Why are you whispering?"

"Patrick is in the shower and I don't want him to hear me," Ben said. "I only have a couple minutes to talk to you. This is crazy."

"What's happening now?" Stella asked, pulling a bottle of wine out of the refrigerator and pouring a glass. She and Ben had spoken since he went to California, but only in quick spurts so he could check in on Jake.

"They want him for this role," Ben said. "We're meeting a talent agent and a lawyer for dinner. This is crazy, right? How can I let him do this? He can't live in California, our home is in Vermont."

"Slow down," she said. "Did they tell you how long the filming is? Are you sure he's going to want to do it?"

"Positive," Ben said. "I've never seen him so excited about something. There's no way I can make him turn this down, Stel. But how do I make this work?"

"One step at a time," she said. "Just like we have told the boys for years when they are facing something scary."

"I have a job," he said. "And two other kids who need me."

"Dan is doing just fine in New York," she said. "And Jake barely needs anyone other than Jenna. Those two won't even notice that you're gone, if we're being honest."

"What do I do about work?"

"That I can't answer," she said. "You'll have to talk to the Board, I suppose."

His sigh sounded heavy, even through the phone. "I can't say no to him."

"This is going to change his life," she said. "Unless maybe the show bombs? There's still a chance no one will watch it, and he'll be back home before we know it."

"That's a horrible thing for me to hope for, but it might be the best scenario," he said. "He can always come back this way for college in a few years, if this is something he wants to pursue."

"See how tonight goes," she said. "And go from there."

"Good advice, as always," he said. "He's about to come out now, so I'll have to run. Everything else is good there?"

"Things are great," she said. "I just grabbed a pizza to share with Jake and Jenna, if I can find them."

"Good," he said. "I've got to run. Tell Jake I'll try to call him later."

She hung up the phone and sipped her wine as she looked at the kitchen. It was spotless, as usual, but she wasn't used to it being so empty. The noise of the boys and Ben was absent, as were the backpacks thrown on the kitchen chairs or books left on the table. Normally, Patrick and Jake would come home from school together and regale her with stories from the day while having a snack at the island. Patrick would settle in at the table for homework while she started dinner, and Jake would disappear for a few hours, no doubt with his girlfriend Jenna. The past few days, Jake had done a quick pop-in after school before taking off, and the quiet was driving her crazy.

***

"You seem off," Heather said, as the two sisters at at the bar at a local restaurant. They had decided to meet up for dinner to cure Stella's boredom, and so Heather could hear the latest news from Califirnia.

"I am," Stella said with a sigh. "I don't know why."

"I do," Heather said with a knowing look.

"It's not Ben," Stella said.

"Yet he's the first thing to pop into your mind," Heather said. "You know it is. What's the latest with you two?"

"Still the same," Stella admitted. "We go back and forth between what we should be to each other."

"You should be in a relationship or not," Heather said. "You need clear boundaries. If he doesn't want to be with you, he should set you free so you can date someone else."

"And if I don't want that?"

"Stella, you can't do this to yourself," Heather said. "You've waited all these years. You need to live your life."

"But he's the one I want to be with," Stella said stubbornly.

"And maybe he would come to his senses and think the same if he knew that," Heather pointed out. "But you don't push him. He has the best of both worlds right now."

"He's the one who wanted to be public and get married," Stella said. "I pushed to keep it between us. If we ever did let everyone know, and then something went wrong? I'd lose them all."

"You can't live your life preparing for something to go wrong," Heather said. "You're denying yourself happiness. There has to be more to this."

Stella hung her head, ashamed to answer. When her sister poked her in the shoulder, she turned back to her. "I still worry that it's just convenience," she admitted. "And I'll take him any way I can get him. I don't want to rock the boat. Now please, change the subject."

"Fine," Heather said with a huff. "How are things going in California for him and Patrick?"

"Patrick was offered the role and an unbelievable amount of money," Stella shared. "We're all still reeling from it. They are going to fly home tomorrow and then go back on Sunday. He starts filming next week, and the schedule will be intense. They want him to do acting lessons, plus filming the show, and they'll have him do school with a tutor. It's going to be hard on him."

"And you, having him and Ben gone," Heather said.

"I just can't help but think…"

"What?"

"Well, Jake leaves for college in the fall," she said. "Dan is already gone, and now Patrick will be in California. With Ben, most likely. Where does that leave me? There's no place for me if the boys, and Ben, are all gone. What do I do with myself, then?"

"You've been taking care of them all for so long now," Heather said. "Have you ever thought about what would happen when the boys grew up? Or had a conversation with Ben about it?"

"Not in a long time," she said. "He told me the cottage is mine forever, no matter what. But we never really got into any details. I just can't see myself kicking around lonely while they're all gone."

"The most logical thing would be admitting to the boys that you're in love with Ben and going to California with him and Patrick. But if we aren't going to talk about logic, then you need to find something else to do with your time. You don't need to work, so that's a good thing," Heather said. "I don't believe you that this has been a paid gig anyway, but I know you invested well with Grammy's money."

"It's not like you have to work either," Stella argued.

"No, but I enjoy it," Heather said. "It gives me a few hours away from the house and the responsibilities. I'm not a born homemaker like you."

"And I had other shortcomings that you did well at."

"Don't say that," Heather said, softly chastising her. "I feel terrible that I was able to have children, and you weren't."

"It's not your fault," Stella said. "And I have the boys, so I really have no complaints."

Stella ducked into an open stall, relieved to end the conversation with her sister. Her sister knew what a painful topic it was for Stella. Growing up, everyone had assumed Stella would have a bunch of babies herself, but fate had other ideas. Dwelling on it only caused her pain, and she preferred to focus on what she did have and be grateful for her unorthodox family.

Heather liked to pick at things like a scab, and wasn't happy with Stella and Ben's refusal to have a public relationship. Heather was constantly stating that she didn't understand the need to stay private, and she fully blamed Ben for that decision. The last thing Stella could handle on a night where she was already feeling vulnerable was her sister pushing her hard on any of the feelings she would rather not explore.

***

The next few days passed in a funk, with no clear reason for her bad mood. Even Jake, who normally was easygoing and good company, started avoiding her. It wasn't until late Friday night, when Ben walked in the front door, that she felt lighter. Which then set her off again, because her mood shouldn't be dictated by his presence.

"Hi," Patrick called out, bounding into the room like a puppy. "We had the most unbelievable week. I can't wait to tell you all about it, but I'm starving. It takes forever to fly home from California."

"I made some sandwiches and put them in the refrigerator," Stella said, accepting the hug from the teenager. "I figured you would be hungry, because there is never a time that you aren't."

"I love you," he called out as he walked into the kitchen.

Ben approached her slowly, looking worn out. "How are things?"

"Fine," she said, hating the tone she heard and forcing herself to soften it. "How was the travel?"

"Exhausting," Ben said. "Patty fluctuated between studying the script and wanting me to help him practice and then freaking out about the thought of leaving Vermont."

"It's a big change for a young kid," she said. "Is it official then? He's moving out there?"

Ben nodded, but didn't look happy. "We still have to work out some details, and I need to talk to the school. But we are flying back on Monday so he can be ready on set Tuesday morning."

"It probably would have been easier to just buy whatever you needed out there," Stella pointed out. "Rather than flying this whole way to pack more clothes."

"I needed to see Jake," Ben said. "And go into work and the school first thing Monday to get those things settled. Trust me, the last thing I wanted was a whirlwind seventy-two hours. I tried to get them to give him a week, but they said he's already behind and they need him to start right away."

"Our little Patrick, on a TV screen," Stella murmured. "It's so weird to think of."

"He looked like a natural," Ben said. "Want to come into the kitchen and hear about it? I'm sure he's bursting with the need to talk to you."

She nodded and followed him into where Patrick sat, a plate of food already halfway gone. He grinned up at her with a milk mustache before wiping it away with a napkin, and she had a pang of nostalgia for his toddler days. Why did he have to grow up so fast?

Ben made himself a cup of coffee and sat at the table, listening as Patrick told Stella all about the people he had met and what he had done. When Jake and Jenna came in, the three teenagers moved into the living room so he could tell them about it, and Stella moved to sit with Ben at the table.

"Are you sure you're up for this?" she asked quietly.

"What choice do I have?"

"I could go with him," she offered. "You could stay here and work. Or we could trade back and forth."

"I feel like I need to get him settled first," he said. "But I will keep that in mind. I hated it out there, it's so different. So many people and cars, and it feels like there's no air."

"I'm sure it will be easier when you're not in a hotel," she said. "Maybe you can find a house with a little land."

"The studio is renting a place for us, at least for the filming of this season," he said. "It's only eight episodes to start, and they can double it if it does well. But we won't know that until it starts airing, so that gives us a break. If it gets picked up, then we really have to consider what we will do."

"Meaning what?"

"I either have to quit my job, or consider other options," Ben said. "Swapping with you might work for a few months, but I was thinking maybe either Jake or Dan could move out there? It's not ideal, but there are several good colleges there that would work for either of them, and they're old enough to be Patrick's guardian. And then we could fly out once a month to check on things."

"Jake would just be eighteen," Stella said. "And I don't see him moving across the country without Jenna."

"Which leaves me, you and Dan," Ben said with a sigh. "I hate to ask it of Dan, but it may come to that."

"I really wouldn't mind going with Patrick," she said. "There's not much for me to do around here with you and Patrick gone, especially once Jake goes to college. Maybe it makes the most sense for me to be with Patrick."

Ben sipped his coffee, then sat staring into the mug for a few minutes before meeting her eyes again. "The problem is," he said. "I really didn't like being thousands of miles away from you."

Chapter 13

"Dad, we need to talk," Jake said, standing in the doorway of Ben's home office. "Can I come in?"

"Of course," Ben said. "Want to go sit somewhere more comfortable?"

"No, this is fine," Jake said, settling into one of the two leather chairs Ben kept in the corner for reading.

Ben moved to sit next to him, taken aback by his son's somber behavior. Jake was normally the quietest of his three boys, but he seemed tenser than usual. "What's up? Are you ready to go to school next week?"

"No," Jake said, shaking his head. "That's what I needed to tell you. I let the school know last week that I won't be able to attend after all."

"What?" Ben stared at him in shock. Jake had been talking about attending the University of Vermont for the last year. Jenna had received a scholarship offer that would pay her full tuition and board, and the two were ecstatic that it meant they could go to school together. It was only a short drive from their home in Windsor Peak, so both Ben and Stella could keep an eye on them.

"We're getting married," Jake said. His shoulders were high, as if he were bracing himself for a bad reaction.

"You have plenty of time for that," Ben said. "Jake, you and Jenna have been talking about college forever. You can get married later, when you're both settled into a career."

"No," Jake said. "We can't. She's pregnant, and I'm not making her go through that alone."

Ben felt the air leave his lungs, and he leaned forward to put his elbows on his knees. He had prepared all three of his boys to avoid this exact scenario and couldn't believe this was happening. "Jake—"

"I know," Jake said quickly. "Trust me, I know. But she's happy. We're happy. I want this."

"You're too young to know what you want," Ben said, running a hand over his face. "Jake, this is a huge responsibility. You have no money, no place to live. What's the plan?"

"I'm going to keep my construction job," Jake said. "It pays well. And Jenna is going to keep her job at the market for now. We both enrolled at the community college. Jenna has enough AP credits to get her associate's degree in accounting before the baby is born. And I can do a business degree, and then we can both either transfer for our bachelor's or take turns. She's so smart, it makes sense for her to get hers first so she can be a CPA. But we can do this. She's been so alone ever since her grandmother died. You know how hard it's been for her. And now I can be her family. We can all be her family."

"Where will you live?"

"Her grandmother left her the house, you know that. We talked about whether we should sell it and ask you about living here, but I don't want to intrude," Jake said. "Jenna has a little bit of money put away that her grandmother left for her, and I can work enough to pay the bills." Jenna had lived with her grandmother, who had passed away the previous year, and had no other family that Ben knew of. Her parents hadn't been seen in years, and he doubted they even kept in touch with their daughter. Ben and Stella had offered to take her in, but the local school and some legal advice from Pete had helped her to stay in her grandmother's home even though she was a few months from turning eighteen.

"Of course you could stay here," Ben said. "I'm not going to throw you out on the street. But if you think you can manage a house on your own, I think that's a good place to start. Please let me know if you get in over your head before it's too late."

"I'm sorry, Dad. I know I disappointed you," Jake said, his head hanging low.

"Son, you're doing the right thing here," Ben said. "I'm disappointed for you and Jenna that you need to grow up so fast. But I'm proud of you for stepping up and taking responsibility. This isn't how I pictured your life going, but I know you'll make the best of it. And we love Jenna, you know that."

"I do," Jake said. The teen kept his eyes down, and Ben suspected he was fighting back tears. "She loves you guys, too. She wanted to be here with me, but I told her I needed to face you man to man."

"I'm worried about what it says that you'd be nervous about facing me," Ben said.

"Not nervous," Jake said. "Well, maybe. But not scared of you. I just felt like I was letting you down."

"You couldn't if you tried," Ben said. He stood and gestured for his son to do the same so he could hug him. "I'm always here for you. And even though I'm way too young, the idea of a grandchild is a happy one."

Jake stepped back and wiped his eyes quickly, then gestured to the door. "I'm going to pick Jenna up. We're going to run to town hall and do this."

"Today? Without Stella knowing? You can't do that," Ben said. "Can we wait a few days? Have your brothers come home? And we can do something small, just us if you don't want to have friends there as well."

"Really?"

"Yes," Ben said, feeling more certain when he saw the look in Jake's eyes. "You and Jenna should celebrate, not rush. Why don't you go call Stella and then we can make a plan. Let her know that I'm going to look into flights for her and Patrick to come back for the weekend rather than me flying there to trade places with her."

***

Ben stood with the small crowd outside the airline's arrival doors, waiting for Stella and Patrick to arrive late Friday afternoon. There were more people there than usual, a fact he recognized a second too late, when they swarmed his son the moment he walked through the door. Patrick looked over at Ben and grinned, signing autographs and posing for pictures with young women.

"He can't go anywhere without this happening," Stella told him as she and Ben exchanged a quick hug.

"It's getting worse, that's for sure," Ben said. "Last week he had to sneak out the back door of a restaurant. And that's in California, where they expect to see famous people."

"I think we underestimated how his life would change," Stella said. "Can you help him get out of here? I can't believe I have a wedding to plan in less than twenty-four hours."

Ben laughed and moved to help Patrick disentangle from the young women clinging to him. The show that he had been cast on was a monster success, and overnight, it seemed that everyone knew who Patrick Burrows was. Ben was uneasy about it all, but Patrick was loving every second of his new life. When the series had been an instant hit Patrick had officially withdrawn from their public school system, and now was working with a tutor to finish high school. At the lawyer's suggestion, they had used some of Patrick's income to purchase a home near the studio. The last year and a half had been tough, switching between coasts constantly so he could maintain some normalcy.

Stella chatted as they drove home, telling Ben about her adventures in California over the last ten days. She had enjoyed visiting him monthly, and yet Ben knew she was happy to be back where she belonged. Neither of them wanted Patrick to know how hard it was on them to live so far from Windsor Peak, knowing it would take away from his excitement. But Ben and Stella had started having conversations about how they felt about him living alone when he turned eighteen, both needing that light at the end of the tunnel.

When they parked in the driveway, Dan and Jake were settled into rocking chairs on the porch, awaiting their baby brother. Patrick raced ahead of Ben and Stella, hugging his brothers before sitting in the third chair. The house seemed brighter, with his three boys together, their laughter ringing out across the air. This was exactly what Jake had wanted for his last night before getting married, to have a quiet family night and spend time with his brothers. And it was exactly what Ben's heart needed, to see his three boys together again.

***

The wedding ceremony passed in a blur, at least for Ben, who watched through a sheen of tears. His Izzie would have loved to be here, watching her son become a husband and soon to be a father himself. Even with how young they were, Jake and Jenna were perfectly matched and glowed with happiness. A local judge had come to perform the ceremony, asking Ben and Stella to stand together as witnesses, Dan and Patrick the only other people in attendance. Jenna and Jake had decided against having their friends, who were all packing up to leave for college, which made the ceremony intimate and perfect.

Ben felt Stella's small hand in his as he wiped at his eyes for the tenth time, and the squeeze she gave him showed her support. He looked over at her, tears streaming down her face unabashedly in a show of love for the couple, and his own heart gave a small stutter. How many years had they wasted, next to each other, holding each other up, yet denying their love to everyone else?

The question and strange feelings kept him on edge as they enjoyed a meal together before Jake and Jenna departed to spend their first night as a married couple at the local Inn. Ben had gifted them the night at Stella's urging, so they could mark the occasion before moving on to their real lives. Patrick has one-upped him, presenting them with an all-expense paid trip to Hawaii, which stunned everyone.

"Hey, if I have it, the least I can do is give a nice gift," he said shyly, blushing as everyone gaped at him. "Besides, Jenna deserves a nice treat. She has to live with Jake from now on."

Jenna had leaned over and kissed him soundly on the cheek, making him blush more and the rest of the table laugh. Dan sulked for several minutes before presenting his own gift, which was a weekend in New York, staying at his small apartment. Jenna was equally thrilled and thanked him effusively, bringing a smile back to Dan's face.

Once the newly married couple departed for the Inn, Dan and Patrick decided to head into town to see what friends they could find. Ben knew full well that Dan was seeking out the girlfriend he had left behind, but knew better than to say anything. Dan would learn at his own pace, much like Ben himself.

Stella held up a bottle of wine and gestured to the porch. "Want to finish this with me and look at the stars once I've cleaned up in here?"

"Sounds perfect," he said, trailing behind her. A nervous energy had taken over him, and he wondered if she could feel it too. Or was it just him that was aware of this change happening between them? Was there a chance she didn't share his feelings?

He took a step towards where she stood at the kitchen sink, washing a serving tray. Her hands were wet and covered with bubbles, and she looked up in surprise as he got close to her. Before he could lose his nerve, he took her by the shoulders and kissed her. He heard the soft gasp from her lips just before his own touched hers, and it encouraged him to continue. Her sudsy hands reached around him, soaking through his shirt as he pulled her closer.

"I need you, Stella," he said, resting his forehead against hers. "I think I'm in love with you. It hit me like a Mack truck when we were watching the kids say their vows, and you took my hand. I've been an old fool, and I know it. Will you give me a chance to fix it?"

"I think I need that wine," she said. "Let's go sit down."

Chapter 14

Waiting for Ben to speak was agony, but Stella knew she had to let him lead this conversation. For years now, she had taken the pieces of him that he offered. Stolen nights together without professions of love, a relationship that only they knew about. Isobel felt further and further away as the days turned into years, and it was hard to remember why they had to keep things between them private. But the longer it went on, the less secure Stella felt in his feelings for her.

"Years ago, when I was fighting with Izzie's parents over custody," he said finally. "The one thing that Joan was adamant about was that you should not take Isobel's place. I don't know why, or what she had against you other than you being alive and Izzie not, but she stayed mad for years. Every few months I would get a letter from her, telling me that if you didn't move out, she would start the custody process. I would have to go talk to her, convince her that the boy's having a steady presence in their life was the right thing for them. And assure her that you and I were not involved."

"Why didn't I know about this?" Stella was shocked. She knew that Joan had pressed Ben about it early on but had no idea it had continued.

"I knew it would cause you pain," he said. "And I didn't want you to think you should leave. I loved having you here, and the boys wouldn't be who they are without you. I thought that if you knew about her threats, you would end things between us, and I couldn't live with that."

"I had no idea she hated me so much," Stella said.

"I don't know that it was you, specifically," Ben said. "Any person who was in what she considered Izzie's spot would be her enemy. And when she was dying, she made me promise."

"Promise what?" Stella stared at him, knowing already what he would say. Joan had passed away just before Patrick began kindergarten, a brief battle with cancer had ended with hospice after just a few months, and Ben had taken the boys to spend the last few days with her.

"That I wouldn't get involved with you," he said. "That I wouldn't fall in love again."

"That's absurd," Stella said. "You're still a young man. No one should have asked that of you. And you shouldn't have promised it."

"I only planned to keep half of it," he said. "But the guilt over the last few years has made me inadvertently let her dictate my life from beyond. William had given me his blessing a long time ago, thanking me for giving her peace as she died, but he never expected me to keep the promise."

"Why would you only keep half of it?" Stella couldn't help but ask.

"It was a technicality," he said. "At that point, I was already in love with you. So, falling in love was out of the question. She didn't ask me not to love you."

Stella stared at him, hyper-aware suddenly of everything around them. The chirp of crickets in the grass, the soft noises the horses made in the barn, her own heart thumping against her ribs, and the way that Ben searched her eyes, waiting for a response.

"Are you saying—"

"That I love you," he said. "I'm saying it's been this way for so many years, but I was refusing to let myself see it. I can't believe I'm saying it out loud now. I don't want to keep going the way we have been, I want the world to know how I feel. I don't want another minute to go by without claiming you as my own. We kept our relationship secret all these years worrying that it might impact the boys, but we should have been honest. And now that I can honestly say that I can't live without you, I want us to be together. The right way."

"Think about Patrick," she said gently. "If he thought he was keeping us apart, he would go crazy. And he's so happy, we can't take that from him."

"We can both go to California," he said. "There's no reason one of us has to stay here, if Jake is living at Jenna's and Dan is at school."

"You have a barn full of horses who would say otherwise," she reminded him. "Not to mention a house, and I think Jake and Jenna will need more support than you realize."

He reached over for her hand, which she gave to him. "We need to find a way to work this out," he said. "Please. I'll get someone to care for the horses, and we can come home once a month to check on things."

"Benji, I wish it were that simple," she said. "It kills me that it's not. But we've lived like this for almost seventeen years now, and now is not the right time to rock the boat. What if we tried being open about the relationship and something went wrong? I can't risk losing your friendship and losing them."

"You wouldn't," he said. "Why would you even say that? You know me better than that. And you certainly know how much the boys love you."

"But they also love you, and you're their dad," she said. "If things turned sour between us, of course they would choose you."

"That's never going to happen," he said, a familiar stubborn set to his eyes. "First of all, I know that we'd be together forever. And secondly, I will always be your friend. I told you that the cottage was yours forever, and that will never change."

"Oh, that wouldn't be awkward at all," she said with a quick laugh. "Your ex living a few feet from the kitchen where you're having a meal with a new girlfriend."

"I am being sincere when I say that I love you, and that I want to spend the rest of my life with you," he said. "Are you saying you don't feel the same?"

"I don't doubt your sincerity. And of course I love you," she said. "But I have doubts about how this would work. We've had our nights of passion, and there's no doubt that we have chemistry. And you're my best friend. On paper, it would work out perfectly. But I'm scared of so many things."

"Tell me what they are," Ben said. "At least one, so I can help."

"What if it's not all you think it is," she whispered. "What if you think you love me because I'm here? Because we know each other so well?"

"That's how I know I love you," he objected. "Because you're the person I always want to share things with. And when Joan made those threats, and I had to picture my life without you, I couldn't."

"I'm still worried about the kids, and how this would rock their worlds," she said. "I know you think they'd take it in stride, but I'd be replacing their mother. My entire place in their lives would change, and that's a lot when they already have a lot on their plates. Dan is away at college and still struggling over his breakup with Kendra. Jake is newly married and learning to be a husband and father. Patrick is away from his home, figuring out how to deal with his fame and wealth while living in an unfamiliar place. They all need you. They need us."

"We should sacrifice our own happiness for theirs?"

She sat staring out at the night as his words swirled in her head. This was what she had wanted for so many years now, making it painful to try to deny it. Tears slipped from her eyes as she considered all the possibilities, and Ben stood, gathering her in his arms. They held each other for what felt like hours before he pulled her into his lap on the rocking chair, kissing her softly at first, then with more desire.

Pressing gently on his chest, she pulled back to look in his eyes, seeing nothing there other than love and tenderness. "We'll wait another year, and then tell them," she said. "I'll come out to California as much as I can, and we can see how we do really taking this seriously."

"Deal," he said, jumping to his feet with her in his arms.

"Where are you going?" she asked with a laugh as he ran towards the door.

"Upstairs before you change your mind," he said.

"Not your room," she said quickly. "They could come home at any minute. My cottage."

***

"Dad, where did you go last night?" Patrick asked, between bites of the pancakes he was shoveling in.

"What do you mean?" Ben asked, shooting a furtive look over at Stella as she carried over a plate of bacon.

"Your door was open when we got home, and you weren't there," Patrick said. "Not like you to be out late."

"We went over to Heather's," Stella said. "They were playing cards, and we missed curfew."

Dan and Patrick laughed and went back to discussing their exploits the night before, while Ben shot her a look of thanks. She sat to eat with them, listening as Dan teased Patrick about his groupies in town, and Patrick gave it back to him for his puppy dog stares at Kendra all night.

"Danny, why don't you just talk to the girl," Ben said. "I don't understand why you broke up with her to begin with."

"It just wouldn't work," Dan said. "And besides, it's fine. I wasn't looking at her."

Patrick laughed and clapped a hand on the table. "That's the best thing I've heard all night. You did nothing but look at her."

"That's enough," Dan growled at his brother. "You couldn't even see me through the crowd of girls around you."

"Where exactly were you?" Ben asked.

"There was a party by the lake," Dan said. "Mostly high school kids, but a few people I graduated with."

"Like Kendra," Patrick said.

"I used to like you the best," Dan said. "I'm questioning that now."

Patrick carried his plate to the dishwasher, still laughing. "Dad, do you mind if I take your truck to the gym? I need to work off some of these calories."

"I'll take you," Dan said. "I have some time before I need to head back to New York."

"We have to leave for the airport at one," Ben called out as they headed to the door. "Don't be late."

The door closed behind them, leaving Stella and Ben in a sudden silence. Stella moved to stand up, but his hand on hers had her sitting back down. "You okay?" he asked, his voice soft.

"I think so," she said. "You?"

"I have no regrets, and I stand by everything I said last night," he said. "I want this to work."

"At least we both have some time to think about it," she said. "You'll be in California for the next two weeks, and I'll be here."

"I wish you would come with us," he said.

"No," she said, shaking her head. "I don't have time to get things in place here. It's only two weeks. We can make it."

Ben nodded, but didn't look happy. "I guess that's true. But when I come home, I'm going to convince you to tell them. I know I agreed to a year, but I can't keep pretending I don't want to kiss you when they're in the room."

"If you help me clean up the kitchen, we'd have at least an hour before the boys come back from the gym," Stella said. She laughed when he jumped to his feet, stacking plates to carry to the sink. She did the same, and in no time, they had the space spotless. Ben tugged on her hand, pulling her toward the stairs, but she pointed out the door. "My place."

"Okay," he said, laughing as he followed her. "Whatever you say."

***

Hours later, the house was empty, and Stella felt more out of sorts than ever before. She was used to being in the home when everyone was off in different directions, but the finality of it was throwing her off balance. Jake and Jenna were settled into her grandmother's house, excited about their upcoming trip. They didn't need her, and she wouldn't intrude on their first days living together. Dan had driven back to New York alone, looking sullen and in a foul mood, but had refused to discuss it, so she didn't want to push him by calling. Ben and Patrick still had hours left in the air, which left her truly alone.

Ben's words the previous evening and again this morning were rattling around in her head, seeming to get louder with each hour that passed. If he loved her and she loved him, why was she worried? The boys were old enough to understand that she wasn't trying to replace their mother, and surely no one in town would care. If she could only quiet that little voice inside her head so she could hear her heart, maybe she could finally have the life she had always dreamed of.

Chapter 15

"Ben, something terrible has happened," Stella's voice came through the phone line, followed by a choked sob. He jumped to his feet and grabbed his car keys, as if he was in Vermont and not thousands of miles away in Patrick's dressing room in California.

"What is it? Are you okay?" He jumped to his feet and started pacing the small space. Patrick had had it set up with a space for a small desk that Ben used to do some work, as well as a comfortable couch for watching movies, playing video games, or napping, which Patrick did frequently. Fortunately, he was filming on set now, so Ben didn't have to worry about disturbing him.

"I'm okay," Stella said, another soft cry following the words.

"Is it Charlie?" Jake and Jenna had their son three months before, and the entire family was in love. The tiny infant had his grandfather, uncles, and Stella all wrapped around a pudgy finger.

"No, he's fine," she said. "He's in New York with Jake. It's Jenna, Ben. Have you had the news on?"

"No, we only just got to the studio," he said. "I was logging into my email when you called. What is it?"

"There was a terrorist attack this morning. Dan just called to tell me they can't find Jenna, and believe she was caught in it," Stella said.

The words hit him like a freight train. Sweet, innocent Jenna? The girl with golden hair and bright blue eyes that had a smile for everyone? She couldn't possibly be taken from the world in such a cruel way. "She must be at a hospital," he said. "I'll start making calls from here."

"I'm saying prayers and have all the women from church doing the same," Stella said. "I'm going to drive down to get Charlie so that Jake and Dan can search for her."

"I'll fly there," he said. "I don't want you to go."

"Benji, that would take at least twelve hours," she said. "I can be there in four, maybe a little less. Dan has a school friend with Charlie now, but we'll all feel better when he's with me."

"I don't want you to walk into a city that is under attack," Ben said. "Please, let me find someone else to go."

"Ben, I'm a big girl," she said. "And the boys need me. You can trust me."

"I do," he said. "But I can't lose you."

"You won't," she said. "The attack happened miles from Dan's place, at the subway station where Jenna would have gotten off for her training. I won't be in any danger, I promise."

"The boys—"

"I know," she said, cutting him off. "I talked to Dan. He swore they would be careful and avoid any public transportation."

"I need to get there," Ben said.

"Stay put for now," she said. "If you jump on a plane, we'll have no way of contacting you if we find her."

"When you find her," Ben corrected her. "Stay positive."

"I'm trying, Benji. But if you heard Jake screaming when Dan called me—"

"I can imagine. I'm sorry," Ben said. "I hate this for all of you. I'm going to try and call Dan now."

"You might not be able to get through, so keep trying," she said. "I'm heading there now and will call you as soon as I know more."

Ben tried to call his son's, but both phones went straight to voicemail. He started calling everyone else he knew that might be able to get him information, hoping someone would be able to help. He was talking to the town sheriff when Patrick came into the room. The teenager frowned at his father but waited until he hung up before speaking.

"What's up?"

"Nothing to worry about, Patty," Ben said.

"I can tell you're upset about something," Patrick said.

Just as he spoke, Ben's phone rang, showing Dan's number on the screen. He held up a finger to Patrick as he answered. "Dan. Any news?"

"No," Dan said. "I don't know what to do. Jake and I are just going from hospital to hospital and checking with the police. We can't find her."

"Are there unidentified victims? Can you ask that?"

"I did," Dan said. "The hospitals all say they have unconscious victims who haven't been identified, but no one fits the description. Jake has a picture of her that he let the police copy, and they gave us a bunch to hand out."

"That's good," Ben said. "You'll have to keep looking. Stella is on her way, you know that?"

"Yes," Dan said. "I have a friend at my apartment with Charlie. She babysits all the time and didn't mind. She'll stay with him until Stella arrives."

"Is it safe for you two? And Stella?"

"The police said they believe this was a targeted attack," Dan said. "But they have most of the city shut down while they investigate. No one really knows anything. But I can't convince Jake to sit and wait. He is desperate to find her."

"Of course," Ben said. "Can I talk to him?"

"Dad," Jake's broken voice came over the line. "I need to find her."

"I know, son. Try to stay calm, and listen to your brother," he said. "We're saying prayers, and Stella is on her way. As soon as I can, I'll be there."

"She has to be okay," Jake said. "This is all my fault."

"It's not," Ben said. "There's nothing you can do now to change what happened, so stop that thinking right now. Focus on finding her and stay positive."

The call dropped and Ben stared at the phone for a moment before turning to Patrick. Sharing the news with him brought them both to tears, and he embraced his youngest son tightly. "They'll find her," he said, his voice sounding gruff.

"I can help," Patrick said, wiping his face with his sleeve. "Let me do something."

"We can't go there right now," Ben said. "There are no flights into New York airports, and we don't want to be in the air when they find her."

"No, I can help from here," Patrick said. "Hang on."

He disappeared from the dressing room and ran back in ten minutes later. "Do you have a picture of her?"

Ben frowned, then glanced at his laptop. "I think we have some from when Charlie was born," he said. "But I don't know where we can print it."

"That's okay, just email me one, and copy my agent," Patrick said. "Then come with me."

Ben quickly selected a photo and sent it off, then followed his son out of the room. There was a small crowd gathered near the offices, and they all stopped talking when Patrick appeared. Ben recognized the public relations executive that was assigned to the show, Patrick's agent, and a handful of others who were part of the network.

"Are we ready?" Patrick asked.

"Yes." Ed Stanley, the head of the public relations team, put a hand on Patrick's shoulder. "We have a camera set up right outside, and we'll send it to the major news networks. That will be quicker than trying to get the press here. There were a few reporters on set for different interviews, so I'll have you talk to them briefly after we record this. Will your father be joining you?"

Patrick looked at Ben and then shook his head. "No, let's just keep it me. He's not used to this."

Ben followed the crowd as they passed through the doors, where even more people were waiting. A camera operator that Ben recognized from the set was patiently waiting, the camera on his shoulder, as a sound technician clipped a microphone to Patrick's collar.

"Can we get hair and makeup?" Ed called out, and Patrick shook his head.

"We don't have time for that, and it doesn't matter," Patrick said. "Let's just do this."

"It's your image—"

"This is my sister we're talking about," Patrick said, his voice sounding steely to Ben's ears. "I'm not wasting any more time."

Ed stepped back, and Ben felt a surge of pride at how in control of the situation Patrick was. He spoke with calm confidence into the camera, explaining where Jake thought Jenna would have been at the time of the explosion and asking anyone with any information to call the number on the screen. When he finished, he stepped back and huddled with the team again before turning to Ben.

"You ready to go?"

"Go where?"

"To New York," Patrick said. "We're either going to find her or be there for Jake."

Ben climbed into the waiting SUV behind Patrick, and was surprised when Ed followed them in. The other man shrugged at Ben's expression. "I'm from New York," he said. "I might be able to help. The studio provided a private plane, so I thought it would be better for me to join you. One way or another, having another set of hands will help."

Ben nodded and clipped his seatbelt on, putting his head back against the rest. None of them had packed a thing, and he wasn't entirely sure that they would be allowed to land when they got there, but he was happy they were going to try. He wanted his entire family together in this crisis, and if that meant jumping through hoops to get to his family, he would do so.

Fortunately, Patrick's employers had taken care of everything and had them land at a private airport just outside the city seven hours later. They disembarked and were swept into another waiting car, which followed a police escort into the city. No one told them anything, so they were shocked when they were delivered to a hotel in Manhattan, where Jake, Dan, Stella and a sleeping Charlie were waiting in a suite.

"I'm going to get on the phone in the room next door," Ed said, after shaking hands with the boys and kissing Stella on the cheek. "See if anything came through on the tip line that we set up. If you hear anything, just yell and I'll be right in."

Ben embraced Jake and felt the tension from the day seeping out of his body. He cried with his son, hearing similar noises as Dan and Patrick greeted each other and then Patrick fell into Stella's waiting arms. Jake was pale, his eyes red and empty, and his voice raw when he tried to speak. He looked broken, and Ben's heart ached at the sight of him.

"No news is good news, right?" Ben asked gently, trying to bolster him up.

"I don't think so," Jake said. "You know she would have tried to reach me by now."

"But what if she's unconscious?" Patrick asked from across the room. "Ed was saying how many hospitals there are, and they were probably moving so fast because they didn't know if something else would happen. She has to be okay."

"What do I do, Dad?" Jake's voice broke on the question, and Ben felt his eyes fill again. His middle child, who rarely asked for anything when he could do it himself. The one who made an effort to solve problems for other people, and loved construction because it gave him a way to help others fix things. Who had stepped up and changed his life plans to be there for the girl he loved and take responsibility for their mistake. Could he really be learning life's hardest lesson at such a young age?

"We need to pray," Ben said. "And wait."

"Don't you think I should be out there looking for her?" Jake's voice was ragged, the pain evident.

"I think it's better to stay put," Ben said. "We have the police looking, and all the hospitals are starting to send updates. I wouldn't want you to be on the wrong side of the city when we find out where she is. Let's sit tight for now."

Jake returned to his seat, elbows on his knees and hands on his head. His brothers sat on either side of him, silent but present for him. The sign of solidarity was almost enough to bring Ben to his knees, but before he could give in to his grief, he met Stella's eyes. She nodded to the kitchen, indicating he should follow her into the small space.

As soon as they were behind the wall, she fell into his arms. "Oh, Benji," she cried softly. "We can't lose her. She just had a baby. She was so happy."

"I hope she's being worked on somewhere, and they just haven't had time to figure out who she is yet," Ben said.

"But you don't think that, do you?" Her tear-filled eyes met his.

He shook his head slowly and embraced her again. "No," he said. "I don't. But if he can have this little bit of hope before his world comes crashing down, I want to give him that. And what if I do suggest she's gone, and then I'm wrong? I can't do that."

"No, we'll just have to wait, and hope for the best," Stella said. They held each other for a moment longer before she pulled back and looked at him. "I've missed you."

"Same."

"You look tired."

"Thanks," he said with a dry laugh. "It's been a day."

"I worry about you," she said, waving away his attempt at humor. "This travel is getting to be too much."

"We can't worry about it now," he said. "Let's get through this, and then we can figure something out. Maybe we should tell the boys about us now instead of waiting longer, and you can come to California with me."

"Patrick is almost eighteen," Stella said. "And we don't know how much longer the show will run. I don't want to disrupt their lives when we could be back to normal any day now."

"What's normal?" He glanced over her head at the door and leaned down to kiss her quickly. "I have a feeling our lives will never be anything close to normal again."

"Another good reason to wait," she said. "If the worst is true, Jake will need us more than ever. We can't be flaunting our love in his face when he has just lost his wife. But we'll figure it out. We always do."

Chapter 16

"Can I talk to you both?" Jake's voice broke through Stella's focus on the dough she was kneading. Ben had been reading the paper at the kitchen table, keeping her company. She had thought they were alone in the house, but Jake must have come in quietly. Ben pushed his chair back and stood to hug his son, talking to him quietly as he did.

She dropped the dough into a greased bowl and covered it with a towel before washing her hands, then finally crossed the room to hug Jake. He had lost weight in the last few weeks, since losing Jenna, and she could tell by the dark circles under his eyes that he wasn't sleeping.

"Come sit down," she urged him. "I'm going to make you a cup of tea."

"No, thanks," Jake said. "Please, sit with me."

"Where's Charlie?" she asked, glancing toward the front door.

"I had Patrick come over," he said. "I wanted to be able to talk to you two without distraction."

"What's going on?" Ben asked, leaning closer to Jake.

"I enlisted."

"You what?" Stella stared at him in shock as the words came out.

"I have to go fight back," Jake said. His eyes filled with tears and he appeared to be fighting them with a deep breath.

"They took her from me. From Charlie. I have to make them pay."

"Jake, no," Stella said. "You have to be with Charlie."

"I will be," he said. "They have childcare on post. I just need to do boot camp first and then he can come with me. I was hoping you could watch him for a few weeks. Please, Stella. I know this will be hard because Dad and Patrick are leaving, but I need this."

"Jake," Ben said. "We completely understand how you must be feeling. When I lost your mom, I would have done anything to make that grief go away. But nothing I did would have changed things. The only thing I could do was focus on being the best dad for you all, because I was all you had."

Stella bit her lip, trying hard to ignore the dagger those words brought to her heart. Focus on Jake, she told herself. There would be time later to think about Ben's comments.

Jake was shaking his head. "I can't do that, Dad. She was special, and they took her away. I can't sleep, I can't eat. It's all I can think about."

"Some counseling—"

"No." Jake cut his father off with a sharp word. "That won't help. This will. I need to go punish the people who did this."

"Is that really what you think she would want?" Stella asked, placing a hand on Jake's arm. "Think about it. She was so loving and kind, violence wouldn't be her answer."

"It's done, Stella. I have already signed the paperwork, and I leave tomorrow. I just need to know if you'll watch Charlie for me, or if I need to figure something else out."

"Of course I will," she said. "You know how much I love him."

Jake stood to leave, and although Stella tried to will Ben to get to his feet, he remained in his chair, staring at the table. She ran down the hall to catch Jake before he opened the door and wrapped her arms around his waist. "You promise me that you'll stay safe."

"I can't promise that." Jake said, his voice pained. "But I'll try my best."

"You have a little boy to come back to," she said. "Never forget that."

Jake pulled a picture out of his wallet, of himself sitting behind Jenna, who held a newborn Charlie. "I'm bringing them both with me," he said. "I'm doing this as much for him as for Jenna. He can't live in a world where people like her are killed."

"Do you want me to come over and help you pack everything up?"

"No, thanks," he said. "I'm almost done. I have to leave early tomorrow, so I thought he and I would come back later and stay here?"

"Of course," she said. "His room is all set up already. Thankfully we had the crib set up when we decided I would watch him while you both worked. I'll just need some clothes and toys, anything you think he might need."

Jake nodded and swiped away a tear, then pulled the door open to leave. "I'll be back in a few hours. And I'll tell Dan and Patrick about this."

Stella watched him leave and quietly closed the door behind him, pausing to gather her thoughts before going back to see Ben. The last few weeks had been so hard on all of them, and the hits just kept coming. Finding out that Jenna had not survived the bombing, and helping Jake plan a funeral for his young bride. Watching as he adapted to being a single parent, when he had barely started learning to do it alongside his wife. It had been emotional and difficult, and this blow might be more than any of them could handle.

Ben was pacing in the kitchen when she returned. "I could make some calls," he said. "I know the Senator. I'm sure we can get this turned around."

"And then what?" she asked, moving to turn the kettle on for tea. "He'll be angry at you and find a way to do it anyway. He's an adult, Ben. We can't stop him."

"He has his own child to worry about," Ben said. "He needs to be here for Charlie."

"I can do that," Stella said. "You know that's not a problem."

"We just finished raising kids."

"First of all, you never finish," she said. "Secondly, what is the alternative? Force Jake to stay here, make him resent us and his own child?"

"He might come around and see that we helped him make the right decision," Ben said, a familiar stubborn look on his face.

"Or he could hate us forever. Benji, you of all people know what he's feeling right now. Why don't you talk to him?"

"I've tried," he said with a sigh. "He shuts it right down. Refuses to talk about what happened, or about Jenna at all, never mind about how he's feeling. You know he's always been the most difficult to get anything out of and that was before this."

"I know," she said. She poured boiling water into two mugs and dropped tea bags in before crossing to sit next to him at the table. "I know this isn't really the time, but I have to say this now to get it off my chest."

"What?"

"Earlier, you said to Jake that you were all they had," she said. "I know you didn't say that to hurt me, but it did. Because I've been there for the boys every step of the way."

"I'm sorry. I didn't mean it that way. I just meant as their surviving parent," he said.

"I know I didn't give birth to them, and I don't want to take Isobel's role, but I feel like I've been a stepmother to them in many ways. Even if they don't know about our relationship."

"You have been," he said. "And if you want to tell them about us, let's do it. I've wanted to for years."

"I know," she said, reaching over to touch his hand. "This isn't the time. I just didn't feel like you were viewing me as your partner in this when you made that comment to Jake."

"You're absolutely right," he said. "If I'm being honest, a little part of me is worried they come to you over me most of the time. I know how much they love you, and I didn't mean to undervalue your role in our family. You're the heart of it."

"Thank you," she said. "Now I need to figure out how to conjure the energy to take on an infant on my own."

"Why don't you both come to California?"

"Taking Charlie away from his pediatrician is a bad idea," she said. "He's so young. I don't want to travel that much with him. Plus, us being here will remind Jake that he has a home to come back to."

"We need to start thinking about whether we want Patrick to be out there alone when he turns eighteen," Ben said with a sigh. "I really hate it out there, and he knows that. I think it might cause him more stress having me there than living on his own would, but I hate the idea of him being so far away and alone."

***

Jake arrived back late afternoon with a car full of gear that his brothers helped him move inside. Based on the questioning looks Dan and Patrick were shooting in Stella and Ben's direction, Jake hadn't yet told brothers why they were moving. Once everything was settled, they retreated to the front porch, where Stella could see them sitting, heads huddled close as Jake shared his plans.

By the time they all came in for dinner, Charlie was up from his nap and settled into the baby carrier that Stella had found in the nursery. Having his tiny body snuggled against her helped keep the tears at bay as she finalized Jake's favorite meal, and even more so when she saw the red-rimmed eyes of all three boys. They all looked devastated, and the quiet of the room was overwhelming.

Once they were all sitting, Dan cleared his throat and turned to his father. "I was thinking," he said. "Since Stella will have Charlie here, and a lot on her plate, that it would be easier if you could be home as well. I was waiting to surprise you with the news, but it seems like a good time."

"What news?" Ben asked, pausing with a forkful of food halfway to his mouth.

"I applied to UCLA for law school," Dan said. "And I got in, with almost a full ride. I can live with Patrick and go to school, so you can stay here."

"That's very generous of you," Ben said. "Are you sure that's what you want?"

"It's one of the top law schools in the world," Dan said. "Patrick's show will run for at least another year, probably longer. He'll be eighteen soon enough, but I'd like to be together, if he's okay with having me."

"Of course I am," Patrick said. "That would be awesome. And Dad can pay for your tuition out of my money, since you'll be doing me a favor."

"I'm not letting my little brother pay my tuition," Dan said with an eye roll.

"It's your advance, or whatever lawyers call it," Patrick countered. "You can be my lawyer when you graduate and work off those hours."

"We'll figure it out," Dan said. "If it's okay with you, dad? And Stella?"

"Yes, it's more than okay," Ben said. "I'm going to miss you both, but you're right, it makes more sense for me to be here. And if I'm being honest, I could never set foot in Los Angeles again and be a happy man."

"It's not that bad," Patrick said with a laugh. "And Dan will love all the attention from the girls way more than you do."

"They're children," Ben said. "Both of you, be careful."

Jake laughed a rough laugh and pointed to the playpen Stella had set Charlie in. "They've seen first hand how quickly your life can change."

Patrick quickly changed gears and shared a funny story from a movie premiere he had recently attended, lifting the mood and getting everyone to laugh. They spent the rest of the evening sharing stories from their childhood, with Ben and Stella both stating that it felt like it passed in a heartbeat.

When the meal finished, Jake took his son upstairs to give him a bath and put him to bed for the last time for months. Stella brought him a bottle when she heard them move from the bathroom to the nursery, and she found Jake talking quietly to the baby as he dressed him in pajamas. He looked up and met Stella's eyes, and the pain in Jake's almost brought her to her knees.

"Jake," she said softly, crossing the room to embrace him. "Are you sure this is the right thing to do? Leaving him?"

"It's only for a few months," he said. "Then I can bring him with me where I'll be stationed. I made sure of it."

"But he can't be with you when you go overseas," she pointed out. "And isn't that your whole objective? To go fight against the people who did this."

He stared at the baby, emotions flickering across his face, before slowly nodding. "Yes, it is."

"It's going to be more time away from him than you realize," she said. "You need to be prepared for that. If you change your mind, we can fix it."

"I can't change my mind, Stella," he said, his voice a whisper. "They killed her."

"And killing them won't bring her back," she said softly. "You know that."

"I just felt lost. And this makes me feel like I have a reason to be alive when she's not."

"This right here," Stella said, reaching over to pat Charlie's cheek. "Is your reason."

"He's also why I need to do this," Jake said. "I need to make sure he doesn't grow up to go through something like this. Leaving him is the second hardest thing I'll ever do in my life. But the first was burying his mom, and I need to make that right for him."

Stella stood on her toes to kiss Jake on the cheek before leaving him alone with his son for their last night together for months. She left the room, closing the door behind her to afford them privacy. Walking quickly, she was able to get down the back stairs and out the kitchen door to her cottage before the tears took over.

The next morning, before the sun came up, she was on the porch watching Jake's taillights disappear down the mountain. It felt like a piece of her heart was going right along with him, and by the dejected looks on everyone's faces, she knew they all felt the same. Only Charlie's cries through the baby monitor snapped them out of it, sending them all back inside to tend to the infant. Dan and Patrick were due to leave in a few hours, going to New York to pack up Dan's belongings before heading to California. Stella felt like her whole world was shifting, everything moving just beyond her control. Fortunately, the baby in her arms was enough to keep her on track, at least until her three boys made their way home again.

Part Two

Chapter 17

"Are you alone?" The bartender, Desmond, asked as he handed Ben a menu. The Windsor Palace was owned by Ben's daughter-in-law Kendra, who was married to Dan. She had taken a step back from working at the restaurant nightly to be home with their growing family, and now she focused more on administrative duties during the day. Des manned the bar most nights, and a manager had taken over Kendra's responsibilities during dinner service.

"I am," Ben said. "I'll have a Sam draft, please."

"Sure thing." Des grabbed a glass from under the counter and started pouring the beer, turning back to Ben as he did. "I haven't seen Stella lately."

"Me neither," Ben grumbled. "I can't keep up with her social life these days. She's always running off somewhere with her sister or her best friend. Barely has time for me."

"Out of the honeymoon phase, I guess," Des said with a laugh. "It's been a few years now, right?"

"We've been married for over two years," Ben said. "But together much longer than that."

"Oh, I thought you just got together." Desmond leaned against the counter. "But I didn't move here until after you got married, so makes sense I'd be out of the loop."

"I was widowed when Patrick was born," Ben said. "Stella and I got together a few years later but kept it private until we got married."

"That's quite a secret to keep. Maybe you can give me some advice, because I can't seem to go on one date in this town without everyone knowing," Des said. He glanced over as the door opened and then grinned at Ben. "I don't think you'll be alone much longer."

Ben turned to see his three boys enter the bar, Dan in front and Jake with his service dog taking up the rear. The brothers were attempting to shield Patrick from view as much as possible with their positioning, Ben knew. Although Patrick wore a hat and kept his head down while staying close to his brothers, heads still swiveled instantly. Ben knew that a lot of tourists came with the hope of catching a glimpse of him. Everyone who visited Windsor Peak knew that Patrick was a resident and frequented the Palace with his girlfriend or family. Jake and Patrick were known to take the stage in the evening, putting their vocal talents to work to entertain their small town.

"Hey, dad," Dan said, pulling out a barstool next to Ben. "What are you doing here?"

"Having dinner," he responded. "What about you boys?"

"We're meeting Mike, JJ and Liam for some darts," Jake replied. "Our better halves said they needed a ladies' night, and they brought the babies with them."

"I would have watched them," Ben said.

"This is easier," Dan said. "Kendra is still nursing, and she insists it's good for him to sleep with a lot of noise around him. Says it will make him a better sleeper. And Calle is at home with Charlie, so it's just the two little ones."

"Want me to go be with Calle and Charlie?" Ben asked, happy to have a task. Dan had officially adopted Kendra's daughter, Calle, after they married. Then both he and Jake had babies with their new wives, giving Ben and Stella a total of four grandchildren. Charlie was about to turn seventeen and probably would prefer to be out with friends rather than playing Princess with his seven-year-old cousin.

"Nah," Jake said. "It's good for him. He has a girlfriend now and needs the reminder that he has to make good decisions."

"You should have him changing Izzie's diapers if that's the case," Patrick said, referring to Jake's infant daughter.

Des stopped by to take the drink orders for the three boys, as well as Ben's dinner.

"You want to join us, dad?" Patrick asked as the bartender went to put the orders in the computer.

"No, thanks," he said. "I'll just eat and head home. That way, if Charlie wants to take off, I'll be home."

The boys stood as their friends came in, all greeting each other with fist bumps and back slaps. The noise in the restaurant rose considerably, not just from the six men all talking at the same time. Liam was Patrick's best friend from Los Angeles and co-starred with him in a series of superhero movies that brought them both enormous fame. The two of them together in any setting tended to bring attention, but their fellow co-star Natalie had recently gone public with a relationship for the first time in a long time, bringing a lot of attention to her other half. Mike, who trained Patrick and Liam, was a former professional football player, and his hulking figure made it hard for him to hide. Rounding out the crew was JJ, Desmond's brother and the local sheriff. The newcomers said hello to Ben as they ordered beers, before they all started moving to the dartboards in the back of the restaurant.

"Dad, is everything okay?" Jake held back from the group to ask Ben. Having his son back in Vermont had been an unexpected joy after so many years of him being gone, and their relationship had deepened so much over the last few years. Jake, usually the most reserved of the three, had opened up since falling in love again and seeking help for his PTSD. Now he was more in touch with the emotions of those around him, in addition to his own.

"I think so," Ben said. "Stella has just been gone a lot. I'm missing her."

"Have you told her that?"

"I've tried, but she's hard to pin down," Ben said. "I don't know what's going on, but it's off putting to say the least."

"She loves you," Jake said confidently. "Everyone knows that."

"I know," Ben said. "It's not like I'm worried she's cheating. Something is just off."

"Talk to her about it," Jake said. "It doesn't help anyone to keep this stuff inside."

"When did you get to be so wise?"

"When I finally started living my life the right way," Jake said. "Kind of like you did, when you finally admitted to us about your relationship with Stella."

"We tried to protect you boys," Ben said. "In case things didn't work out. It never meant the feelings I had for her weren't real."

"You can't live your life preparing for the worst-case scenario," Jake said. "I learned that the hard way."

Desmond came from the kitchen carrying Ben's dinner, which he placed down along with a set of silverware. "Can I get you anything else?"

"I'm good, Des, thanks," Ben said. Turning to Jake, he gestured to where the rest of the men had disappeared. "Go play with your brothers and friends. I'm going to eat this and head out."

"Talk to her," Jake said as he stood up. "Don't be a stubborn old fool."

"Who are you calling old?" Ben called to his son's back, seeing Jake's shoulders shake with laughter as he walked away.

***

The lights were off in the cottage that Ben and Stella now lived in together when he pulled into the driveway, but every light in the main house appeared to be on. Dan and Kendra lived there now, with Calle and their baby Declan. Jake lived just across a small field with his wife Shea, son Charlie and baby daughter Isobel. Jake had built the house on the acres of land that Ben owned surrounding their property, and the two families loved being so close. Patrick lived just down the mountain, along with his girlfriend Emma, when they weren't in California or filming somewhere.

Ben had thought having his three boys return to live nearby would be the best feeling in the world, but nothing topped being a grandfather. He and Stella had a special bond with Charlie, after raising him for the first fifteen years of his life. Jake had tried to bring Charlie with him when he moved into military housing, but as Ben predicted, it had fallen apart fast. After months of someone needing to race to help with the baby, and Patrick secretly helping pay Jake's bills when he was overwhelmed with childcare costs, having Charlie in Vermont made the most sense. When Jake had enlisted, no one had expected it to last more than four years, but he had stayed in for nearly fifteen, lost in a cycle of grief and self-blame. The years apart had made things difficult for Jake and Charlie, and Ben was so glad that they had finally found their way back to each other. And that Jake had put down his need for vengeance to live his life again.

"Papa! Your home," Calle cried as she rushed over to hug Ben around the knees. "Charlie and I are watching Tangled. Want to watch?"

Charlie looked up from his cell phone, which was hidden under a throw pillow, to smile at his grandfather. "It's only the hundredth time we've watched it."

"Charlie, it is not," Calle said, putting her hands on her hips. "You say that every time. I just love Rapunzel the best."

"You say that every time," Charlie countered.

"I'm home for the night," Ben said to Charlie. "I can take over here if you want to take off to do your homework."

Charlie hesitated and then saw Ben's wink, indicating that he was fibbing to avoid hurting Calle's feelings, before he jumped to his feet. "Thanks, grandpa. I should get to it."

"But Charlie! We didn't get to the best part yet," Calle said, jutting her lip out.

"I bet Grandpa will sing along with you," Charlie said. "Everyone knows you like the song they sing in the bar the most."

"And the one in the boat," Calle said. "Okay, but next time you have to watch the whole thing. And sing. Promise?"

"I promise," Charlie said. He planted a kiss on her head before pulling on his jacket. "Thanks, grandpa."

"Anytime, bud. Be smart."

The rest of the evening passed in a blur as Calle sang and danced around him before being wrangled into bed. It took three chapters to be read to her and an agreement that she could finish one more before he was able to convince her to stay in her room, and yet she was asleep before he even made it to the door. Her energy was boundless, but when she finally let herself relax, she could fall asleep faster than anyone else he had ever met.

He wandered back downstairs, thinking of how much everything had changed in the last few years. This house, where he had raised the boys, was slowly transforming into one that reflected Dan and Kendra's family. Pictures along the wall were once of his own boys from infancy on, and now were of Calle and Declan, and the four of them as a family. One large photograph on the wall in the living room had been taken the previous Christmas as a gift from Patrick. It had everyone in the picture, with Ben and Stella smack in the center. Suddenly, their little family had turned into a big crowd, and it brought him nothing but happiness.

Ben had fallen in love with the farmhouse the first time he saw it. He and Isobel were newly married, and he had accepted a management position at a local bank. They had grown up in Windsor Peak, but both had lived in neighborhoods closer to town. Isobel had been nervous about the house and the empty acres that surrounded them, thinking they were too remote for her. Ben had convinced her they were an easy bike ride to town, so their future children could have the best of both worlds. Empty land to explore, and convenience to their peers.

Isobel had barely started to put her touch on the house when he lost her, and slowly he and the boys had made it a home. With Stella's help, of course. Somehow, all these years had passed, and he had gone from three screaming babies to young children racing down the halls, then teenagers trying to sneak out, and then young men questioning their decisions. Somehow, they had all come back to be within these walls, figuring out who they were as men and as a family. It made him feel old, if he were honest. Flashing back to three boys trudging down the stairs in their pajamas to go to an early hockey practice, it felt like yesterday. And yet thirty years passed in the blink of an eye.

When Kendra came home a short while later, he made his way back to the cottage. The lights were still off, and he had no idea what could be keeping Stella so late. She had told him earlier that if she had a glass of wine or two with her sister that she might stay over, and not to expect her, but it still felt like a kick to the stomach. Why did he feel like the woman he had spent his life with was suddenly keeping secrets from him?

Chapter 18

Heather was sitting next to her, leaning forward over a notepad that she had placed on the edge of the desk they were sitting in front of. Stella had spent most of their time in the office listening as her sister fired question after question at the man sitting behind the desk, but it didn't feel as though anything had truly sunk in. Thankfully, her sister was committed to recording every word so they could go through it all at a later date.

The last few weeks had been the same, with Stella feeling as though she were walking around in a daze as her sister took charge. She knew she was lucky to have someone like Heather in her corner, and yet the whole situation was so exhausting. All she wanted to do was crawl into her bed, let Ben wrap an arm around her, and cry.

However, he was hundreds of miles away, with no idea that she had left Vermont. She felt terrible lying to him, but until she could come to grips with this herself, she didn't want to bring him into it. Heather was able to handle everything with a confident efficiency that anyone else would have lacked, and Stella would never stop being grateful for that.

When it was time to leave, Heather gathered the stack of paperwork and cards and gestured for Stella to walk through the door. Once they were out in the street, Heather unlocked the car and opened the passenger door before looking at her. "Want to stay here tonight?" Stella nodded, unable to say anything, and Heather hugged her tightly. "This is all going to be fine," her sister said. "You'll see. Let's get to the hotel and get some wine, and we'll make a plan."

"I'm scared."

"I know," Heather said, her voice soothing. "Me too. But I also have faith and confidence that this will all be a distant memory soon enough."

"I wish I had your confidence," Stella said as she wiped away a tear.

Heather hugged her tightly and then nudged her into the car. "A glass of wine and a good night's sleep, and this will all look better in the morning."

The drive back to Vermont passed too quickly, even with all the stalling that Stella had done. Before she knew it, she was back in her small cottage, which had thankfully been empty when she arrived. It gave her a chance to settle her stomach and her thoughts before facing Ben, who had a lot of questions according to his many text messages.

She had always been able to talk to Ben about anything. Even when they were young children, he was the person she had talked to when she was being bullied by a student in class. He quickly took care of the situation and was her protector from that day on. His friendship had been her backbone, and it had been hard to keep this from him. But knowing that it would tear him apart had forced her to do it, at least to grant him a few extra days of peace.

After prepping for his favorite meal, she took a shower and studied herself in the mirror once wrapped in a towel. Her face was showing even more lines than it had been years before when they had started their intimate relationship, and even more than when they had finally told the boys about it and then gotten married. Her hair was streaked with silver, though she still wore it long enough to wrap in a bun most days. Ben loved it when she took it down at night and brushed through it, often wanting to be the one doing it for her. She looked tired and pale, which she knew was due to the last few weeks of appointments. Perhaps she hadn't realized how she had aged, especially since Jake had come home and everything had changed, but it was staring her in the face today.

Ben was still as handsome as ever, maybe even more so. He had aged well, his dark hair simply turning a dignified shade of silver so slowly it hadn't struck her until it was all the same shade. Although his forehead was creased and his laugh lines appear frequently, they had made him look more distinguished. He kept in shape, often working out with his boys, and his waistline had never changed. The man had aged like fine wine, and she felt like a glass of champagne left on the counter.

Sighing, she brushed out her hair, applied some lotion and a minimal amount of makeup to her face before stepping out to find clothes. She came up short when she opened the bedroom door and saw Ben on the bed, clearly waiting for her.

"Hi," she said, hating how he voice sounded. Unsure, confused, scared.

"Hi yourself," he said. He placed the book he had been holding down next to him and studied her face. "It feels like a long time since I've been able to talk to you. I thought it was best if I waited out of sight to grab you before you could disappear again."

"Like when the boys tried to sneak in after curfew?" She stepped into her closet and pulled on her clothes, hearing his soft laugh from behind her.

"Something like that," he said. "Although this feels more serious than what they were doing."

"That's debatable," she retorted. Taking a deep breath, she turned to face him. "Let's go finish making dinner, and then we can talk."

"Are you leaving me?"

His words stopped her feet and her heart at once. She turned to face him again, shocked by the honesty on his face. "How could you even think that?"

"You keep disappearing without any notice," he said. "You're off with Heather, barely calling or texting me for days. What else am I supposed to think?"

She crossed the room to climb onto the bed next to him, putting her head on the familiar spot on his chest where she had fallen asleep thousands of times. "I love you," she said. "I would never leave you willingly. Besides, I was just wondering when you would realize you've aged so gracefully, and I look like a sack of potatoes next to you. It's more likely that you would upgrade."

"Why would you even say such a thing?" he asked, sounding angry. "You are as beautiful as ever. Don't put yourself down. I love you, and you're the only woman for me now and forever."

"We both know how quickly forever can change," she said. "I wasn't your first choice, and we both know that."

"Stella, what are you doing? We've had this conversation so many times, it's making me crazy. I was twenty-two when I married Izzie," he said. "I had no idea that you had feelings for me. I thought we were just best friends, and I cared about you. But you never told me it was more than that for you."

"Because it wasn't for you," she said, hating the stubborn tone in her voice. This wasn't going at all how she had planned it, but she couldn't stop herself from picking a fight.

"I don't know if it would have been," he argued. "This is so foolish to be fighting about something from nearly forty years ago. I don't think I was mature enough to even consider the possibility that there could be more between us. And I hate when you say this."

"Express my feelings?"

"No," he snapped. "Bring up something from forever ago that I can't change, and I wouldn't change. Because even if I had a time machine and could go back, if I did, that would erase Dan, Jake and Patrick from my life. And I love you, but I would never, ever, for anything, lose them."

"I would never ask that of you," she said.

"But you are. In questioning my relationship with Izzie and why I married her over you, you are," he said. He gently pushed her aside onto her pillow before standing up. "I loved Isobel. She was a wonderful wife, mother, and friend to you and I. She never once expressed any jealousy toward you, and your ongoing feelings toward a woman who died more than twenty-five years ago is ugly. I have to walk away from this."

She heard the front door slam and curled into a ball as she sobbed. Nothing was going the way it should, and she only had herself to blame. Instead of falling into his arms and telling him what had been going on, she had purposely picked a fight so she could put it off longer. She was the worst kind of coward.

"Stella?" Kendra's voice called from the front door. Kendra and Dan had keys to the cottage, as did all of the kids, but the front door was rarely locked. Calle loved to drop in after school and share stories, and Charlie popped in at least once a day at some point.

She took a minute to wipe her face and then emerged from the bedroom, finding Kendra perched on a barstool in the kitchen. She looked worried and frowned when she saw Stella's face. "Are you okay?"

"No," Stella admitted. Crossing the small room, she filled the kettle and put it on the stove before changing her mind and pulling a bottle of wine out of the rack. Kendra took it from her shaking hands and expertly pulled the cork before pouring two glasses and handing one to Stella.

"Spill."

"How did you know something was wrong?"

"Dan just chased Ben down the mountain," Kendra said. "He left here with steam coming out his ears and peeled out of the driveway. Dan was sure there was an emergency of some kind and went after him."

"No emergency, just a fight."

"That's not like you guys," Kendra said, her tone gentle. "Want to talk about it?"

"No," Stella said, wincing when she saw the hurt look in her daughter-in-law's eyes. "And yes. I was a fool."

"Tell me," Kendra encouraged. "Something has been going on with you for weeks. Everyone is worried."

Stella took a healthy sip of the wine and gestured toward the sofa, leading the way to sit. She took one end, Kendra on the other, and they both turned to face the other. Taking a deep breath, she started. "I was putting off telling Ben about what's been going on," she said. "And I picked a fight. It was silly and petty and I'm ashamed of myself that let my old insecurities come through because I was afraid of telling him the truth."

"Do you want to start there? With what's been going on? Or tell me about what you just fought over?"

Stella plucked at the blanket that was hanging over the back of the couch, avoiding Kendra's eyes. "I have always been a little angry that Ben chose Isobel over me, and I leaned into those feelings now."

"Did you and Ben have a relationship back then?" Kendra looked stunned, then relieved when Stella shook her head.

"No," she said. "We had been best friends from kindergarten on. Kind of like you and Dan, and Jake and Jenna. But when Izzie moved to town, he was knocked senseless. And I was so jealous."

"You already had feelings for him?"

Stella nodded. "I had always assumed that when we grew up, he would realize that we should be together. I had envisioned our entire lives together, and suddenly, he was falling in love with someone else. And I couldn't help but like her too, and become her friend, so I could never say something to disrupt that."

"You put a lot of weight into a dream," Kendra said gently. "Especially without telling him."

"I know," Stella said, wiping away another tear. "And look what happened after all that. I won him in the worst way possible, when my friend died."

"That's not how anyone sees it," Kendra objected. "You didn't benefit from his first wife dying, but it did throw you together."

"Sometimes I have to wonder…"

"What?"

"If he loves me for me, or because I was here," Stella whispered, ashamed of herself at the words as they came out. The fear had always been a tight string around her heart, even though she should have left it behind many years ago.

"Stella, anyone can see how much he loves you," Kendra said, reaching over to squeeze her hand. "He's been crazy lately, trying to figure out what's going on. I've never seen him like this before."

"About that," Stella said, bracing herself to say it out loud for the first time. "I—"

"Mama, the baby is crying again." Calle appeared at the front door, baby monitor in hand. "I tried to play with him, but he wants out of the crib, and you told me I should never try to do that."

"I did, Calle, thank you," Kendra said. "Can we pause for a minute? Let me grab Declan and I'll be right back."

"No, you go be with the kids," Stella said, waving a hand. "I'm going to see if I can get Ben to come home. It's only fair that I have this conversation with him first."

"Are you sure?" Kendra looked concerned, glancing between the monitor and Stella.

"Positive," Stella said. "You'll all know soon enough."

"I'm always here for you, Stella," Kendra said. She walked over to hug her tightly. "We all are."

"Me too," Calle said, bouncing over to join the hug. "I can stay and play now if you want. Mama will have to feed Declan anyway and he makes a big mess."

"Come with me," Kendra said. "Stella has some things to do."

Calle frowned but took her mother's hand, casting a look over her shoulder at Stella as she left. Stella tried to force a smile on her face but could tell from the little girl's expression that it didn't work. Now she had another person that she had upset today, and she wasn't done yet.

Chapter 19

Ben pulled into a parking spot on Main Street and glanced around, debating his options. If he went to the Palace, no doubt his boys would be alerted, and he would be surrounded instantly. In no mood to be around people, especially those he loved, he chose the coffee shop. Once he had his black coffee, he sat in a corner, happy to be the only customer at this time of day. They were due to close in an hour, but that gave him time to calm down.

Dan came in before he took his second sip, and Ben was surprised when the door closed behind him, without his other two boys. "They're coming if I text them to," Dan said, reading Ben's expression. "But we thought maybe I could convince you to come up to Patrick's to talk out whatever is going on."

"Why Patrick's?"

"Emma is out with Zoe for a sister's night, and he's home alone," Dan said. "Jake has a houseful, and obviously you don't want to be at my house."

"I just want to sit here alone for a bit," Ben said pointedly.

"That's not going to happen," Dan said. "You can come with me, or I can sit here and figure it out."

"How did you find me so fast? Or even know something was going on?"

"Kendra saw you storm out of the cottage," Dan said. "And then your tires peeling out of the driveway was a not-so-subtle hint that something had happened. She threw my keys at me and had me follow you, and she went to check on Stella."

"How did that go?" Ben couldn't stop himself from asking. Although furious with Stella at the moment, he loved her and was worried about what was really going on to make her act so oddly.

"If you want answers, you're going to have to give some yourself," Dan said, crossing his arms stubbornly. "Here or Patrick's?"

"Fine," Ben huffed. "We can go to Patrick's."

"I'll drive," Dan said. "I'd like to get there safely."

Patrick and Jake were waiting for them, a bottle of whiskey on the counter. Ben poured a glass for himself and took a seat at the island, feeling strangely out of place. He was used to being the one his boys came to when they had troubles, not the other way around.

"What's going on, Dad?" Patrick asked, leaning against the counter opposite where Ben sat.

"It's nothing," Ben said.

"Not nothing," Dan replied. "You flew out of the house and down the driveway like you were on fire."

"And Stella is upset," Jake added. "Kendra already called Shea."

"She's upset?" Ben asked, his eyebrows shooting so high they were probably meeting his hairline. "She goes missing for days at a time and won't tell me where she is or what's happening. Then, when I finally feel like I'm about to get some answers, she pulls out some old bull."

"What old bull?" Dan prodded.

"Jealousy, that's what," Ben said, slamming his glass down on the granite.

"Of who?" Patrick looked surprised as he asked.

"Your mother," he said with a sigh. "This is ridiculous."

"Explain it to us," Dan said. "I've never heard her say anything but nice things about mom."

Ben took a moment to refill his glass and collect his thoughts. "Izzie and Stella were friends," he said. "We all were. We grew up here, and as you all know, there's not a lot of people. There were eight of us in our first-grade classroom, so we were all friends. As we got older, the town grew, and lots of new kids came to town. We joked that Stella was the welcoming committee. She was always the first one to say hi or invite someone to sit with us at lunch. Your mom moved here when we were freshmen in high school, and I took to her right away. Your mom and I started dating when we all turned sixteen, and Stella never let on."

"On to what?" Jake asked.

"That she had feelings for me," Ben said. "I thought we were just friends. But one night after graduation, she did confess it to me. We were all out by the lake having a little too much fun, and Stella kissed me. Told me that she loved me, that she always had. But the next day, she acted like it never happened. I thought she just had one too many, and I didn't want to embarrass her."

"And you were already in a relationship with mom? Doesn't sound like Stella," Dan said.

"I agree, which is why I just let it go at the time," Ben replied. "Years later, after your mom passed, we talked about it again. I was feeling guilty about our new relationship, and she told me about a conversation that she had with your mom."

"What was that?" Jake asked, sipping his whiskey.

"Apparently they had talked about her crush on me," Ben said. "Your mom knew about it, and before we got married, she asked Stella if their friendship would survive. I don't want to know if your mom would have turned me down if Stella had said yes."

"You think their friendship might have been stronger than what you two had?" Patrick asked, surprise written on his face.

"I don't know," Ben confessed. "All I know is what Stella told me."

"Can you share more?" Dan asked softly.

"From what Stella said, they had this conversation the night of your mom's bridal shower," Ben said. "Stella spent the night with Izzie after, and your mom was acting off. When Stella pushed, she said she felt guilty that Stella had just organized this whole shower, and would stand up for her at the wedding, when she knew that Stella had a thing for me."

"That must have been a weird talk," Patrick said.

"Stella said they both cried," Ben confessed. "But Stella convinced her that it was a harmless crush. That I had set an example of what she should be looking for in a partner, but she wasn't secretly in love with me. And that she was happy for us."

"And mom obviously believed her," Dan said.

"I think even Stella believed it," Ben replied. "I don't think she was pining for me all those years, she was always around and I never had that sense."

"But things changed after mom died," Jake said.

"Not right away, but eventually."

"'I don't see Stella as the type that would be jealous,' Patrick said. "Especially of her two best friends."

"That's what's so weird," Ben said. "Why would this come up now?"

"She's avoiding something," Jake said. "Take it from someone who is a master at this. She doesn't want to talk about whatever is really bothering her, so she's throwing some smoke in the air."

"You are an expert at that," Dan said with a laugh. "Or you used to be. Now you're an open book."

"Therapy, man," Jake said with a grin. "Who would have thought?"

"Everyone who had told you that for years," Dan said, rolling his eyes.

"Boys." They both turned to look at Ben, who gave them a stern look that had worked when they were young kids. "Can we focus on me for a moment?"

"Sorry," Jake said. "But I think I'm probably right on this. There's something else going on that she doesn't want to talk about. This is a diversion."

"She has been gone an awful lot," Patrick said. "Did she give you any answers about what's been going on?"

"No," Ben admitted. "And that's what we were talking about when this came up."

"I think you need to go back home," Dan said. "And push for some answers. I hate to admit it, but Jake is probably right. She's distracting you from something else."

"Want us to come with you?" Patrick offered. "Maybe four against one would work."

"No," Ben said, shaking his head. "We need to figure this out, just the two of us."

"But you'll tell us right away if something is wrong?" Patrick asked, looking concerned.

"I will," Ben said. "As soon as she says I can share. If it's something personal that she wants to keep to herself, I have to respect that."

"She's always been open with us about everything," Patrick argued. "If something is wrong, we should know."

"Let's not get worked up yet," Jake said. "Let Dad talk to her, and we can go from there."

"Fine," Patrick said on a sigh.

"Are you driving me?" Ben asked Dan. "Since you forced me into your car."

"You were driving like a lunatic," Dan countered. "But yes, I'll drop you back at your car. Unless you want to just get it in the morning?"

"Let's do that," Ben said. "It will be faster. And I've had more whiskey than I should have."

"I'll ride with you too," Jake said. "I can walk home from your house and catch a ride back here tomorrow to get my truck. Better safe than sorry."

Ben hugged Patrick as they said goodbye, and noticed his youngest son held on a little tighter than usual. Stella was such an important part of all three boys lives, but she was the only mother that Patrick had ever known. Ben knew Patrick would be worried until he had answers, and it made him more determined than ever to get to the bottom of what was happening with his wife.

***

Stella was in the kitchen when he arrived home, pouring herself a cup of tea. Her eyes suggested she had been crying for some time, which was a sucker punch to the gut for him. He hated the idea of her crying alone, and because of him. Without saying a word, he crossed the room and took her into his arms, relieved when she went willingly. Her arms wrapped around his waist, her head on his chest, and it was like she was the perfect puzzle piece to fit him.

"I'm sorry," he said finally. "For a lot of things, but right now for walking out when we should have continued the conversation."

"No, I'm the one who's sorry," she said. "I never should have said that to you. I was wrong."

"Please, tell me what's really going on," he begged her. "I'm going crazy imagining all the things that could be going on."

"Let's sit," she said. "Do you want some tea?"

"No, I think I'll have something stronger," he said. "I think I might need it."

They settled in front of the fireplace in their matching chairs, set side by side facing the fire and the television above it. They sat in the same places each night, playing along with a game show, or laughing at a comedy, or guessing who did it in one of their legal dramas. This time, the tv was off, and the room felt heavier somehow.

Stella took a breath and met his eyes, her own welling up at the same time, causing him to reach for her hand. "I found a lump in my breast," she said. "Last month in the shower. I thought it was nothing. I've always had what they called lumpy tissue, and it's always been fine. That's why I didn't tell you right away. I didn't want you to worry."

"I worried anyway," he responded. "You've been acting so distant and spending so much time away from me. How could I not worry?"

"I'm sorry," she said, a tear slipping down her cheek. "I really am. Once I started seeing doctors, the panic set in. A part of me felt like if you didn't know, it wasn't really happening. Heather made appointments for me and took me, so I wasn't alone. And I wasn't lying to you about spending time with her."

"Multiple appointments? Please tell me what's going on." Fear was clawing at his chest, making it hard to breathe. Her tears kept his own at bay, because he knew if he broke down, she would suppress her own emotions to help him. That's just who she was, always putting someone else in front of her own needs.

"I have cancer, Benji," she said so softly he could cling to hope that he was hearing wrong.

"Cancer?" he repeated, his voice even softer than hers.

"Yes," she said, nodding. "I had a biopsy done, that's why we spent the night in Boston. I didn't want to come home still sore and not be able to explain."

"How long did you plan to keep this from me?" Ben asked, torn between the questions running through his head. From the look on her face, he knew it was the wrong one to ask. Selfish of him, to think of his own feelings over hers.

"I kept hoping that I would get good news, and then I wouldn't have to scare you," she said.

"But I would have been there with you," he said. "I should have been with you to support you through this."

"Heather was," she said. "Please, don't get caught up in what has already happened. There is a long road ahead, and I need you with me."

"You're right," he said, nodding his head. "Tell me everything. We're in this together, and there's no outcome other than to beat this. I don't care where we have to go, or what doctor we need to see, I'll be at your side. And you know Patrick can get you in with the top medical professionals in the world, so wherever we need to go, we will."

She nodded and took a shaky breath, then a long sip of her hot tea. He hoped it was to compose herself before telling the story, and not to push down feelings about how he was handling this. He knew he was doing this wrong, but losing Stella was not an option he would accept.

"We went to Dana Farber in Boston, which my doctor here recommended," she said. "They can coordinate my care so that I can get treatment here. I'd like to be at home for most of it."

"But wouldn't it be better down there?"

"They'll be involved the whole time," she said. "And I'll go there for surgery."

"You need surgery?"

She nodded again and seemed to shrink inside herself. "I need to have a mastectomy."

The words hit him hard, and he took a moment to absorb them before speaking again. "Then what?"

"Chemotherapy," she said. "Which I can do here. The surgery I will do in Boston."

"Do you have a date for that?"

"Two weeks from Monday," she said.

"Why the long wait? Shouldn't they do it quickly, before it spreads?"

"They wanted to give me a little time."

His head snapped up. "For what? Is this dangerous?"

"No," she said, shaking her head. "Just to wrap my head around everything. And to talk to you. They didn't seem to think there was any danger in waiting, and they have a full calendar anyway."

"We can pull some strings. Waiting isn't a good option, Stella. We need to attack this."

"Let's sleep on it and see how we feel in the morning," she suggested. "The boys don't even know yet."

"We need to tell them too," he said. "Tomorrow is soon enough. There is one very important piece we need to focus on."

"What's that?"

"You're going to be okay," he said. "You have to be."

He stood and offered her a hand, which she took. Once they were both settled into bed, he pulled her closer, needing her more than he ever had before. She was his heart, his strength, and his reason for living. He needed the reassurance that she was still here, with him, and that he wasn't losing her now or ever. For tonight, at least, he would try to keep his questions and unspoken fears to himself and focus on holding his wife.

Chapter 20

Listening to Ben's breathing slow down was usually enough to lull Stella to sleep, but not tonight. She was lying with her head on his chest, listening to his heartbeat under her ear. It was so solid, so reassuring, that she couldn't bring herself to move. Sleep had been eluding her for days now, as she agonized over her diagnosis and the idea of telling Ben and the boys.

The thought of the upcoming day weight heavy on her. The news would crush the three boys, and she could already predict what their responses would be. Dan would start researching, needing facts before allowing himself to feel anything. Patrick would want to fix it quickly and would offer to fly in the best medical team or take her where she needed to be. She had no doubt he would have his entire team trying to find the best plan for her, but she needed to convince him to let her do it her way. Jake would look at it with a clinical detachment, the most used to losing people. She worried about him the most, knowing this could set him back enormously with the grief and PTSD that he had fought through. He had made such strides since coming home and falling in love with Shea; she hated the thought of what this would do to him.

Realizing sleep wouldn't come anytime soon, she slipped out from under Ben's arm and pulled on her robe. It was too cold to sit on the small porch, so she settled into her chair in the dark living room. This little cottage had been her home for nearly half her life, and seeing Ben's things next to hers still caught her off guard sometimes. Even with a few years of marriage behind them, it was still hard to believe that this was real. Seeing his hat on the hook by the door next to her purse, or the book he was reading on the end table next to hers, still gave her a small thrill. It caught her off guard sometimes that this was how their lives had turned out, and how easily they had adapted to living together.

In the morning, she would be forced to really accept her fate and look the future in the face. For now, she wanted to visit her memories and let them offer her comfort. And most of all, she wanted a private moment to have a quiet, albeit one-sided, conversation with her best friend. Izzie would know how to handle all of this, and she needed to feel her presence tonight more than ever.

***

The boys arrived early, summoned by a text from Ben that was sent before they had even woken up. Dan and Kendra arrived first after getting Calle to school. Declan was just starting to move around, and Kendra quickly set up a playpen to plop him in, much to his annoyance. However, when Jake and Shea entered and put little Izzie in with him, the two babies were content to play together. Patrick and Emma were the last to arrive but came carrying boxes and coffee from the bakery.

"Piper sent enough for a small army," Emma said, laughing softly as she unpacked the boxes. "We thought we would get here first, since you both had kids to get off to school."

"We have babies," Shea said. "We're up with the sun. And I'd normally be in school already, but I took the morning off to be here."

"Calle had to be in school early," Kendra shared. "She joined the crafting club, so you can all expect homemade gifts for your next birthday."

They all piled pastries on plates and grabbed cups of coffee from the carrying trays, chatting easily amongst themselves, having no idea what was to come. Stella had picked up on some tension from the three boys, but they had tried to cover it well. She knew Ben had talked to them the night before, and didn't want to keep them waiting any longer to find out what was happening. Once everyone was settled, she cleared her throat, and they all turned to look at her.

At the sight of their faces, she nearly lost her courage. She loved them all so much, and the idea of breaking their hearts was difficult. Ben moved to her side, taking her hand, and looked at his family.

"Stella has cancer," he said. Stella heard the gasp of everyone in the room, her own mixed in with theirs. She had expected to share the news in a more delicate fashion, rather than hitting them over the head with it, and felt a surge of anger that she pushed away. He was only trying to help, and she needed to be grateful for that rather than mad at how he did it.

"What?" Dan asked in a sharp voice, exchanging looks with his brother. Kendra placed her hand on his arm, stopping him from speaking further.

"Stella, we're all here for you. Ben, you as well. We'll do whatever you need. Can you tell us more?" Kendra reached for a box of tissues behind her and passed them to Stella, who hadn't realized she was crying.

"How bad is it?" Patrick asked, looking shellshocked. Emma had moved closer to him on the small sofa, taking his hand as they waited for Stella to respond.

"They believe its early stage," Stella said. "I found a lump in my breast and had it checked here by my doctor. She wanted to do a biopsy, and Heather pulled some strings to have me go to Dana Farber in Boston to have it done. We went back last week for the results, and again this week to make a plan."

"What do they suggest?" Shea asked. Jake was silent next to her, his service dog at attention by his knee. Stella knew when the dog rested his head on Jake's knee that he was experiencing stress, and the dog was trying to offer support.

"They offered to do a lumpectomy," Stella shared. "But the oncologist said the safest plan would be a mastectomy. We did some testing while we were in Boston, and it seems that it will reduce my risk of recurrence. Since I already…"

"Already what?" Dan asked when her words trailed off. His fingers were drumming on the table next to his coffee, his shoulders tight and high near his ears as he waited for her to answer.

"Well, it just makes more sense to have the surgery," she said. "Make sure they get everything. And that should eliminate any future battles with cancer."

Ben frowned next to her, as if knowing she was leaving something out, but not knowing what it was. "She's planning to have the surgery in Boston," he said. "Then treatment here."

"Treatment?" Patrick asked, his eyes darting from Stella to his dad.

"Chemotherapy," Ben said.

"But you said it was early." Patrick stood and began pacing in the small room.

"We won't really know much until the surgery," she said. "They test the lymph nodes and surrounding tissue to make sure they got the whole tumor. But the chemo will make sure it's all gone."

"There must be risks to it, though," Dan stated. "We should look into this more before we decide anything."

"Let me make some calls," Patrick added. "I know there are some amazing doctors in Boston, but let's get a second opinion. Maybe they made a mistake."

"They didn't make a mistake, Patty," Jake said, his voice gruff. "You know Stella better than that. She wouldn't be telling us this if she wasn't sure."

"But she's upset," Patrick argued. "And none of us were there with her. I just think we need to make sure."

"We can't pretend this isn't happening," Jake snapped back. "That's what you're trying to do."

"Please, boys," Stella said. "I can't have you fighting. I know this is upsetting news, but everyone is very optimistic."

"I think we all need a little bit of time to absorb this," Kendra said gently. "But in the meantime, what can we do for you, Stella?"

She smiled gratefully at Kendra, who she had known the longest and had been considered family long before she and Dan had reconnected and married. "I'm okay."

"No," Emma said, shaking her head. "I know that all too well. I spent years telling people I was okay when I wasn't. But I didn't want to burden anyone with my own feelings, so I pretended. You're surrounded by people who love you. Don't push us away and try to handle it alone. It's okay to accept help."

"There's nothing happening for the next two weeks," Stella explained. "Once I have the surgery, I'm sure I'll need help."

"We'll put our heads together," Kendra said, nodding to the other two women. "I'm sure there's a way we can support you now. Both of you."

Ben smiled at her, the first time he had smiled all morning. "I'm sure you will, Kendra."

"Help each other through this for now," Stella said softly. "I know this is a lot to handle, and I'm so glad you boys have someone to help you through. And your dad will need you three to lean on."

"We'll do whatever you need," Dan replied quickly.

"Stella, can I make some calls? Maybe there's another option that they haven't thought of," Patrick pleaded with her.

"Honey, I've talked to them at length. I promise you, this wasn't a decision made lightly. I am in the best possible hands, you can trust me on that."

He crossed his arms, a stubborn look in his eye that she recognized from his childhood. Patrick didn't like to be told no, and being surrounded by people who didn't want to deny him anything made it an unusual occurrence for him. She would have to talk to him again privately, and get Emma on her side to help him understand that all she needed was his support.

Kendra stood and moved to hug Stella, whispering words of support in her ear as she did. Everyone else followed suit, Jake the last. Rex stuck close to him, making it clear to everyone in the room that his handler was not coping with the news well. Shea's eyes followed Jake worriedly, then turned to exchange a quiet word with Kendra.

"Jake, I need you to listen to me," Stella said after hugging him. She held on to his hands and waited until his eyes met hers. "I'm okay. I will be okay."

"You can't know that," he said, an angry edge to his voice. "No one can know that. You can be fine one day and gone the next, and then what?"

"That's true for all of us," she said gently. "Worrying about that now isn't good for you. Or for me. We both need to stay positive. And I want you to promise me that you'll go see your therapist as soon as possible."

He nodded, and Shea did the same behind him. Stella knew he was in good hands with his wife, and saw that Dan and Patrick were both listening carefully as well. "I will," Jake promised. "I have an appointment today anyway, I was going to ask you to watch Izzie. But maybe Kendra could?"

"Don't be silly," Stella said. "Having Izzie here is the best medicine for me."

"Are you sure? I know today wasn't a day for you to watch her," Shea asked. "I can take the whole day off."

"No, we'll be fine. Ben will be here, and Kendra is right next door. But some time with the baby will be good for us both," Stella said.

"We need to tell Charlie," Jake said, the hurt look returning to his face. "How are we going to do that?"

"Do you want me to talk to him?" Stella offered.

"No," Jake said. "You're already going through so much. And this is a chance for me to help him through something big. I'll figure it out."

"And you'll tell him that I'll be fine?"

"Stella, I can't make promises to my son that I don't know I can keep," Jake said. "I can't put him through that if something goes wrong."

"Nothing will go wrong," Patrick snapped. "Stop saying that."

"Life can pull one over on you, Patty," Jake bit back. "We all learned that early on."

"That's enough, boys," Ben said. "Stella doesn't need stress in her life."

Emma linked her arm with Patrick's, leaning against him so they melded into one person through Stella's tear-filled eyes. She was so happy they had all found someone and that they were able to share their love with the world. All three had started with issues they needed to overcome and had come out the other side and made them stronger for it. She hoped the same would be true for her and Ben, that they could fight this battle side by side.

"Why don't I stay with you today," Kendra suggested. "You've been promising to teach me how to make your cinnamon bread, let's do that."

"We've got some things to discuss here," Ben said.

Stella watched a silent exchange happen between Kendra and Dan before Ben's oldest stepped forward. "Dad, I needed your opinion on a few things today," he said. "I was hoping you could come down to the office. And I know Patrick mentioned he was hearing a weird noise from his dishwasher, and was hoping you could take a look."

Patrick started to speak, but a look from Jake stopped him. "Now that you mention it," Jake said. "I could use some help with the fence. I was going to wait until Charlie got home, but if you're available, maybe you could swing over and help."

Ben glanced around the room, as if calculating the motivation behind the words. Stella put her hand on his arm, pulling his attention back to her. "I'll be fine. We've talked about this enough already, and if Izzie will be with me, I don't want to spend the whole day thinking about what's coming. I want to enjoy my granddaughter and teach my daughter-in-law how to cook."

"I didn't say that I needed to learn how to cook," Kendra said, a confused look on her face.

"Oh, you're adorable when you're clueless," Dan said, kissing her on the nose.

"I'm not a bad cook," she exclaimed, putting her hands on her hips.

"Of course not," Dan said. "That's why we grab most meals from the restaurant or Palace Plates."

"Zoe is a professional," Kendra sniffed. "You can't compare me to her."

"Alright, everyone, get out of here," Stella said. "I'll be fine, and I'll text you all later with the details of the surgery. I'm meeting with the oncology team here in a few days, and I'll update everyone after that."

"Should we come?" Dan asked, glancing at his brothers.

"No," Stella said firmly. "Your father will come, and maybe my sister. That's enough people."

"Heather has done enough," Ben said. "I'll be there."

Stella started to object to his dismissal of her sister and decided to save the fight for another day. If she wanted her there, she would be there, regardless of Ben's feelings. This was her life, and she needed to stay focused on that, rather than trying to make things comfortable for everyone else.

Chapter 21

"Dad, why don't you ride with me?" Dan asked as they all walked out to the driveway.

Ben glanced back at the cottage that he had just been rushed out of, and shook his head. "This is ridiculous," he said. "I'm not leaving. She and I have things to figure out."

"Dad," Patrick said, stepping forward. "Just come with us for the day. I think she needs a little time too."

"But we don't have time! She needs to start fighting this," Ben nearly yelled.

"A few days probably isn't going to matter," Dan said. "Having the right mindset is more important than rushing into something."

"I hate to say it, but Dan's right," Jake said. "Mental strength is a huge component in survival."

"Don't say it like that," Patrick snapped.

"Don't acknowledge that she's fighting for her life?" Jake fired back. "This is serious. Actual, real-life cancer."

"Like I'm not taking it seriously?"

Ben stepped between his two sons. "Okay, I'll go with you, as long as you agree not to fight all day."

"We won't," Dan said, staring at his brothers until they mumbled their agreement. "Let's go to the golf course. We can use the virtual driving range and work out some frustrations."

"I thought you had legal things to consult me on?" Ben asked, walking towards Dan's SUV.

"Yeah, I was going to make something up," Dan said with a chuckle. "This is easier."

"I think we should go to the library," Ben said as he buckled his seat belt. "Let's do some research on this. Maybe we can make some calls, make sure that she's in the best hands. There are a few other hospitals that specialize in cancer. One of them might have a more experienced doctor."

"Or we can let her go with the one she's comfortable with," Dan suggested. "We know nothing about him. Or her. Maybe we should trust her judgement?"

"You're right," Ben said. "We don't know. Where's my phone? We need the doctor's name so we can do some digging."

"Dad, we aren't doing that," Patrick said. "You have to trust what she wants. She said she's comfortable with this plan. That's what you need to deal with."

"But what if there's a better one?"

"There isn't," Jake said. "You heard her. This is what she wants. You have to accept that and be on her team. That doesn't mean taking it over and dictating how things go. Sometimes you need to be the support player."

Dan pulled into the parking lot just outside the building that housed the virtual golf. In Vermont, they played more golf this way than out on the course, and they all had fun with it. "Let's put this aside and play eighteen," he suggested. "Put our phones away and not talk about it. We all need to let this sink in for a bit before we make any rash decisions."

By the time they finished their round, it was past lunchtime. "Let's go get something to eat," Dan suggested. "We can talk there."

Ben nodded and got back into Dan's car for the short drive to town, where they parked in front of the Windsor Palace. On a weekday before the ski season, there were fewer tourists loitering hoping for a glimpse at the local celebrities, so they were able to get inside easily. They chose a table away from the windows, and accepted menus from the waitress despite all knowing the options by heart.

"This is a nice surprise." Zoe, the head chef at the Palace and Kendra's partner in the catering business, stopped at their table. "What brings my favorite Burrows men in?"

"We just played eighteen out at the course," Dan told her. "Grabbing a bite before some of us go pretend we have a job."

"Not a bad way to pass the day," Zoe said with a grin. "I made some fresh chicken noodle soup this morning if anyone is looking for some comfort food. And we have pot pies ready to go in the oven."

"You're killing me," Patrick moaned. "I want all of that and can't. Please tell me you have something amazing that I can eat and not have to work out for six hours after."

"I have bruschetta chicken," Zoe said. "I made it with you in mind, you'll love it."

"Perfect," Patrick said, smiling at her. "I knew you loved me."

"I'll get back there so I can make your food myself when the order comes in," Zoe said. "Enjoy your lunch."

"Okay, so let's talk about this," Ben said, leaning across the table. His mind was racing with all the questions he had regarding Stella's diagnosis and plan, and he needed to run through them all. Before he could continue, the waitress came to take their order, and the mayor stopped at the table to say hello.

"I'm sure we can all be a part of it," Patrick was saying to the mayor. "Let me talk to Liam and Nat."

As the mayor walked away, Ben looked at Patrick. "Be a part of what?"

"You heard him," Patrick replied. "He wants us to be a part of the town's birthday celebration."

"Of course he does," Dan said. "You three being confirmed to be here will increase the tourist traffic and money spent in town. Let's make sure you don't already have something else on your calendar, and that you want that kind of attention."

"It's just being on stage to kick it off," Patrick said. "Doesn't sound overly time consuming."

"You say that now, and then he'll throw ten other responsibilities at you," Dan said.

"You'll be honorary mayor for the weekend," Jake said with a laugh. "And for sure have to attend the official birthday ball at the Inn."

"Boys, can we drop that for a minute?" Ben asked, frustrated that the conversation kept going off the rails. "I really need to figure out this stuff with Stella."

"There's nothing to figure out, Dad," Patrick said patiently. "She told you the plan. You just have to get on board with it."

"That's not how I work," Ben said, knowing he was being stubborn. "I work with numbers all day. I like facts and solid proof, not just feelings about a doctor. I want to know that she's in the best possible hands."

"You're spinning in circles," Jake said. "Trust me, I get what you mean. I would always prefer to be a part of the battle plan than to be told what to do. But sometimes you have to put your faith in someone else and believe they are making the best possible decision."

"And at the end of the day," Patrick said. "It's her that's actually going through this. Not you. Or us, for that matter. We are all here to support her and I'll do anything she asks, including pulling strings to get her the best possible care. But I won't do it unless she asks me to."

"I can't lose her," Ben said softly. The fear was clawing at his chest, demanding that he do something. Anything. "And I can't just pretend that I'm not terrified, or that I'm okay just being on the sidelines as she fights for her life."

"But you are," Dan said, his tone gentle. "No matter what. Even if you handpicked the doctor, you'd still be an observer. You can't take the cancer out of her body and put it in yours."

"Remember the time we went camping?" Jake said, changing the subject so suddenly Ben's head spun. "You planned everything. Found the perfect campground, mapped out the drive to get there, told us what to pack. It was supposed to be the perfect week away from everything. And remember what happened?"

Dan and Patrick were laughing as Dan responded. "Stella hated it," he said. "She lasted one night in a tent and then made you rent one of those cabins."

"Which you both got to enjoy, while leaving us three outside in the tents," Jake said. "And it rained all week, so we were always wet and cold."

"What does this have to do with her having cancer?" Ben asked.

"You can't plan everything," Jake said. "Even when you do, and you think it's perfect, something can go wrong. I learned it a million times over in the military. And that trip was proof of that. You thought you had everything figured out, and it was a disaster."

"Not a total disaster," Ben said, smiling at the memory. "Stella and I got to spend a week in a romantic cabin in the woods without you three suspecting a thing."

"You were involved even back then?" Dan asked, shock written on his face.

"Yes," Ben said, nodding. "It started a long time ago."

"Why not just tell us?" Patrick asked. "You knew we loved her and would have been happy."

"That's a good question," Ben said. "In hindsight, it was foolish. But in the moment, we were both afraid. Not only of your responses, but what it would look like to the town. What would happen if something went wrong. There was a lot we worried about, when all we should have considered was our own feelings."

"We would have loved her no matter what," Dan said. "But if you had married her, she would have officially been our stepmom. That would have been nice."

"I always struggled with how to explain her to people," Patrick admitted. "She's not my mom, but she raised me. It was confusing as a kid, so yes, I agree. That would have made things much easier."

"It's crazy to me that you would even think that you wouldn't work out," Jake said. "You're clearly meant for each other."

"We all do foolish things in our lives," Ben said. "This was mine. Or ours, I suppose. Time just went by so fast, and it didn't make sense to rock the boat. Every time we thought we would tell you guys, something happened. Your grandmother was against it from early on, so that kept us quiet for years. Then Patrick was discovered, and that threw a wrench into plans."

"How so?" Patrick asked.

"Nothing that's your fault," Ben assured his son. "But we knew if you thought you were keeping us apart, it would make the whole thing less happy for you. And you were so excited about it, we couldn't take that away."

"She could have come to Los Angeles with us," Patrick pointed out.

"Yes, but then Jake and Jenna told us about being pregnant," Ben said. "And Stella was worried to leave them.

They didn't have anyone else here to turn to if they had trouble. And then Jenna died, and that changed things again."

"I feel bad that we took over your life like that," Jake said. "I was selfish to leave Charlie here. You should have been able to live your lives at that point."

"You were no more selfish than me," Ben said. "We both lost wives and dealt with it in our own way. I let Stella do most of the work raising you three, but then didn't give her the credit she deserved. I should have married her and let her be your official stepmother, and I didn't push for that. I'll always regret that."

"I'm surprised she didn't push for it," Dan said.

"Me too," Ben admitted. "I think that's why I let it go for as long as it did. I guess I'm fundamentally lazy, and didn't want to risk messing up a good thing. But if I had been more persistent, maybe I would have gotten to the bottom of why she didn't want to say anything. I know my own reasons, but never really understood hers."

"And yours were because of Grandma Joan?" Dan asked.

Ben nodded. "And respect for your mom."

"But we wouldn't have thought of it as disrespectful to mom," Jake said. "It was just a different type of mom. Stella was the one there taking care of us. The one we went to when we were sick or upset. Our mom couldn't do that stuff, but that doesn't make her less important. Just different."

"True," Patrick said. "Especially for me, because I don't even have a faint memory of her like they do. Stella is the only one that I had, but growing up, I never put it together. I hope that wasn't hurtful to her."

"What?" Ben asked, looking around the table.

"That we didn't treat her as a mom," Patrick said. "Even though she was. In every way possible. It shouldn't have taken you getting married for us to think of her that way. And even saying stepmom now feels weird, because she's it for me."

"For all of us," Dan said.

"All the more reason why we need to make sure she gets the best possible care," Ben said. "Let's put our heads together and make sure of that, and then we can deal with all of this later."

"We're not doing that," Jake said firmly. "She asked us not to, and we're going to listen. You should too. Trust her."

"Even though it's life and death?"

"Especially then," Jake said. "That's when you put your faith in the best of the best. And that's what she is."

Chapter 22

As she watched everyone head out the door to go about their day, Stella felt herself flashing back to when the boys were little and going to school. It had always been chaotic, trying to get three of them fed, dressed, and out the door. By the time the door closed behind them, she was exhausted, and her day had just begun. That was how she felt at this moment.

Kendra, the only person remaining, studied her from across the room. Smiling gently, she crossed and put her arm around Stella's shoulders, guiding her toward the bedroom. "I want you to lie down for a little bit," she said. "I'll make you a nice cup of tea, and we'll put on some soft music. Just take a little time for yourself, Stella."

"I should…"

"Nothing," Kendra said firmly. "Your house is spotless. Nothing needs to be done right now that can't wait. I'll be with the babies, and I'll be right here if you need me."

Kendra pulled a soft throw from the foot of the bed and covered Stella as she put her head on the pillow. It made Stella feel like a child herself, being cared for so tenderly. She blinked back tears again, which Kendra caught.

"Don't cry," Kendra said softly. "You've been so good to me over the years, it's an honor to be able to take care of you now."

"You're the daughter I never had," Stella whispered, squeezing Kendra's hand.

"And you were my second mom long before Dan came to his senses," Kendra said with a soft laugh. "Let me go make that tea. You rest."

Classical music floated down the hall from the kitchen, and she could hear Kendra moving around. The two babies were babbling and squealing as they played together, the sounds joyful and warm. Before she knew it, her eyes were sliding shut and sleep finally came.

***

According to the clock on the bedside table, it was just after eleven when Stella woke up. It felt, however, as though days had passed. A cup of tea, now cold, was next to the clock, and the curtains had been drawn, so Kendra had been back into the room. Through the closed door, she could hear the muffled sounds of someone moving and the two children playing. She allowed herself a few luxurious moments of pretending all was well in her world before pushing back the blanket and shuffling to the bathroom.

When she emerged from the bedroom, feeling more prepared to face the day, little Izzie clapped her hands and cried out. Kendra had been changing Declan on the couch and smiled at her as she went to pick up the baby, accepting wet kisses and a pat on the cheek from the little girl.

"Someone's happy to see you," Kendra said.

"It's like coming home to a puppy," Stella said. "Every time you walk in, it's like they had been missing you for years."

"So true," Kendra said. "And your timing is perfect. These two are going to have lunch and then go for a nap, so you and I can get to baking."

214

"Are you sure you don't have something else to do today? You have two businesses to run, after all."

"Zoe is down there keeping an eye on everything at both spots, and I have a manager for the restaurant. It's nice to have a partner in Palace Plates, so we can share the responsibilities," Kendra said. "I have a feeling Zoe and JJ will start having babies soon, so I'll take this time with Declan and cover for her when it's her turn."

"Does that mean you and Dan are done?"

"No," she said quickly. "I just know JJ is anxious to start a family, and now that Zoe has finally admitted she's in love with her husband, I won't be surprised to see them be next."

"I wish Patrick and Emma would settle down," Stella confessed. "I see her with these two, and it's obvious that she will be a fantastic mom."

"They will," Kendra said confidently. "They are perfect together. His schedule is so crazy. I bet as soon as he films the next one and has a longer break, they'll start talking about it."

"All this young love around us," Stella said with a smile. "It's making me realize just how old I am."

"You are not," Kendra said. "You and Ben are practically newlyweds yourselves. You have a long life ahead of you."

Stella nodded and turned to the kitchen, carrying Izzie. "Let's see what we have for lunch for these little ones."

Kendra followed, pulling out the two highchairs that could be hooked onto the kitchen table. She settled Declan in, then took Izzie to place her next to him. The two babies happily attacked the cereal that Kendra put in front of them and gobbled down the jars of food that Stella had pulled from the cupboard. Before long, they were heavy eyed and ready for naps, Declan in one pack and play, Izzie in another right next to him that Kendra had quickly set up.

"Ready to bake?" Kendra asked, turning to Stella. "Or would you rather lie down again?"

"No, let's do this," Stella said. "You said the magic words. Now Ben and all the boys will be nosing around later, looking for cinnamon bread.

"I tried to make it on my own once," Kendra said as they gathered ingredients. "Dan said it somehow tasted like I burned the cinnamon, but the dough felt like it wasn't cooked. I thought I followed the recipe exactly."

Stella laughed as she pulled out two mixing bowls. "Dan is just used to mine, and nothing else will ever be the same. No insult to you, of course."

"Well, in his defense, I'm not much of a baker," Kendra said. She tied an apron on and picked up a wooden spoon, grinning at Stella. "Help me, wise one."

They chatted about local gossip as they mixed ingredients, Stella correcting Kendra gently when she nearly mixed up the measurements for sugar and salt. Once they slid the loaf pans into the oven, Kendra glanced over at the two sleeping children and then gestured to the porch. "Want to sit outside while they cook?"

They both pulled on sweaters and stepped outside, where the sun had warmed the porch enough to make it feel like spring was approaching. They each took a chair and sat quietly for a moment before Kendra reached for Stella's hand. "I meant what I said earlier. I love you like I love my own mom, and I'll do anything for you. I know this must be overwhelming, but the one thing you can count on is having us all in your corner. Is there anything you want to talk about?"

"I'm just scared." The words slipped out before she could stop them, and she swiped away yet another tear. "I feel like I really just started living, and now it could all be snatched away. And to think of what would happen to the boys if I didn't make it is hard. They're doing so well, and starting families of their own, and now this."

"They won't lose you," Kendra said, sounding confident. "But that's not your weight to carry. You can only do so much, Stella. You can't worry about all the what-if's, or how everyone else feels. You just need to think about the right now. What's the next step?"

"Surgery," Stella said. "Actually, meeting the oncology team to have my plan in place for after surgery."

"Talking to them will help, I'm sure. My friend Tina is a nurse at the hospital. I'm sure she knows people over there. If you have any questions, I can always ask her," Kendra offered.

"Thank you. I did think of her when I was making the plans, but I know she works in a different department. I'm sure I'll recognize a couple of the people, even from neighboring towns. I've been here a long time."

"Do you have some favorite memories of your life here?"

"Oh, sure. Especially the night that I found you and Dan out in the barn, well after midnight. I don't want to ask what was happening there," Stella teased.

"I'm sure we were studying," Kendra said, straight-faced. "I did need a lot of extra help with my homework, and he was so smart."

"Really, though, I have so many memories here. From childhood in town to all these years living here, and right up until a few weeks ago," Stella said, laughing softly. "I think of that as my pre-cancer days. Those were mainly happy memories. Outside of losing Isobel, and my own parents, of course."

"Those early days, when she died, must have been hard."

"I'm sure you can imagine, with Calle and Declan, what Ben was facing with three little ones," Stella shared. "And suddenly realizing he was alone in it."

"It was good of you to step in to help."

"I never thought twice," Stella said. "And I had my own motivations. Not to say that I wished ill on Isobel. I would have been involved in the boy's lives no matter what. But the circumstances made me more than the honorary aunt I became when Dan and Jake were born."

"I can't imagine their lives without you," Kendra said. "You are such a strong part of my childhood."

"It was a gift. Being a part of this family was the best gift I've ever been given." Stella looked around her, at the property where she had spent the best years of her life. Raising her best friends' children, who felt like her own. "It was a blessing and a curse, you know? I got everything I wanted in one swoop, but I lost someone I loved. I dealt with that guilt for a long time. And I have to wonder if this diagnosis is karma finally coming for me."

"Stella, you couldn't possibly have known what would happen to Isobel," Kendra said. "And I know you. You wouldn't have wished that on your worst enemy, never mind your best friend. Why would karma be after you for doing the right thing? If you hadn't stepped in here, you would have gone on to have a family of your own. I'm sure Isobel was looking down on you, so happy that her boys had you to rely on."

A cry from inside the house ended the conversation, to Stella's relief. She didn't want to revisit the past and the old feelings. And she certainly didn't want the three boys to think that she had celebrated the death of their mother. She had struggled with the guilt of taking over her friend's life for so long; it felt like her treasured secret she wasn't willing to release to anyone.

***

Ben returned late afternoon, looking frazzled and frustrated. He had two large bags in his hands, which he carried to the kitchen and dropped onto the counter. After hanging up his jacket, he kissed her on the cheek and sank into the chair next to her.

"Are you okay?" she asked him when he remained quiet.

"Yes," he said. "But it was obvious the boys were just giving me busy work all day. I can't be mad about it, but none of them wanted to talk about it or help me do research."

"Honey, there's no need to do research," she said gently. "That's what the doctors are for."

"But what if there's a better doctor out there? Or better treatment?"

"Ben, I have to ask you a question, and I want you to really think about it before you answer."

"Okay," he said, the word coming out slowly.

"You understand what the mastectomy is, I know that. I want to make sure that you'll still…"

"Still what?" He frowned, looking confused.

"Want me," she said in a whisper.

"Stella, are you serious?" He stood and moved next to her, going down on a knee next to her chair. "I don't have to think about that, not for one second. You are the woman I love and desire, that will never change."

"But I'll be different," she said, looking down at her lap.

"You'll be alive," he said. "That's all that matters. You can't possibly think I'm so shallow that one breast would make me not love you."

"I just had to make sure that wasn't what had you so upset."

"I'm upset because my wife has cancer," he said. "I'm upset because you're sick and I want to fix it. I don't want anything bad to happen to you, ever. If I could take this on myself to spare you, I would happily. That's why I'm upset. I feel useless."

"You aren't," she said, finally meeting his eyes. "You're the person I need the most. I need your support and love, and your confidence to get me through this. I'm so scared, Benji."

"Mr. and Mrs. Burrows." A young woman in pale pink scrubs, hair in a tight ponytail, approached them with her hand extended. Ben realized who she was a split second before his wife said her name. Finley Monaghan was the sister of local sheriff JJ, who was a close friend of his boys. She also lived in the apartment above the Windsor Palace, because her twin brother worked behind the bar for Kendra most nights.

"Finley," Stella said, her voice warm. "Please, call me Stella. It's so nice to see you. We haven't seen you since JJ and Zoe's wedding."

"I've been working or sleeping," Finley responded. "Desmond spends all his time downstairs at the bar, so I pop down most nights. Especially to get dinner. What's the point of having a sister-in-law who's a fantastic chef if I don't mooch some food?"

"It's funny we haven't run into each other there," Ben said. "We seem to send up there a few nights a week, either to visit with the boys or to have dinner."

"I'm a little bit of an introvert," Finley shared. "I tend to disappear when the crowds show up. After being around people all day here, it's nice to have some time alone. Follow me, I'm going to take you back to Dr. Lincoln's office."

They followed her through the door, into a quiet hallway. "Once you finish with him, I'll give you a complete tour," Finley said over her shoulder. "He is a stickler for time, and I don't want to risk getting you to him a few minutes late. And since I know you, I'll fill you in on him quickly."

Ben increased his pace to make sure he heard, since Finley's voice dropped lower as she leaned toward Stella. "He's brilliant. I would trust him to care for my own mom, so you know he's good. But his bedside manner is, to put it mildly, not great."

They stopped outside a closed door, and Stella reached for his hand. "We don't need to be friends," she said. "We just need to beat this."

"I hope it's okay that I'm one of your nurses," Finley said. "If you'd rather, I can have you switched to someone you don't know."

"Don't be silly," Stella said. "It makes me feel better to have a familiar face."

Ben nodded, and Finley turned to rap on the door. A gruff voice called out for them to enter, and Finley opened the door and motioned for them to go in. The doctor behind the desk looked far too young to be as brilliant as described. His sandy hair was hanging messily over his forehead, and his glasses looked too big for his face. He wore simple blue scrubs, which were wrinkled and looked too big for him.

"Please, come sit," he said, barely taking his eyes off the computer screen. "Nurse, are you staying?"

"I can," she said. "Or I can be close by for when you're done."

"Stay." Finley's cheeks flared red at the abrupt word, but she took a seat next to Stella.

"Mrs. Burrows," the doctor said. "I'm Dr. Evan Lincoln. I'll be overseeing your chemotherapy after your surgery. I understand you're having that done in Boston. They reported that you will have a port placed during the surgery. Do you understand what that means?"

Stella nodded. "Yes. They said it would make the chemo process easier."

Finley nodded her support and murmured agreement, but the doctor spoke over her. "Yes, it will. When your treatment is complete, I can remove it here. Did you discuss reconstruction with the team in Boston, or will you do that here?"

"We discussed it," Stella said.

"Excellent." The doctor flipped through some papers on his desk. "You had a hysterectomy at twenty-two, which is unusual. Was that trauma related?"

Ben frowned, trying to see the papers the doctor had in his hand. It was obviously someone else's chart, not Stella's. "I think you're–"

"Yes." Stella said the word softly, ducking her head down.

Ben stared at her, trying to figure out what was going on. Stella hadn't had a hysterectomy. What was happening?

"That takes away the possibility of cervical cancer also being in play, which we would normally screen you for. And you've been in good health ever since. I see no reason for concern here." The doctor closed the papers and folded his hands on top of them. "My plan is to be aggressive with the chemotherapy. I've spoken to your doctors in Boston and they agree, one fast, hard course and you should be in the clear. That will change if they find anything different during the surgery. There is a risk that it could have spread to your lymph nodes, which would force us to adjust. You understand all of that?"

"I do," Stella said. Ben's mind was still spinning, and the rapid-fire way the doctor was speaking only added to his confusion. It felt like he was watching a TV show in another language, and he was trying to find some clues to follow along.

"I'll manage any and all symptoms," Dr. Lincoln said. "Nausea, anxiety, pain, sleeplessness. Please make sure to tell me immediately. I'd rather prescribe you something than have you suffer. That only makes it harder to get through, and we want you to be ready for battle. I'll give you medication with each infusion that will help with the nausea, but if you need more, I'm happy to get you a prescription."

"Thank you." Stella said, nodding at him.

"Nurse Finley will be your primary," he went on. "We like to have each person in our care have one familiar face for their treatments. That way, she can monitor you for any of the things I mentioned, and ideally, you'll feel comfortable confiding in her if you are having side effects. If for any reason you would prefer a new nurse, all you have to do is say the word."

Stella frowned and reached over to pat Finley's arm. "We'll be just fine."

"Obviously, you can be with her throughout," Dr. Lincoln said, addressing Ben for the first time. "Or a friend. One person can accompany her each visit."

"I'll be here," he said quickly.

"Or my sister," Stella added. When Ben looked at her, surprised that she wouldn't want him at each one, she squeezed his hand. "Only if you can't make it. I don't want this to be a chore for you."

"It won't be," Ben said stubbornly.

"If you don't have any questions, I can let Nurse Finley take you around the unit so you can get familiar with everything," Dr. Lincoln said.

"I had one question," Ben said. When the doctor nodded, he continued. "What are the survival rates of this?"

"Extremely high," Dr. Lincoln said without hesitating. Ben purposely avoided Stella's eyes as he waited for the doctor to finish, feeling like he just jinxed her with the question. "Stella's cancer was caught very early. She was diligent in her self exams and follow through. It does not appear to have spread, and what we will do here is more preventative than anything else. We are fighting the rogue cell that may have slipped through, more than battling active tumors."

"Do you think waiting to have the surgery is a mistake? Should she go now?"

"No, I don't. The tumor appears small, and slow growing. I don't believe there is any risk of metastasizing in the few extra days between now and surgery."

"Thank you," Ben said, finally looking at Stella, who had her arms crossed and looked upset. He stood to leave, reaching to shake the doctor's hand. "I appreciate your time."

He followed Stella and Finley out of the room, and half listened as the nurse toured them around the area. He saw the small rooms where patients received their treatments. Each room had a comfortable recliner, along with a second comfortable chair for the accompanying family member. They also had a table where cards could be played or jigsaw puzzles put together, a television, and a selection of books on a shelf. Finley had explained that they could request food or drinks at any time, and they would be brought right in to them. Each room was quiet and peaceful, and so private that Ben never saw another person as they walked around.

They followed Finley back to the waiting room, where she showed them the door that Stella was to use when she arrived. "We don't want you to be sitting out in the waiting room," she explained. "You just come here and ring the bell, and I'll be right there to let you in. If you need any help from the car, just call me on the way and I'll meet you outside."

"I'm sure I'll be fine," Stella said.

"Keep the option open," Finley advised. "You never know how you might be feeling day to day. Do you have any questions for me before I send you on your way?"

"No, I don't think so," Stella said. "Ben, do you?"

He shook his head, his brain still going a million miles a minute. He needed to get his wife alone so he could ask the questions he had. Finley wouldn't be able to answer any of them. Once Stella had said goodbye, they walked in silence to the car. By the time he had clipped his seatbelt in and started the car, he could feel blood thumping in his ears.

"I know you have questions," Stella said, cutting him off before he could speak. "Can we get home first?"

He nodded and shifted into drive, but eased off the gas pedal when he saw her grab the door handle. Killing both of them because he was driving like a lunatic wouldn't solve anything. He purposely kept his speed at just a few miles above the speed limit, making the drive seem endless.

Once they were in their own home, Stella held up a finger and went to the kitchen, pulling out a bottle of red wine and two glasses. She carried them back to the table between their chairs and gestured for him to sit. After handing him a glass, she poured herself one and then sat. "Okay, let me have it," she said.

"Let you have it? I don't want to fight, Stella. I'm just very confused."

"About the hysterectomy?

"Yes, about the hysterectomy! Why don't I know about that? Is it even true?" He gripped the glass so tightly it was a shock it didn't break, so he forced himself to put it on the table. "Stella, this is a huge thing to have kept from me."

"It really wasn't, though," she said. "You were away at college when it happened. Isobel knew about it, but how do I talk to my male best friend about my uterus? Especially a male best friend that I have feelings for?"

"You could have talked to me about anything," he said stubbornly. "I would have wanted to be there to support you."

"And I would have given up every single dream at the same time if I had told you."

"What does that mean?"

"I was in love with you," she said. "All I could think about was having a family with you. I was secretly hoping that you would end up with me, even though every sign said that you would marry Izzie. And when I lost my ability to have your children, I was already grieving that. To have you see me at my lowest, to know this happened, would have been too much."

"I really don't understand any of this. I can't believe I didn't know about the hysterectomy," he said. "Or the accident, for that matter. Never mind your feelings about me."

"Let me start at the beginning," she said. "When you were away at college, I was here, taking classes at the Community College. You were all the way down in Rhode Island, which was far away back then. And you had just moved back for your junior year when the accident happened."

"Tell me about it," he asked.

"I was driving home late one night, after a babysitting gig," she said. "A car crossed over the lane and hit me head on. I flew off the highway and was trapped in the car for almost an hour until they could get through all the metal. My pelvis was crushed. I was bleeding heavily when I got to the hospital, and they told my parents they were taking me into surgery immediately. They told them to do anything they needed to do for me to survive. I came out without a uterus. The damage was too significant to save it, they said."

"But..." his voice trailed off, not able to come up with all the questions that raged through his head.

"It was a long road for me," she said. "I wrote to you from the hospital and pretended everything was fine, but it wasn't. I had to learn to walk again, once I had finally healed enough to get up. Isobel came home one weekend unexpectedly and found out, and then she came back all the time."

"I remember that," he said. "I thought it was weird that she was making the drive each weekend, and her parents weren't questioning it."

"They knew what was going on," she said. "They knew I needed the support. I was in a very dark place for a long time. All I wanted was to be a mother, and it was taken away from me in one instant. I honestly didn't know how I would keep moving after that news. Izzie knew that, and she pushed me constantly. Talked about adoption, or how many kids are in the foster system that need homes. She kept telling me there was more than one way to be a mom, and we would figure it out."

"Little did she know how right she was," he said quietly.

Stella wiped a tear away and took a healthy sip of her wine. "Which is why I struggled with the guilt of it for so long. It was like the Universe had found the way to give me everything I wanted, but it was at her expense."

"Let's recognize that what happened to Izzie was going to happen, no matter what," Ben said. "What do you think she would have wanted? If she had known beforehand, what do you think she would have planned for?"

Stella shook her head slightly but didn't speak. She grabbed another tissue and wiped her eyes, then sipped her wine. "She had a premonition."

"She what?" The words came out sharper than he would have preferred, but he couldn't stop them.

Stella flinched, but nodded. "Through the entire pregnancy with Patrick, she had a bad feeling. She kept asking the doctor if everything was okay, and she told me over and over again that she just felt like something was going wrong."

"She never said a word to me," he whispered. Why had his wife kept that from him? It must have been torture for her, all those months of worry.

"You had your hands full," she said. "Two toddlers, a pregnant wife, a big job. And your dad had just passed away, so she was worried about you. She made me promise not to say anything. But she made me promise one more thing."

"What?"

"That I would be there for her children," she said. "And for you."

"Is that what this was? Or has been all these years? Your obligation to your dead best friend?" Ben fought to breathe, stunned by her admission. Everything he thought he knew was upside down, and he couldn't see the way through to the truth.

Chapter 23

"How are you feeling?" Heather asked Stella within seconds of sitting across from her at the Windsor Palace. The surgery was scheduled for the next day, and Heather had been worried enough to insist on meeting for lunch.

"I'm okay," she said. "A little nervous, but ready to get this over with."

"How is Ben dealing with it all?"

"Not great," Stella admitted. "He's been a nervous wreck since I told him and seems to be grieving me before I'm even gone. It's making me more anxious."

"Did you tell him that?"

"No," Stella said, shaking her head. "We've had a lot of other things come up that have taken precedence."

"Like what?"

Stella was saved from responding immediately by the waitress, who came to take their order. Once that was settled, she took a sip of her iced tea and met her sister's gaze. "We have been talking about Isobel quite a bit."

"That seems grim," Heather responded. "Talking about the wife he already lost when facing your diagnosis."

"It's more than that," she said. "I told him about Izzie's premonition while she was pregnant with Patrick. And about the promises I made to her. He was very upset."

"At which part? You can't control what his wife chose to tell him or keep from him," Heather pointed out.

"But I chose to keep it from him," Stella said. "Even after we got involved. And certainly, after we got married."

"More than twenty-five years had passed by then," Heather said with a dramatic eye roll. "You had raised three kids with him by then. Four, really, if we count Charlie. Which I do. At what point were you supposed to bring up his dead wife?"

"That's a harsh way of putting it," Stella said, wincing at her sister's bluntness.

"But that's what it is," Heather said. "She had been gone for that long before you got married. Does he really think that was top of mind for you to confess to him before taking your vows?"

"I think he's hurt that she didn't tell him," Stella said. "And that I didn't share it after Izzie died. I just moved in and fulfilled my promises to her and never shared that part with him."

"Let me ask you something," Heather said, crossing her arms on the table and leaning closer. "If Izzie hadn't asked you to do that, what would you have done differently?"

Stella frowned and tried to put herself back into the mindset of her mid-twenties, single self. She had been living alone, in a small apartment owned by her grandmother, and commuting to Burlington for work. The job was entry level at the local newspaper, and she had little interest in the industry, but it paid her bills. She had felt lost, and unsure of herself, while all around her, friends were finding their way.

"I don't think I would have done anything different," she said. "I tried to tell him that. The promises didn't even come into my mind until about six months after she passed, when I was up rocking Patrick in the middle of the night. I felt like I could feel her around us, as if she soothed him back to sleep. And it came back to me in a flash. Before that, I was so grief stricken and busy with the boys, I didn't have time to think of it."

"See? It's not like you intentionally kept something from him."

"We're just struggling in a few ways," Stella said. "Me keeping the diagnosis from him, plus the Izzie stuff. And he found out about the hysterectomy that I had."

Heather sat back in her chair. "You never told him about that?"

"No," she said, shaking her head. "He was away at college. I was in a car accident, and I kept it all from him. I was embarrassed, I think, at that loss. I never properly grieved my lost dreams. I can recognize that now. And part of that was keeping it a secret."

"I'm surprised he never noticed the lack of feminine products," Heather said. "Although there was so much testosterone in the house, I guess it's easy to overlook."

"Plus, I was out in the cottage," Stella said. "It's not like he went through my cabinets."

"He's upset about a lot of things that happened a long time ago," Heather said. "He needs to focus on the here and now and let that stuff go."

"Easier said than done."

"Do you want me to talk to him?" Heather offered.

"No," Stella said quickly. "Please don't bring any of this up with him."

"But where does that leave you?"

"I don't know," Stella said with a sigh. "Still feeling guilty that I stole my best friend's family?"

"Stella," Heather exclaimed. "You did no such thing. You couldn't possibly have known what would happen to Izzie."

"But I was so jealous," Stella whispered. "What if somehow the universe made that happen for me? I had always dreamed of being a mother, and then I lost my uterus because of a drunk driver. And I had loved Ben for my entire life, and suddenly, he was free with three babies that needed a mother figure."

"You can't believe that," Heather said, shock on her face. "Why wouldn't the universe help you fall in love with someone else, or lead you to a child that needed to be adopted? Why would it choose to take her out of the equation? Nothing you did could have caused this to happen."

"I just…" Stella's voice trailed off as she tried to figure out how to explain to her sister what she was feeling. How she had been feeling for all these years. But it was impossible.

"You're anxious about the surgery, and everything seems worse than it is," Heather said.

Her sister sounded so confident that Stella wanted to cling to the words and pretend all was fine. Push these feelings back down, into a hidden chamber of her heart that she didn't allow to open. But her life seemed to be falling apart due to it all spilling out, and she felt more lost than ever. Her happiness seemed to be based on lies, and fixing it seemed impossible.

"I'm sure you're right," Stella said finally.

"I always am," Heather said with a wink. "Let's put this out of your head and focus on healthy thoughts. Get through the surgery and then we can figure out the rest. Are you and Ben heading down to Boston tonight or tomorrow morning?"

"Tonight," Stella said. "We don't want to worry about weather or traffic in the morning. We'll head down around three this afternoon, have a late dinner, and be ready to go in the morning. I wanted to leave earlier, but I promised Charlie that I would see him before we left. He'll come straight from school, and then we'll get on the road."

"I hope you can get some sleep tonight."

"Me too. But that's all I'll be doing tomorrow, so if I don't, that's okay. I'm glad I can at least get Ben settled in at the hotel, so he has a comfortable place to wait while I'm in surgery," Stella said.

"He won't stay at the hospital?"

"I told him not to," Stella said. "It could be hours, and it will just make him more anxious. Especially with all these memories about Isobel swirling around us."

"You're going to be fine," Heather said. "That's all there is to it. I can still come, if you want me to?"

"No, I'll need you when I get home. Save your energy for that," Stella said.

The sisters finished their lunch, talking about local gossip and old family stories, Heather doing her best to lighten the mood. Stella appreciated her sister more than ever. She had stepped up in so many ways over the last few weeks and continued to be a safe landing place for Stella's emotions. The first few days after surgery, Heather would be the one helping to care for Stella, and she knew she would be in good hands. Now she just had to make it through the surgery, and maybe her world could reset itself.

***

The driveway was full when she got home, with not only Dan, Kendra and Ben's cars but also Jake and Patrick's. She could see them all through the window, all collected in Dan's kitchen, as they had done for so many events over the years. Her eyes clouded suddenly as she flashed through the years of birthday parties and nights of homework and girlfriend issues. All celebrated or solved in that kitchen, together as a family most of the time.

Choking back tears, she was debating pulling out of the driveway before they spotted her, but Shea parked behind her before she made up her mind. She could see the moment Shea realized Stella was in the car, the way her eyes darted between the kitchen window and Stella's car. When Shea knocked on the driver's window, Stella forced herself to open the door and climb out. Without a word, the younger woman embraced her, holding tight as she patted Stella on the back.

"It's going to be okay," Shea whispered. "I know it is."

Stella felt the tears flow and only managed to nod slightly in response. Shea simply held her as she cried, making her feel

236

like a child again. When the sobs quieted, Shea took a step back but held on to her hands.

"Is this all too much for you? I can go in and distract them while you sneak around to the cottage," Shea offered.

"No, they want to see me before the surgery," Stella said. "I'm just very emotional."

"Of course you are," Shea said. "You're facing major surgery. And a terrifying diagnosis. But I really think you'll be fine. Come Christmas, we'll be looking back at this as a memory."

"I hope you're right," Stella said. Squeezing Shea's hands, she managed to smile at her daughter-in-law. "Thank you. You've been such a blessing to our family. I want you to know how much we love and appreciate you. You brought Jake back to himself."

"He did most of the work," Shea said. "I just helped him find some of the tools. I'm the lucky one, becoming a part of this crew. There's nothing quite like the Burrows family."

"That's very true," Stella said, half laughing and half sobbing. "And we should probably get in before the rest of them start wondering what's going on out here."

The noise in the kitchen immediately silenced when they walked in, until Shea put a hand on her hip and pointed at everyone. "You all be normal," she said. "This is weird. You're never all quiet at the same time."

Kendra hugged Stella with one arm, the other holding Declan. "I hope you don't mind, but we didn't tell Calle," she said. "It's hard to explain to a little girl, and we didn't want you to have to worry about her."

"That's fine," Stella said. "I'll see her in a few days when I get home."

Dan approached and kissed Stella on the cheek. "We're all looking forward to that," he said. "Are you sure you don't want one of us to go with you? Or all of us?"

"Yes, having Patrick there would help get you all the attention," Kendra said, winking at her brother-in-law.

"Trust me, they are hoping that he will come," Stella said. "I can't tell you how many times I'm asked if I'm related."

"I can come," Patrick said quickly. "Emma and I both can, if you want."

"No," Stella said. "You stay here. I'll be fine."

"I can call and—"

"No," she said, cutting him off. "I don't need any special attention."

"Are you all packed?" Emma asked, swiftly changing the subject. She put her arm around Patrick's waist and leaned on him in a show of support.

"I am," she said. "Ben and I will hit the road as soon as Charlie gets here. I promised I wouldn't leave without seeing him."

Jake was quiet, sitting by himself at the table, his service dog on the floor by his feet. Stella moved toward him, reaching for his hand as she got closer. "Come with me for a minute," she said.

He walked down the hall with her to what used to be Ben's office and was now Dan's. She sat in one of the two chairs in the corner and patted the other, which Jake sank into. Rex sat at his master's feet, his head on Jake's knee, nudging his hand until it stroked the dog's soft fur. Jake looked as if the weight of the world was on his shoulders, and her heart broke as she looked at him.

"Jake." She waited until he looked up at her. "I'm going to be okay."

"You don't know that," he said. Suddenly, he was the three-year-old little boy who had just lost his mom. The five-year-old who didn't want to leave Stella's side to go to school. The teenager falling in love for the first time. The shell of a man, recently widowed, who was telling her that he had to leave. All flashed before her eyes in an instant, making her realize how fast time had passed.

"I don't," she said. "You're right. But I promise I will do everything in my power to come back to you."

"You're the only mom I've known," he said, choking a little on the words. "I don't remember her, but you were always here for me. When I came home again, all I wanted was to let you fix things for me. Like you always did."

"I know this is hard for you. You've lost so much already, and I don't want to be causing you this pain."

"I'm scared," he said. "I can't lose you."

"I love you, Jake. I'm proud to have been able to be a part of your life all these years," she said. "And I know that no matter what happens, you'll find a way to pick yourself up and make it through. Because you've done it so many times, and now you have an amazing wife in your corner, and two children to get you through."

"Three," he said quietly. "We aren't telling anyone yet, but Shea is pregnant. I wanted you to know before tomorrow."

"Oh, Jake," she said, tears springing to her eyes again. "I'm so happy for you."

"I need you here, because we're going to be outnumbered and I don't know how you did it," he said, laughing slightly. "Especially the three of us."

"I want you to stay positive," she said. "I won't be able to focus on healing if I'm worried about you. Can you do that for me?"

He nodded, and her heart wept. For all he had lost, for the worry he was feeling, and for her own fears. If only she could go back in time, fix all that had been broken. But all they had now was a result of what had broken and had been repaired into this. A beautiful family and life, which was what she needed to focus on as she started this battle.

Chapter 24

"I'm sorry." The words came out of his mouth the second he got on the highway heading south. They had a longer send off than he had wanted, and he suspected Stella's emotions were high as he watched her hug each of the boys. Especially Charlie, who had openly cried and fallen into his father's arms as soon as Stella let go and escaped to the car. Jake and Charlie had been clinging to each other as Ben pulled out of the driveway, feeling as though he was leaving his heart behind. But then he had looked over at his wife, looking so small and scared, and he had realized what his role was now. He had to be what she had been to him for so many years, and he needed to start now.

"Did my sister call you?"

"No, why?"

"I'm the one who should be sorry. I dumped a lot on you, and that wasn't fair. Keeping it from you, or telling you after all these years," she said. She wiped her eyes with a tissue and sighed. "I'm so sick of crying."

"I shouldn't have pushed you so much about Isobel," he said. "And everything that happened so long ago. It isn't worth fighting over now."

"Maybe it is," she said. "But at the same time, it led us to where we are now. That's what I realized when I was talking to Jake."

"What?"

"That if I could go back and fix all his hurts, it would take away what he has now. And I loved Jenna, we all did. But what would it mean for who he is today if things had been different? And with us. If I could go back and tell you those things, would it have changed things?"

"It would have changed one thing," he said.

"What?"

"I would have been more comfortable being open about our relationship earlier on if I had known that Isobel gave her blessing," he said. "It would have been easier to fight back against her mom, and against a lot of my fears. And I wouldn't have worried so much about you having a baby of your own."

"You worried about that?"

"Of course I did," he said. "How could I not? You were always the one we expected to have six kids and be a fantastic mom. You talked all the time about how you couldn't wait. You babysat for everyone in town, for that matter."

"But I had the boys," she said. "Even though they aren't mine."

"I wanted you to have your own, but I was afraid to push you on it. I brought it up that one time, and then you never said anything again," he admitted. "I have to admit, I was a little relieved when you didn't bring it up again. After what happened with Isobel, if you had gotten pregnant, I would have been terrified."

"That's understandable."

"See, you're even understanding about my selfishness dictating your life choices," he said. "You can be mad at me too, you know."

"Ben, that choice had been made for me long before we were intimate," she said. "If you aren't mad at me for not telling you about the hysterectomy, or about Izzie's fears, I can't be mad at you for what you didn't do."

He took her hand and was happy when she dozed off a short time later. She hadn't been sleeping well for days, and neither of them had gotten much sleep the night before. The anticipation of the surgery hung over their heads, keeping both awake. The revelations of his late wife's predictions and the promises she elicited from Stella had rocked him to the core. Although Stella had told him repeatedly that she had always loved him, hearing Izzie's words had made him look at everything differently.

The road sped by as Stella snored lightly in the passenger seat. As the Boston skyline approached, she woke, and they both stared at the view without saying a word. The next twenty-four hours were looming ahead, and he knew they would determine his future. Tonight, his only responsibility was to take Stella's mind off the impending surgery. Tomorrow, when she was wheeled off to the operating room, he could let his fears run wild.

***

"Mr. Burrows?" A young man wearing a surgical cap and blue scrubs was pulling on a white coat as he approached Ben in the waiting room. After pacing the small confines of the hotel room, taking himself out to breakfast, working out in the gym, and trying to distract himself by shopping for flowers for his wife, Ben had finally settled into the waiting room. The flowers were next to him, on a small table, as he jumped to his feet.

"Yes," he said. "Ben Burrows. Stella's husband."

"Dr. DiNolo." They shook hands briefly before the doctor crossed his arms. "Your wife did fantastic. She's in recovery now, you'll be able to go see her shortly."

"She's okay?" Ben felt the relief course through him, making his knees feel weak.

"She's great," Dr. DiNolo assured him. "We're going to do some testing to make sure we got it all. I'm confident we did, but it's best to hold off that confirmation until the lab does their work. We should know in a day or two."

"How long will she stay here?"

"That depends," the doctor said. "I would expect three days. We did the reconstruction today, which we had discussed with her at length. That plus the mastectomy, especially given you traveled to be here, I'd like to give her some extra time. If she's anxious to leave sooner, and her pain is controlled, we can discuss that."

"Great, thank you," Ben said. "Will someone let me know when I can see her?"

"Absolutely." The doctor shook his hand again and then left to talk to a nurse behind the desk, pointing to Ben. He nodded once in his direction before disappearing behind a closed door.

Ben sank back into his chair and put his head in his hands, so overcome with emotion, he wasn't sure what to do with himself. She was alive. She was going to be alright. He fumbled with his cell phone as he pulled it out of his pocket, knowing that everyone back home was anxious for news. After sending a group text to his family, he dialed Heather's phone number.

She answered on the first ring. "Ben?"

He could hear the fear in her voice and spoke quickly to ease her fear. "She's fine. The doctor just came out and told me everything went well."

"Oh, thank God," she said, a sigh of relief coming through the phone with the words. "Have you seen her yet?"

"No, but it should be soon," he said. "I'm just waiting for the nurse to get me. I'm just so glad she made it through without any issues."

"You and me both," she said with a soft laugh. "I've reorganized my kitchen cabinets five times this morning, because I stress cleaned yesterday and this was the only thing I could think of to do."

"We can relax now," he said. "I'll call you later, after I've seen her."

"Please do."

Heather said goodbye and hung up, so he read through the text messages quickly. Everyone, even Charlie, who wasn't supposed to have his phone in class, had responded instantly, expressing their happiness over the news. The phone rang before he could read through them all, Dan's face flashing on the screen.

"Hi, Dan," he said. "Did you get my text?"

"I did," Dan said. "I just wanted to check on you."

"I'm alright," he said. "Better now."

"I think we all feel that way. What a relief to have this behind her."

"Absolutely. And if I never see another hospital waiting room, it will be too soon."

"Try to be patient," Dan encouraged him. "Focus on Stella. Get rest for yourself, because when she comes home, she needs you."

"Yes, sir."

"Dad," Dan laughed. "I'm serious. You have to stay healthy for her sake. Especially once she starts the chemo. I saw Finley, and she told me that infection control is really important. I didn't bring it up with Stella, because I don't want her worried that she can't see the kids once she starts. But you really need to do what you can to avoid getting sick."

"I will," he said, sobering at the thought that this journey wasn't over. It was just beginning.

Over the next half hour, he fought the urge to go bother the nurse at the desk. He wanted to insist on being brought right in to see his wife, but knew alienating the staff wouldn't help. When she received a phone call and then waved in his direction, he jumped to his feet and rushed to the desk.

"I can take you back," she said. "But you forgot your flowers."

"Oh, thank you." He rushed back and grabbed them and then met her at the door the doctor had gone through. "Thank you for getting me back here."

"I'm sorry you had to wait. I know that's hard," she said. "But we like to make sure the patient is awake and comfortable before we bring anyone back. Everyone reacts to anesthesia differently, and we like to stay with them until they are stable."

"Was she not?"

"Oh, she's been doing great," the nurse assured her. "Just a little nausea, but that seems to be under control now."

They walked down a long hallway, which opened to a large room. There was a nurse's station at the center, busy with doctors and nurses. The exterior walls were divided into individual berths, the front open to the nurse's station. Ben tried to keep his eyes forward but could tell the beds were all full of people in the same position as Stella. Just coming out of surgery, in pain, some unsure of where they were.

When the nurse stopped and gestured for him to enter a room, his heart hitched at the sight of Stella in the hospital bed. She was asleep and looked smaller than usual. He took the chair next to her, resisting the urge to touch her. After a few minutes, a new nurse appeared in the doorway.

"She's a little sleepy," she told Ben. "But should be waking up soon. We're just about ready to move her up to a regular room."

"So soon? Shouldn't she be monitored?"

"She will be upstairs as well. It will be quieter and more comfortable. Her vitals are great, and we have her comfortable."

He nodded, unsure of himself. Why had they refused to let any of the kids come with him? They wouldn't have panicked at the sight of her in the hospital bed, or the thought that something could go wrong when there wasn't a doctor close by. Telling himself to get a grip, he turned back to his wife and was relieved when she reached for his hand. Even though her eyes were closed, it was a sign that everything was going to be alright.

***

Three days later, he was up with the sun, packing up the belongings Stella had carefully set up for him. His clothes from the closet, toiletries from the bathroom, charging cords by the bed. Everything she had thought to pack for him, and set up for him, while she should have been thinking of herself.

He sat heavily on the bed, realizing how different his life would have been without her. He had been so hurt and angry over not knowing about the conversation between Stella and his late wife and could have wasted the last few days with her. If something had gone wrong, his last memories would be of disagreement and anger, which was not a good representation of their relationship. Why did it matter if Izzie had asked her to look out for him? Even if he had known about their conversation, it wouldn't have changed a thing. He would have still fallen in love with her once he opened his eyes to her as a woman, and not just his best friend.

Resolving to be a better husband and partner, he went back to packing. The sooner he could get her home, the faster he could be the husband she deserved. On his final sweep of the room to make sure he didn't miss anything he found four things he would have left behind. He had to laugh, realizing this was what Stella talked about when she said all her boys were unable to see what was right in front of them. How could he miss his slippers, or the book he was reading?

***

Stella was up and dressed when he arrived, her things neatly packed in the small overnight bag she had asked him to bring to the hospital once she was settled in a room. He had no doubts that she hadn't forgotten anything, and it made him smile.

"What are you so happy about?" she asked, after letting him kiss her hello.

"I was thinking this morning about how lucky I am to have you," he said. "All of us. Me and the boys, and now their families. We don't realize how much you do for us."

"What brought this on?"

"I was packing the room this morning, and I would have forgotten half of my stuff," he admitted with a chuckle. "I was thinking about how you had taken care of me, even when we were here for you. You remembered everything I needed and made sure I was comfortable. I would have forgotten half of it there if I hadn't checked three times, and I walk in here, and you're so organized and ready."

"I always find something one of you was sure you had packed up," she said, smiling at him. "You can't find the milk in the refrigerator half the time or tell if the dishwasher is dirty

249

or clean. I can't imagine how you would figure out preparing for a trip with those observation skills."

He laughed and sat next to her on the bed carefully. "How are you feeling?"

"Better," she said. "Sore, and I'm sure if the pain medicine wore off, it would be much worse."

"Any word from the doctor about the lab tests?"

"Not yet," she said, shaking her head. "He said they were a little backed up, and they'll send the results to Dr. Lincoln. I have some time before I start chemotherapy, so it's okay."

"I'd still like to know sooner than later."

"And we will," she said, patting his hand.

A nurse knocked on the door and entered with papers in her hand. "You ready to get out of here?"

"More than ready," Stella said.

"Were you able to fill those prescriptions?" The nurse looked at Ben, who nodded. "Great, so you'll have pain pills for the ride home. You'll want to take some in two hours, even if you aren't feeling pain yet. Stay ahead of it for the ride. You don't want to be catching up while in the car. Now, we showed you how to empty the drains earlier. Would you like me to show your husband?"

Ben looked at Stella, surprised. He had been here almost constantly since she woke up, and he had no idea there were drains in place, or where they were. But Stella shook her head quickly at the nurse. "I'll be alright, and my sister will help."

"I can help," Ben argued, feeling useless.

"No, it's fine." The look on Stella's face suggested the subject was closed, so he kept his mouth shut.

"I packed you some extra supplies in case you need to change your dressings," the nurse continued. "Again, you might need help with that as well."

Stella nodded but didn't say a word. Ben was looking back and forth between them, trying to figure out what was happening.

"Any questions?" The nurse was looking at Stella, so Ben bit his tongue to ask the many that were running through his head. He thought he was more than ready to bring his wife home, but now he realized he might be out of his depth. He had no idea how to deal with bandages or drains.

"I might—"

"We're all set," Stella said, cutting him off. "Thank you for everything."

"Did you valet park?" The nurse asked Ben, pulling him back to reality.

"I did. That's what they said would be best today."

"Great. Why don't you head down with her bag, and I'll follow in a minute with Stella in a wheelchair. I don't want her to be waiting down there too long." The nurse smiled at him, so he stood and headed out of the room. They'd have several hours in the car to get to the bottom of why he was left out of the important instructions.

Chapter 25

"I brought you some coffee." Ben set the steaming mug down on the nightstand and then sat gently on the side of the bed. "Are you ready to get up? I could help you."

"Heather will be here any minute," Stella said. "She'll help me get ready for the day."

"I'm already here," he argued. "I could do it."

"It's okay, Ben. Heather is already on her way, and she is used to doing all of this."

"But I should be the one helping you." A stubborn tone had taken over, and she could see the temper rising. "I don't understand why you're pushing me away."

"I'm not," she said softly. "There are just some things that I'm more comfortable having her do for me. That's all. It's nothing against you."

"It sure feels like it is."

"I don't know how to convince you otherwise," she said. "I'm here with you. You are the one taking care of me in every other way. I just like her help with some of the stuff that I'd rather you not see."

"But why?" He stood and started pacing the room, stopping after a minute to stare at her with his arms crossed over his chest.

"I can't explain it," she said. "Just know that it's nothing against you. I love you. I'm so grateful for all you are doing for me."

"But you don't want me to help in any way that matters," he said flatly.

"That's not true," she argued. "You're making all of my meals. Or at least heating them up since Kendra and Zoe filled the freezer. You're here all day to get me anything that I need, so I only have to get up to use the bathroom. You're taking care of all my medicine to make sure I get what I need. You're keeping me company. You get up in the middle of the night to make sure I'm okay when I go to the bathroom. That's all important, Benji."

"It doesn't feel it." He left the room before she could respond, and she was ashamed of herself for letting him go. But the other option, of letting him see her with bandages and drains, felt just as terrible.

***

"You're being cruel," Heather said. She had listened to Stella's story about the morning with a disapproving frown on her face before sharing her opinion. "He just wants to help. He loves you."

"I know," Stella said. "But look at this! How could he see all of this and still look at me the same way after?"

"You're not serious?"

"I am," Stella said, but with far less conviction. Was she being ridiculous?

"Stella." Heather sat down next to her on the bed. "He's going to love you no matter what. You think some bandages and a drain will turn him away from you? How shallow do you think he is?"

"He's not," Stella said. "But maybe I've always tried to have him just see the best parts of me. I might be the shallow one here."

"Does he see you in the morning, before you've done your hair and put on makeup? When you have morning breath?"

"Yes," Stella admitted.

"What about when you had the stomach flu last winter, and you couldn't keep anything down?" Heather continued. "Who took care of you then?"

"He did, and then I did the same for him."

"Did you think less of him after seeing him sick?"

"Of course not," Stella said.

"Then why would you assume he would think that of you?" Heather stared at her, and when she didn't answer, she carried on. "You took vows. You promised to love each other through everything and every day. The hard times and the sicknesses. Good times and bad, Stel. You don't get to choose which you share with him, you're a team. You are making him out to be less of a man than he is."

"I don't mean to," Stella said. "I'm just afraid."

"Of what?"

"Losing him," Stella admitted. "I wasn't his first choice, remember?"

"That's absurd," Heather said, standing to pace. "Do you think he doesn't love you enough to see all of this and still want to be your husband?"

"How could I possibly know?"

"He shows you!" Heather practically shouted. "Every single day. When he asks your advice on something. When he makes you a cup of coffee in the morning or pours you wine without asking at night. He brings home flowers for you and buys you thoughtful gifts just because he sees something you would like. It may be as simple as a new book, but it shows he pays attention. That man loves you like crazy and you're making him sound shallow. You're lessening what you have together, and it's not fair. Would you love him less if the situation were reversed?"

Stella hung her head, ashamed. Her sister was right, of course, but it was hard to move past. The insecurities were ugly, and yet she couldn't find a way to shed them.

***

"I'm not sure I'm ready for this," Stella whispered to Ben. They were walking up to the door that Finley had told them to use for her first day of chemotherapy. She would also have a quick exam by Dr. Lincoln while she was here to save them from driving back into Boston. He had seen her once already and removed the drains, for which she was grateful, and said she was healing well. She hoped for more good news today.

"Hi," Finley said in a cheerful tone as she opened the door. "I saw you coming in from the parking lot. The first day is the worst, I swear. Every time you come from now on, it will get easier. And then on the last day, you'll be a little sad that you don't have to come anymore."

"I find that a little hard to believe," Ben muttered.

"I did too, when I first started," she responded. "But it's true. We all cry and hug and promise to stay in touch, but most people do like to forget about this time once they've had a good report at their first checkup. But we still get a lot of Christmas cards and have some patients who come back and volunteer."

"What do they do as volunteers?" Stella asked. She hadn't seen anyone on their previous visits that looked like they weren't an employee, patient or family member.

"We have some patients who don't have anyone to keep them company," Finley said in a quieter tone. "The volunteers come and sit with them. No one should be alone during this. Even if the patient just wants to sleep, the volunteer will just sit and read. It gives comfort, knowing someone is watching over you."

"That's so nice," Stella said.

"You won't have that problem," Finley said with a smile. "You probably have people fighting over who gets to come with you."

"And you know you'll be seeing me around town, so I won't forget to stay in touch," Stella replied.

"Here we go," Finley said, waving them into the small room. "This is your spot for today. They are all identical, but I'll try to keep you in the same one for every visit."

"I'm sure any of them are fine," Stella said.

Dr. Lincoln came to the door before Finley could reply, and Stella saw a stormy look pass over the nurse's face. "Mrs. Burrows," he said. "Are you ready to get started?"

"As ready as I could ever be."

"We checked your port at your last visit," he went on. "I'm glad you decided to have that placed during surgery, it will make things easier for you. Would you mind if I checked the incisions before you begin? I don't want you to have to stay after you've completed treatment."

"No, not at all," she said. She shot a look at Ben, who remained in his seat with a stubborn look on his face. The doctor drew the curtain, and it was obvious her husband was not being pushed out. He had yet to see her without a bandage of some type, and her stomach started churning.

"Are you okay?" Finley asked, a concerned look on her face.

"Yes, fine."

The nurse helped her remove her sweater and unbutton the shirt she had worn underneath, exposing the dressing. She closed her eyes as Finley worked quickly to remove the tape and bandages. She could feel the doctor approach and heard him make an approving sound.

"This looks great," he said. "We can remove the bandages today, but you'll still wear this bra for another two weeks, at least. Is your pain improving?"

"Yes," she said. She felt Finley start to help her with her clothing and rushed to help cover up.

"Great," he said. "I'll take a quick look in two weeks, but if you have any new pain or concerns, just let me know. I'm very pleased with your recovery so far. And you feel ready to start treatment today?"

"I'd like to get it over with," she said.

"We still haven't heard back about her lab results," Ben interrupted. "Have you seen anything?"

"Oh, I did." The doctor pulled up his iPad and consulted it. "The margins were clean. It does not appear to have spread, but this will make sure of that."

"What a relief," Ben said, smiling at her. "Does that mean what you had planned when we met last time is still going to be the right treatment?"

"It is," Dr. Lincoln said with a nod. "No changes needed. Unless Stella struggles, in which case we will look to see if we can make some adjustments. I'll let nurse Finley get you started now, so you won't be here all day."

Finley scowled at his back as he left, but smiled at Stella. "I'm just going to grab everything. I'll be right back."

Stella watched as the nurse chased after the doctor, and they appeared to have a heated exchange before Finley turned and stomped away. The other staff at the nurse's station looked amused as they watched and seemed to tease Finley when she came back out, carrying IV bags. She blushed but kept walking, closing the curtain behind her when she got back to Stella.

"Are you okay?" Stella asked.

"Me? I'm fine. Are you?"

"It looked like Dr. Lincoln rattled you a bit," Stella said.

"Oh, he can be difficult. He thinks I talk too much," Finley admitted. "That I keep patients here too long. But I like to make sure they're comfortable and feel okay before they leave. You're not a number to me; you're a human with emotions. And especially you, Stella, because of all our family connections."

"I think you're a wonderful nurse," Stella said. "I'm sure he sees that, too."

"Doubtful," Finley said as she hung the first bag on the hook behind Stella. "Just between you and me, I think he might be a robot."

"A handsome robot," Stella teased, satisfied when she saw the flush rise up Finley's cheeks.

"Is he? I hadn't noticed."

***

Three days after her second treatment, a clump of hair came off in Stella's hand as she shampooed. Even with the frequent warnings her support group and Finley had given, it still hit her hard. She stared at it for a long time, tears streaming down her face, before the water turned cold and forced her to move. She brushed carefully, seeing more come out, causing fresh tears to start.

"Honey," Ben called from behind the door. "You okay in there?"

"Fine," she responded.

“I'm going to run into town,” he said. “I'll bring back lunch.”

“Heather is coming over,” she said quickly. “Maybe you could give us some time alone?”

“What do you mean? I can bring enough for her,” he protested. “Can you come out here? I hate talking to you through the door.”

She fixed her hair quickly, trying to hide the missing pieces, before going out into the bedroom. He looked upset when she came out fully dressed, and she knew before he spoke what he was going to say.

“How much longer are you going to hide your body from me? Getting dressed in the bathroom rather than coming in here seems extreme, doesn't it?”

“I just need some time to adjust,” she said. “And I'm still a little sore.”

“But not so sore that you need me to help you?”

“What does that mean?”

“It means other than the one time in the hospital when the doctor examined you, you haven't let me near you, let alone see anything.”

“Why do you need to?” she shot back. “Can't you let me come to grips with it first?”

“And you don't think it would help your view of it to know that I love you as you are? Scars and all?”

"I lost a piece of myself," she said. "And no, I didn't want you to see my incisions. You can barely handle it when I cut my finger in the kitchen, never mind this."

"But I want to be there for you, and I can't do that if you keep me at arms distance."

"There's a big difference between not walking around topless and keeping you at a distance," she argued. "I'm right here with you. You've been next to me every day since I had the surgery."

"Are you saying that I'm here too much?"

She sighed, not sure which of them was trying to pick a fight at this point. "Maybe it would be better if you went to do something on your own today. Visit the boys, spend some time away from here."

Ben stared at her, hurt written all over his face, before turning and walking out. She managed to text Heather before collapsing on the bed, unable to find any way to feel better about what she had just done.

Ben sat on the couch, his three boys sitting across from him on the matching sofa in Patrick's living room. Emma was busy in the kitchen, waving them off when they asked her to join them. Ben could see the worry on his son's faces but had to get the weight off his chest before it exploded.

"What happened?" Patrick asked, his voice soft.

"I don't know," Ben said. "Everything was fine, and then suddenly she didn't want me there anymore."

"There has to be more to it than that," Dan said. "Start at the beginning."

"She's emotional," Ben said. A slam from the kitchen jerked all of their heads toward the kitchen, where Emma shrugged and mouthed that she was sorry. The boys turned back to Ben and waited for him to continue.

"But what started it?" Dan asked again. "You guys have seemed fine. We've seen you every day, and there hasn't been a problem before now."

"I don't know," Ben said again. "She was showering this morning and then told me to go out for the day. Said her sister was coming over, and she wanted me to go out. I don't get it."

"So, it wasn't a fight. You're just upset that she wants some private time with Heather?" Patrick asked.

"You make that sound shallow," Ben said with frustration. "But she's never asked me to leave before when her sister was coming over. I offered to bring back lunch for them, and she shut me right down. I'm her husband. I should be with her."

Another slam from the kitchen, this one louder. They all stared at Emma, who was red-faced and looked as though she was struggling not to say anything. "My love," Patrick said in a sweet voice. "Do you have something to add here?"

"I do. Thank you for asking," Emma said. She crossed the room and perched on the edge of a chair close to Ben. "You're being incredibly selfish."

Ben heard his son's synchronized sharp intake of breath, but he kept his eyes on Emma. "Why do you think that?"

"First of all, saying she's emotional as if it's a weakness is just wrong," Emma said. "She has every right to be upset and emotional. She's in a battle for her life. You all could learn something from her, because she's warm and loving and not afraid to show what she feels to those around her. Hiding your emotions is not a strength, no matter what you think."

"Even if it makes it harder to communicate?" Ben crossed his arms and sat back further.

"It only makes it harder to communicate if you aren't listening," Emma countered. "Because she's telling you everything you need to know in order to support her. If your own emotions are making it impossible to see what she needs, that's your issue, not hers. And if you're scared of what she needs emotionally, you need to man up."

"I'm not," Ben protested. "I've been trying to be there for her. She keeps hiding from me, not the other way around. Changing in the bathroom and not wanting me to see her after the surgery, for example."

Emma's eyes narrowed, and Ben resisted the urge to sit back further in his chair. "She's going through something major right now," she said. "Her body has changed, and she needs time to adapt to that. And it's still changing as we speak, with the drugs going through her system. It's perfectly normal to need time to adapt."

"But I'm her husband! I love her no matter what," he said. "I'm not trying to gawk at her. I just want her to know that I think she's beautiful in every way. I love her for who she is, even more than how she looks."

Patrick's phone rang, and he held up a finger before stepping out of the room. Emma's eyes tracked him as he left before turning back to Ben. "You've been very kind to me," she said. "And Stella welcomed me unconditionally when I came into your lives. She could have held me at arm's length, or been suspicious of me, but she didn't. She embraced me and made me feel like an actual person, after years of not feeling that way. Whatever she is feeling right now, it's valid. You need to put your own feelings aside and look at it from her perspective. Be the husband she needs you to be, not the husband you think is best."

"She's right, dad," Jake said. "You can't expect her to act the way you would, or you think she should. Everyone's process for handling grief is different."

"Some of us just leave for over ten years," Dan quipped, causing Jake to punch him in the arm.

"What grief? She's alive," Ben said, ignoring their wrestling on the couch.

"She lost a part of herself," Emma said. "A part of her womanhood."

"But she had the surgery to reconstruct," Ben said. "She's exactly like she was before."

"No," Emma said gently. "She's not. And that's what you need to see."

Patrick stuck his head out of the office and gestured for Emma to join him. They all watched, puzzled, as she disappeared and then reappeared a moment later. "Jake and Dan, Patrick needs a private word with you," she said.

"That was weird," Jake muttered. "He could have told us that himself."

Emma rolled her eyes. "He had to talk to me privately first."

"What's going on?" Ben demanded as the men closed the office door behind them.

"Don't worry about it," Emma said. "Do you want some more coffee?"

***

Jake and Dan said their goodbyes and left to get back to work, seeming distracted or upset when they emerged from Patrick's office.

"Are you okay?" Ben had asked Jake after hugging him. His middle son looked strained, and his service dog was clearly trying to offer comfort.

"He's fine," Dan said firmly, pushing his brother towards the door. "We just both have to get going."

"Daniel Burrows," Ben said. "What are you hiding from me?"

"Nothing. Jake and I just realized we're late, and since he's driving me back to work, so we're twice as late."

"You sure you're alright?" Ben tried again with Jake, who nodded briefly before walking through the door.

"Dan—"

"I've got it, Dad. Don't worry. I know what he needs right now," Dan promised, closing the door behind them.

Ben was rattled by Jake's behavior and wondered what was happening in Patrick's office. His youngest son still hadn't come out, and Emma was doing her best to keep Ben's attention away from the door. She poured him fresh coffee and offered him the television remote, which he declined. Better to sit with his thoughts, as miserable as they were.

The front door opened and Patrick's trainer, Mike, walked in, followed by his girlfriend, Natalie, who was Patrick's co-star in a movie franchise. They both greeted Ben before hugging Emma, the women disappearing into Patrick's office quickly.

"What in the world is going on?" Ben asked Mike, gesturing at the closed door.

Mike shrugged and held up the coffeepot. "No idea. I didn't know she was coming with me until I was halfway down the driveway, and she came running out. I try not to ask too many questions. I think that's the secret to a healthy relationship. You want any more of this?"

Ben shook his head, and then turned as the door opened yet again, with Patrick's other co-star Liam coming in wearing workout clothes. Shea's sister Holly, who lived with Liam, was at his side, and disappeared into the office after saying a quick hello to everyone. Within minutes, the three women came back out, kissed their significant others goodbye, and ran out the front door.

"You really have no idea what's going on?" Ben asked. "That was weird."

"They always hang out," Liam said, sounding defensive.

"At nine in the morning?"

"Holly was hungry," Liam said. Ben tried to study his face to see if he was lying, but it was no use with a professional actor.

"Mike," Ben said. The trainer was his best bet if he was going to crack someone. "What's really going on?"

Mike held up two hands and backed toward the stairs, which led to Patrick's basement gym. "I'm just here to work these guys out," he said. "I think I'll go stretch."

Patrick finally emerged from the office, avoiding his father's eyes and only looking at his friend. "Ready to work out?"

"Patty, what is going on? Your brothers were acting weird, and then Emma and the other girls running in and out of here," Ben said. "I'm worried. Does this have something to do with Stella?"

"Dad, can you just trust me for now? I promise, it's not anything bad," Patrick said. "Please, don't ask a lot of questions I can't answer right now."

"Why don't you work out with us?" Liam suggested. "It would be good for you and take your mind off things."

"I can't keep up with you guys," Ben said. "I can barely get through the workouts Mike does with me at the gym."

"All the more reason to do it," Patrick said.

"Because you guys would spend hours of your day in the gym if you weren't being paid millions to take your shirts off on a movie screen?" Ben saw the hurt look on Patrick's face and felt ashamed. "I'm sorry, that was rude."

"It was," Liam said, nodding. "But also true. I'd love to just sit on my couch with Holly and eat ice cream. But that wouldn't pay the bills."

"Dad, just come hang out with us," Patrick suggested. "Give Stella some space and take a little time to calm down."

Ben followed them to the basement and sat while Patrick and Liam got on treadmills and bikes. Mike stood between them, holding a jump rope, and making adjustments to both machines.

"Hey, go easy," Liam said. "We're just starting out."

"This is easy," Mike said with a laugh. "These two whine a lot, Ben."

Mike and Liam started teasing each other, but Ben noticed that Patrick wasn't participating. He looked distracted and worried, similar to how Jake had looked before he left.

Something was obviously going on, and he needed to figure out what it was. Pushing himself up and out of the chair, he stepped onto the treadmill next to Patrick.

"You want to change, Dad? I've got a whole cabinet full of workout gear in the bathroom," Patrick offered.

"No, I'm fine. I'm just going to walk at a leisurely pace rather than sit on my duff," Ben said. "Gives me a chance to check in with you."

Patrick sighed and glanced around the room, as if looking for an escape. "I think I'll just listen to some music," he said finally, putting his earbuds in.

***

Ben gave up after less than an hour, realizing Patrick wasn't going to give him any information or even look in his direction again. Ben couldn't decide if his son was mad at him or hiding something, but either way, sitting around in the gym was making both of them uncomfortable. He waved and headed up the stairs, trying to think of what he could do for an afternoon. Seeing the stable manager in the paddock gave him an idea, and he quickly made his way out to see him.

"Travis," he called out, catching the attention of the other man as he led Emma's horse around the ring. "How's it going?"

"Good, sir," Travis said. "Just getting some exercise in since it's so nice out."

"I was wondering if you needed help? I'd love to take one of the horses out," Ben said.

"Absolutely. Want me to get one saddled up for you?"

"No, you keep doing what you're doing," Ben said, waving him away. "I'm perfectly capable of doing that. Any preference who I take?"

"Any from Patrick's riding crew," Travis said. "We have six rescues right now, and Whiskey here will only let Emma ride, but you can choose any of the others."

Ben nodded and headed into the barn. The rescues were timid when he first entered, but they accepted sugar cubes from him and eventually let him stroke their noses. The horses that Patrick kept to ride were all itching to get out of their stalls, and he chose a mare he had ridden several times. "Hey there, Beauty," he crooned. Emma had named the horse after her favorite book as a child, and the horse fit the name. She waited patiently while he got her ready and danced happily when he led her out of the stall and into the sunshine. He slid onto her back and set off into the woods, toward the familiar trails he had ridden with his boys. And Stella, most recently, when they took a picnic out to enjoy by the river.

They took a challenging path, which Ben knew would require his complete focus. This was what he needed, to put everything else out of his mind and focus only on the task at hand. His problems would wait, as would whatever had gotten into Stella and his son's. Sometimes the best ideas came to him when he wasn't thinking of them, and he hoped that would be the case today. By the time he returned to the barn, he hoped to have some clarity and ways to improve as a partner and a best friend to Stella. He couldn't lose her, not to cancer, and certainly not to his own inability to see what he was doing wrong.

Chapter 27

Stella had expected a quiet morning with her sister. When the first knock came late morning and revealed Emma, Natalie, and Holly at the door, she had been surprised. When Kendra and Zoe appeared, then Shea, she was overwhelmed with emotion. All of these women had dropped everything to be there for her.

"You should be at work," she said to Shea through tears.

"No, I should be here," Shea said, hugging her tight. "When I get a message that you need girl power, of course I'm coming. What's going on?"

"We have a surprise on the way," Natalie said, winking at Shea. "Should be soon."

"What surprise?" Stella asked, looking around at the room full of women, who all avoided her eyes.

Kendra and Zoe busied themselves uncovering all the food that they had brought from the restaurant. Zoe turned on the oven and popped a tray into it, then pulled out a bowl and started mixing ingredients from her bag. Shea was passing out mugs of coffee to the other women, who were sitting around in the small kitchen. Heather was next to Natalie and looked a little star-struck by her presence.

"I've heard so much about you," Heather was saying to Natalie. "It's nice to finally meet you."

"Hopefully, you've heard good things," Natalie said with a smile.

"Oh, yes," Heather gushed. "Patrick told me he would call you, but I had no expectation of all this."

"Why did you call Patrick? And why did he need to call Natalie?" Stella asked, in shock as the women settled in around her.

"I thought he could help," Heather replied simply. "Sometimes having a superstar as a nephew comes in very handy."

"Like when you needed that reservation at the sold-out spa," Emma said teasingly.

"Those poor clerks," Heather said with a laugh. "They were expecting you two, and they got me and Andy. I tipped well to make up for it."

"I'm sure it was fine," Natalie said. "And knowing Patrick, he probably went there the next week to make up for it."

Emma blushed and nodded. "We did," she admitted. "We went for a massage under a different name and surprised them."

"See? It all works out," Natalie said.

The doorbell rang, and Stella glanced around at the people around the room. She had no idea what to expect but stayed in her seat as Emma moved to open the door. A small man in an expensive-looking suit entered, followed by a much taller, younger man who was dressed almost identically.

"Pierre," Natalie crooned, walking over to kiss the short man on the cheek. "You're so good to come up here on a moment's notice."

"I would think of nothing less when two of my favorite people need me," Pierre replied. "Where should Anthony set my things?"

"In the bedroom, I think," Emma said. She led the taller man into the bedroom, then rejoined them. Anthony followed her out, disappearing out the front door and returning moments later carrying two large leather cases.

"What in the world is happening?" Stella asked.

"My darling, you must be Patrick's mother," Pierre said. He pulled her close to kiss her on both cheeks. "Stunning."

"Stepmother," she replied, brushing past the compliment. The last thing she felt was beautiful, and she knew he was going to be overly effusive over someone Patrick loved.

"Pierre is the top hair stylist in New York," Natalie said. "He did my hair for the Met Gala last season, if any of you saw that. I've been known to fly across the country for him to fix a problem for me."

"And despite what looks like a simple hairstyle, Patrick will spend hours in Pierre's chair," Emma said with a laugh. "I think he was there longer than me the last time we were in New York."

"He worries about thinning," Pierre said in a mock whisper. "But that is not happening. Just don't tell him our secret. I enjoy the time with my hands in his hair. Sorry, darling."

"I don't blame you," Emma said, laughing. "I feel the same."

Stella put her hand to her head, feeling self-conscious and battling more tears. "Speaking of thinning," she said. "I feel that you've wasted a trip here if you came for me."

"Nonsense," Pierre said. Anthony came in on his third trip, carrying more cases, and Pierre waited until he passed to continue. "My own mother went through this, so I dropped everything to be here when Patrick called. The very best thing we can do is confront this head on. Which I know is a terrible choice of words, but it's the best I can do."

"What do you mean?"

He took her hands in his and met her eyes. His gaze was direct and strangely comforting in that way, since so many people had avoided this since her diagnosis. Most people didn't know what to say or do, so they gave her platitudes and avoided talking about it. Now this stranger was in front of her, clearly unafraid. "We're going to shave it," he said. When she gasped, he squeezed her hands tighter. "And then we will find you the most amazing hair pieces you could imagine. I brought everything I had, and I can send Anthony back for more if we need to. Patrick chartered a plane to be at our disposal, and a helicopter to get into the city quickly. He thought of everything and told us to spare no expense for you."

"I don't know if I'm ready," she whispered.

"We never are," he said. "My mother wasn't. But when we finished, and she was able to claim that part of her, she was happier. This is how you take control. Cancer will take a lot from you, including your hair, but this is one way you can beat it to the punch."

Kendra stepped closer, catching Stella's eye. "I'll do it too, if you want."

Stella gasped. Suddenly, all the women were nodding and making the same offer. "Not her," Pierre said, pointing at Natalie. "I know she wants to, but I can't allow her to. She has a contract that specifies what she can and can't do with her hair, and this is definitely on the list of not."

"I can deal with them," Natalie said.

Stella shook her head. "None of you are shaving your heads," she said. "But I love you all for offering."

"Are you sure?" Shea asked. "Because I thought shocking Jake with a blond coming home would be fun."

"I'm positive," Stella said. "Let's get this going."

Pierre pointed at Shea before leaving the room. "We can still make that happen," he said. "We'll find something for everyone to have fun with."

Once they were in the room, Stella saw that Anthony had pulled a chair into the bedroom, facing away from the mirror. She sat, and Pierre hunched down in front of her. "Do you want anyone in here with you?"

"No," she said, shaking her head and wiping away a tear. "I don't want anyone to see me like this."

"Here's what I see," he said. He moved behind her, placing a cape around her neck. "I see a strong, beautiful, very loved woman who is battling an invisible enemy. She can't fight back; she can't tell it what she thinks of it. But she can do this one little thing and take the power back."

She nodded and took a deep breath. "I'm ready."

The clip of scissors was the only sound in the room, Pierre's fingers soft in her hair. After some time passed, she heard the buzz of clippers and felt them close to her scalp. Over the years, she had many occasions to buzz the boy's hair. She flashed back to one of the traditions she had forgotten from when they were in elementary school. The first thing they had wanted to do when school got out for summer was buzz their heads. They would line up in the kitchen, regaling her with stories of their final day in school, while she clipped off the hair they had let grow longer just for the occasion. It had signaled the start of summer for them, and feeling their soft, fuzzy heads at the end of a long summer day had filled her heart with joy.

"All done," Pierre said. "Do you want to see? Or wait?"

"I'll have to look sometime," she said. "Might as well do it now."

"I'm going to have Anthony come in and clean up," he said. "Come with me."

He led her into the bathroom, blocking her view of the mirror. "Before you look, I want you to remember that it will grow back. And that if you decide that you and I are the only people to ever see you like this, I'll hold it close to my heart as a treasured secret."

"I don't deserve you," she said.

He stepped aside, and she saw herself for the first time. Her head was completely bald, a shiny orb in the overhead light. She clapped a hand over her mouth, surprised to find that she was laughing. "I look like my father," she said. "He

278

was bald the last ten years he was here with us, and now I look just like him. I didn't expect that."

Pierre let her stare for another moment before leading her back to the chair. "Now, we have to choose some looks for you," he said. "But I also wanted to show you how to use some scarves and show you some hats I brought. Like I said earlier, you can use these and wigs so that you and I are the only ones who ever see you without hair."

He showed her how to tie the beautifully colored scarf so that it completely covered her head and made her practice over and over until he was confident that she got it. They moved on to hats then, and a few sleeping caps, which were as soft as the ones the newborn grandbabies had come home in. Pierre had brought options in every color imaginable, so many she knew she would never use them all.

"Now, for the fun part," he said. "Let's get you some hair."

He worked from behind her, so she couldn't see what he was applying to her head until he showed her in the mirror. When the first was on her head, she gasped. It looked so real, she would never have known it was a wig. The blond bob was parted perfectly down the middle, with a brush of bangs over her forehead.

"You look twenty years younger," he said with a smile. "Want to show the girls?"

"I think this is too young for me," she said. "I should go with something more similar to my hair."

"When will you ever be able to match your hair to your mood again?" he countered. "Embrace this. We'll fit you with several, and you can change them out at will."

He opened the door and gestured for her to go out, and the women went from looking anxious to grinning. "You look amazing," Emma said.

"I love it," Natalie said. "You look amazing as a blond."

"I think it's too much," she said, touching it lightly. "So different."

"That's the whole idea," Natalie said. "It's like when we do movies, and we get to play a new character. It's fun to try someone else on and pretend. That's what you're doing, in a way. You can be whoever you want to be. Maybe the blond is a seductress, and you can find a dark option for when you want to kick butt."

"I think she looks like a secret assassin," Kendra declared. "Sweet and innocent looking, until she poisons your tea."

They all exploded in laughter, and Pierre led her back to try another option. Soon they were all modeling different wigs, with Anthony helping everyone in the living room and Pierre continuing to make choices for Stella. When he placed a light pink wig on her head, she groaned.

"There's no way," she said. "It's obviously not my real hair."

"Exactly," he said. "It won't be for a few months, so let's try everything. Who knows when you might want to have some fun?"

They settled on the blond, a curly brunette, a longer dark hair that was already braided, the pink that Pierre insisted on, and the one that was almost identical to her old hair that she pushed for. She knew that he had brought it on purpose, but pretended to fight her on it, based on the fact that it was already styled exactly right.

"I think I'll wear this one tonight," she said as he finished with the one like her hair.

"No girlie, you won't," he said firmly. "You're going to knock your husband's socks off and have so much fun you'll forget all about being bald."

"Pierre," she cried, laughing with him. "I can't surprise him like that."

"Trust me when I say a man loves a good surprise," he said. "And your hubby coming home and finding a smoking hot blond in his kitchen? You'll make his day. And night."

She shook her head, but didn't argue when he fitted it on her head. Or when he helped her with her makeup, teaching her a few things she had never known. By the time she walked back out of the bedroom, in the outfit he had chosen, she barely recognized herself. Or anyone else in the room, she realized, when they all turned to smile at her in their new hair.

"What are they all going to think?" she asked, laughing as she looked around. Kendra had exchanged her dark hair for red, Shea went blond, Emma had taken black curls, Holly a black pixie cut, and Natalie was wearing blue hair that somehow perfectly suited her.

"That they are the luckiest men on the planet," Pierre stated. They all cheered, and Stella heard the pop of a champagne bottle. Anthony made his way around the room, handing out glasses to everyone, before Pierre held his glass high. "I propose a toast. To Stella and her health."

They all clinked glasses and cheered again, and Stella was overwhelmed with gratitude for everyone in the room. And even those not here, since Patrick had organized all of this at the drop of a hat. Heather had clearly known the right person to reach out to, because her day had started with a feeling of doom and was ending with her feeling ready to continue the battle. She felt strong and capable, and even beautiful again. All thanks to the people who loved her.

Chapter 28

Ben felt refreshed after the ride. Cooling down Beauty and brushing her thoroughly had allowed him the chance to catch his own breath as well. They had gone further than he had planned, but the horse seemed to know just what he needed. After following the trail through the woods, they came to a clearing next to the river. It was the same spot he used to take his boys fishing and swimming each summer, and where they had enjoyed many family days. Just being there had lightened his spirits, and he was excited to get home to see Stella. She had been right, as usual, that he needed a little time away to reset his brain and mood.

As he walked slowly through the stable, handing out treats again to the horses he hadn't taken out, he caught sight of a strange woman entering Patrick's kitchen door. He was reaching for his phone to call for help when she turned, and he realized the dark-haired woman was Emma. Puzzled as to why she would have changed her hair so drastically, he decided to skip going into the house and go straight to his car.

When he opened his door, he froze. A woman with short blond hair was in the kitchen, and he had a momentary flash of panic. Did something happen to Stella? Did she have to call someone for help? "Hello," he called out. "Is everything alright? My wife?"

"She's fine." It was Stella's voice, and yet it sounded like it came from this woman. She turned slowly and he realized it was Stella, but with a completely new hair style.

"Stella! You scared me," he said with a laugh. "When did you go get your hair done? I never imagined you as a blond, but I have to admit, I like it. You look fantastic."

She touched the hair and blushed like she used to as a schoolgirl, making him grin. He moved closer and kissed her, then toyed with her hair a bit. She winced slightly and pulled back.

"I have to tell you something," she said.

"You look very serious," he said. "What is it?"

"This isn't my hair."

He swore he was normally quick on his feet, but this was throwing him. It wasn't her hair? "Well, who does it belong to?" he asked, trying to lighten her mood.

"It's a hairpiece," she said. "A wig. Patrick and Natalie had someone fly in from New York to help me."

"But why…" The truth came to him when he saw the flash of pain in her eyes and cursed himself. They had talked about the possibility of her losing her hair, but it was such a minor detail in the grand scheme of fighting for her life, he had forgotten.

She nodded, seeing the understanding in his eyes. "This morning," she said. "When I was so snippy with you. I'm sorry I took it out on you. I just couldn't have you see me like that."

"Stella." He stepped forward and took her in his arms again. "I love you. I don't care what's on your head, or what your body looks like. I love you for who you are inside. For what you have done for my boys. For how you love me. All of that matters. Not the hair, or scars, or whatever else you're afraid for me to see."

She sniffed slightly and then shook her head. "I'm so sick of crying," she said. "And I have heard that blonds have more fun. I guess it's time to put that to the test."

***

"I think something is going on between Finley and Dr. Lincoln," Stella said in a conspiratorial whisper to him. They were at her fifth chemotherapy appointment, and she had grown bored with everything he had suggested to pass the time. They typically played cards, struggled through Wordle together, and spent a bit of time each reading quietly. Stella would often take a nap, and he had been known to doze off at the same time. Gossiping about the staff was the newest distraction.

"I don't think so," he said. "They barely look at each other."

"That's why I think I'm right," she said. "It's all an act for the rest of the staff."

He watched as she waved Finley over and groaned. "You should leave it alone," he whispered.

"Nonsense," she said to him. She smiled brightly at Finley. "Hi, honey."

"Hi," Finley said with a smile. "Are you doing okay? Can I get you anything?"

"I'm doing great," Stella said. "I just had a little question for you, if it's not too personal?"

285

"Fire away," Finley said.

"You and Dr. Lincoln," Stella said quietly. Ben noticed a cloud pass across the nurse's face, but didn't trust his ability to catch these small details like his wife did. "Do I sense a little tension between you two?"

"Probably," Finley said. "Just between you and me, he's a fantastic, brilliant doctor. But that's where it ends."

"What do you mean?" Stella said.

"He's the worst," Finley crossed her arms and glanced out into the hallway. "He dismisses everything I say, even when I know I'm right. He's never polite enough to even say hello or ask how my weekend was. I swear, he's the most antisocial person I've ever met in my life. Just because he's a doctor, he thinks he's better than us. If he wasn't so good to the patients, I'd be asking to work with a different doctor."

The sound of a throat clearing came from behind the curtain, and Ben saw Finley's face grow pale. They all waited in silence until the other person came into view. Dr. Lincoln stepped through the open door, and even Ben could feel the tension now. "How are you, Mrs. Burrows," he asked.

"I'm doing fine," Stella replied, sounding as embarrassed as she looked.

"No more nausea? You're eating well?" The doctor continued questioning her and studiously ignoring Finley, who was as red as a tomato and two feet away from him.

"I'm doing well," Stella replied. "We're doing smaller meals which helps. My daughter-in-law owns a restaurant, and they have sent us enough food to last a lifetime. Maybe you've been there, the Windsor Peak Palace?"

"Can't say that I have," Dr. Lincoln responded. "I'm fairly new to town and tend to keep to myself."

"I'm sure you'd love it," Stella said. "Finley's twin brother works there behind the bar most nights, and he could talk to a tree. He'll introduce you around."

Dr. Lincoln glanced at Finley so quickly Ben thought he might have imagined it, but then he nodded in Stella's direction. "If that's all, I'll get back to it. Let me know if you need me for anything. Or if you have anything else to share." He said the last bit in Finley's direction as he walked out of the doorway, and the nurse looked even more horrified.

"I'm so sorry," Finley said to Stella. "I didn't mean to do that. I didn't think he was even here today. That was so embarrassing. I'm sorry I dragged you into it."

"Are you kidding?" Stella asked, the glee in her eyes visible. "That was the best thing to happen to me all week. I can't wait to get you two in a room together again. This gives me something to focus on."

"Please, don't," Finley begged. "I really like this job and don't want to have to quit."

"Nonsense," Stella said. "You heard the man! He's new to town and needs some friends. And you know just about everyone, and Desmond can introduce him to the rest."

Finley kept shaking her head as she made her way out of the room, peeking down the hall first before darting to the nurse's station. Ben couldn't help but laugh, thinking of all the ways he was sure Stella would try and throw them together now.

"They are adorable together," Stella said, proving him right.

"Really? I was uncomfortable watching them," he said.

"But don't you see? If they didn't have something happening between them, it wouldn't bother them so much," Stella said. "It's like when Dan used to pull Kendra's hair in first grade."

"These are two grown adults," Ben argued. "Medical professionals. Not children."

"You'll see," Stella said. "I'll work my magic."

***

They had settled into an ease with chemotherapy, and Stella had come out of her shell after the day with the hairstylist. Ben had been convinced to go play a round of golf with the boys after her seventh treatment, the end clearly in sight for this fight against cancer. Stella had told him she was feeling tired and could use the day of rest without him puttering around, so he had happily headed out with his sons for the day.

It was nearly five o'clock when he was leaving the golf course, far later than he had expected. Stella hadn't answered his few text messages, and when she didn't answer the phone as he drove home, he got a pit in his stomach. Dan seemed to pick up on his tension as he listened to the phone ring, so he pulled out his own phone.

"You're not supposed to use that thing and drive," Ben said.

"Obviously you're worried," Dan shot back. He turned his attention back to his phone and spoke into it. "Hey honey. Have you seen Stella today? Could you do me a favor and run over to check on her? She's not answering dad's calls."

Dan hung up and tossed the phone into the console between them. "She'll call me back."

"Step on it," Ben said. "I have a bad feeling."

Five minutes later, Dan's phone rang, Kendra's name appearing on the car's screen. Ben hit the answer button before Dan had a chance, but waited for his son to say hello. "Ben, can you hear me?" Kendra's voice came through the car speaker.

"Yes."

"She's burning up," Kendra said. "I'm calling 911 right now. Hurry home."

"Dan—"

"I'm on it," Dan said. He pointed to the screen that displayed his phone screen. "Call JJ."

Ben scrolled through Dan's contacts on the list and hit connect for JJ. The sheriff answered on the first ring. "I just got the call," he said. "I'm going to head up there to see if I can help."

"My dad and I are about to come through town," Dan said. "I need you."

"Where are you coming from?"

Dan told him, and JJ promised to be in front of them. Within three minutes, they were racing through town behind the police car, lights blazing. When they got to the house and saw the fire truck and ambulance in the driveway, Ben jumped out before the car even stopped. A fireman tried to stop him, but he ran past everyone until he got inside and saw Stella.

She was as pale as the sheet on the gurney, other than her cheeks, which were blazing red. They had placed an oxygen mask over her face and had leads all over her chest. Her eyes were closed, and she didn't respond even when he called out to her.

"What's happening?" he asked the closest paramedic. "What's wrong with my wife?"

"Your daughter told us that she's been going through chemotherapy? My best guess is some kind of infection," the man said. "We're going to take her to the hospital. They know we're on the way. I'd offer to let you ride with us, but we're tight on space."

"I'll take him," JJ offered from behind Ben. The paramedic nodded and they continued past Ben with the stretcher. It was all he could do not to throw himself on top of her and beg her to be okay.

Calle was standing on the back porch of the main house, tears rolling down her face. Ben watched as Kendra gathered the little girl in her arms and saw Dan move to be with them. As much as he wanted to comfort his granddaughter, he needed to be with his wife.

"JJ, can we follow them?"

"Let's go," JJ replied. "Dan, I'm taking your dad."

"We'll be right behind you," Dan called back.

"Make sure she's okay first," Ben said, his voice breaking as he nodded at Calle.

***

After an hour of agonized waiting, Dr. Lincoln appeared in the conference room the family had been brought into. Ben had been placed in the crowded waiting room with JJ, not even able to find two empty chairs to sit in. But when Patrick arrived twenty minutes later, the hospital administrator herself had rushed down to find a more comfortable spot for the family to await news. JJ had left, hoping to help create a perimeter for the press to respect once they found out Patrick was inside. Now Ben, Dan, Jake, Patrick and Emma were huddled around the table, and all jumped to their feet when the doctor arrived.

"Hello," he said, briefly acknowledging the people he hadn't met yet. "Mr. Burrows, it appears Stella has contracted pneumonia. It was one of the risks that we went over before starting the treatment."

"How big of a risk? Is this life threatening?" Dan fired off questions so fast the doctor seemed to take a step back.

"Any infection is life threatening when someone is undergoing chemotherapy," Dr. Lincoln replied. "The treatment kills off white blood cells, which the body needs to fight off infection. A healthy body presented with a virus will try to fight it off, triggered by the white blood cells. Someone who is undergoing chemotherapy and fighting off those white blood cells is highly susceptible to infection. And when a patient does get sick, it is harder to fight."

291

"Should we move her to Boston?" Patrick asked. "I can get a medical flight."

"No, let's not rush things," Dr. Lincoln said. "I've been here with her every day and am familiar with her treatment. I have already started her on a strong course of antibiotics, and between that, oxygen, and a lot of rest, I believe she will make a full recovery."

"You believe or you'll guarantee?" This from Jake, who looked ready to snap.

"There are no guarantees in regards to health, unfortunately," the doctor said. "I can guarantee I'll do my best. That's all I can promise."

"When can we see her?" Ben asked.

"Not anytime soon," Dr. Lincoln replied. "She's in the ICU, and she will stay there until she's stable. I'll let you go in for a few minutes at a time, one at a time, once I feel she is up to it. In the meantime, the best thing I can suggest is that you go home. Get some rest yourself, so you don't get sick as well. I'll call you with any updates."

"Oh, we are not leaving," Jake said.

"No, we aren't," Patrick agreed. "We'll be right here."

The doctor nodded and backed out of the room, and they all sat back down and stared at each other. Jake pushed Patrick's cell phone closer to him and gestured with his chin. "Get on that."

"And do what?"

"I don't know," Jake yelled. "Whatever it is you celebrity millionaires do. Get someone here who can save her."

Ben put his hand on Jake's arm, shocked at how rigid he was. Rex, Jake's service dog, was licking his other hand and nudging him with his nose. Jake finally put his hand on the dog's back, and the dog reciprocated by laying its head on his leg.

"Do you think I would sit here and do nothing to save her if I thought there was anything I could do?" Patrick snapped back at his brother. "Tell me, genius, who I should call?"

Jake sighed and ran his hand through his hair before putting it back on Rex's back. Before he could answer, the door opened, and Shea stepped in. "I got here as quick as I could," she said. "Holly and Liam came over. They're going to take the kids over to Dan and Kendra's and watch everyone. Mike and Natalie said they would go help. So, we'll have four adults watching Charlie take care of the three little ones."

Dan laughed roughly. "Thanks," he said. "Kendra texted that she was on her way."

"Are you okay?" Shea asked Jake softly as she sat next to him. Ben watched as his son visibly relaxed in the presence of his wife and was glad she had been able to come.

"Little stressed," he said.

"She'll be okay," Shea said. "I believe that, and you need to as well. Focus on the things you can control."

Jake nodded, and they all settled into silence to wait for news. Kendra arrived and quietly slipped into the seat next to Dan, reaching over to squeeze Ben's hand. Zoe and JJ arrived, with bags full of sandwiches, bottled water, and a vat of coffee. They were taking everyone out when Finley appeared in the doorway.

"Mr. Burrows, I can take you to see your wife now."

Chapter 29

The exhaustion had come out of nowhere. One minute she had a little nagging cough, the next she couldn't keep her eyes open. Through the heavy fog of sleep, she had been aware of Kendra, the emergency responders, and Ben's frantic calling of her name. Once she arrived at the hospital, she had been poked and prodded, and yet all she wanted was to sleep. Finally, she had been moved out of the bright lights and noise where she had been into a quieter, dimmer room. Now she could finally rest.

Just as she was drifting off again, she heard a soft woman's voice, followed by Ben's much louder one. "Okay, okay, I'll only stay for five minutes," he said. "Just let me see her, please."

She tried to open her eyes to see him, but they wouldn't cooperate. He took her hand and leaned over, so she felt his lips on her forehead before she heard him sit. "Stella, honey, it's me," he said. "Are you awake?"

The most she could do was squeeze his hand, and even that took all of her strength. Fortunately, she didn't have the energy to worry about what was wrong with her. That would come later, if she could get at least an hour of sleep. Then she could figure this all out.

"I'm here," Ben said. "The boys too. We're not leaving until we know you're okay. Can you squeeze my hand again, so I know you heard that? There, good. You gave us all quite a scare, but you're going to be just fine. You're in good hands here. Finley even came up to make sure you had the best nurse on the floor. And Dr. Lincoln is involved with everything. They'll get you up and out of here before you know it."

She could feel the weight of his arm on the bed next to her, and the soft stroke of his hand on her cheek. The snuffle she heard could have been him crying, but that would shock her. There had only been two occasions when she had seen him cry in front of other people. One was the day that Isobel died, and the second the day they got the news about Jenna. Ben had always tried to be a pillar of strength to those around him and only let his raw emotions through when he was sure everyone else was supported.

"I love you," he said. "I hope you understand how much. I know I've been difficult, and I've been working hard to stop being selfish and only thinking about my own feelings. Especially when it comes to your cancer. My only job is to take care of you, and I freaked out, thinking that I could lose you. I can't lose you, Stella. You're my everything."

"Sir? We need to let her rest now." The woman's voice came from further away, as if she was talking from the hallway into the room. Stella wanted to tell her to leave him alone, let him stay right where he was, but she couldn't garner the strength.

Instead, she felt the press of his lips to her forehead again. "I'll be back," he said. "I'm going to let the boys come in for the next few visits. They'll go crazy if I am the only one coming in. But I'll be back later. You get some rest."

She heard the click of a door closing a moment later and then silence again. The sleep she had been holding at bay took over quickly, pulling her into the darkness.

***

"This is her room." A woman's voice again broke through the dreamless sleep Stella had been in. Had it been minutes? Hours? Days? She had no idea. "You can only stay with your mom for ten minutes at the most, okay? It was so nice to meet you. I hope she's better soon."

"She's, uh," Patrick's voice stammered. The way the woman was talking, Stella had known that it was Patrick coming in. People always reacted to him the same way, and it rarely threw him. She must look terrible if he was so overwhelmed. When he spoke again, it sounded surer. "Thank you."

The door closed, and she felt him come closer. Like Ben, he leaned over and kissed her before sitting and holding her hand. "Hi, it's me, Patrick," he said. "Dad said you squeezed his hand, so he knew you were awake?"

She squeezed and heard him sigh in relief. "Oh, good. Because I only have a few minutes, and I just realized something. I wish you were feeling better, and we were having this conversation anywhere else, but I have to say this now. That nurse? She just called you my mom. And I almost corrected her. But she's right. You are my mom in every way. Isobel gave birth to me, and you raised me. I'm the luckiest man in the world to have two loving mothers. I'm sorry I never thought of asking if I could call you that before. But I'd like to start now, if that's okay."

Stella used all of her energy to open her eyes. Tears were streaming down her cheeks, and she needed to see her precious boy's face. The youngest, who she had taken in her arms just an hour after he came into the world. She had spent

297

so much time memorizing his tiny little features, especially in the middle of the night, when it was just the two of them. Watching him grow into the man he was today had been one of her greatest pleasures. Once she managed to open her eyes, she saw that he was also crying.

"Are you okay?" he asked. "Should I call a nurse?"

She shook her head and summoned the strength to speak. "I love you, so very much. It's my honor to be your mom."

He cried with her and hugged her as best he could with all her tubes and wires. "Don't tell Jake and Dan that I'm your favorite," he said, making her smile. "I think they know anyway, but why burst their bubble?"

"I'm so tired," she managed to whisper, closing her eyes again.

"That's okay, you rest. I'm going to sit here until they kick me out," he said. "I love you. And I want you to get better soon. I need you there when I get married. Not that it's happening anytime soon, but you know what I mean. I'm going to stop talking now."

***

Dan was next to come into the room, his short conversation with the nurse waking her up. She still had no concept of time, and it was a struggle to wake up for him. He sat next to her quietly for several moments before she heard him clear his throat.

"I hope you're awake enough to hear me," he said. "I don't want to wake you up if you're asleep."

She managed to open her eyes enough to meet his, and give him a weak smile, before closing them again. He sighed in what sounded like relief.

"I haven't been that scared since Calle disappeared," he said. "Or when I was standing out in the hallway, waiting for the police to save her. All those years of having Jake in war zones had hardened me to fear, I think. I was always afraid for him, worried about the news, so I fought off every other connection. Now that I'm back, and I have a family of my own, losing any of you is too terrible to even think about. I hope you know how much I love you, and how grateful I am for all you've done. We all need you to get better. You're what holds our family together."

He sat in silence, holding her hand so she knew he was still there. Dan was always good at providing a safe space for others. His silence was never heavy or tense. It was a warm place, where those around him knew he would speak if necessary, and was always willing to listen. His quiet confidence was why he found such success as a lawyer. People naturally trusted him, and she knew it was warranted.

After his allowed time passed, he stood and kissed her softly on the cheek. "Jake is coming in next," he said. "He's struggling. He needed the extra time to get it together. But he'll be alright, so don't start worrying about him. Focus on getting better, we've got him."

Even though she wanted to stay awake enough to ask him questions, or to demand Jake come into the room this instant, she fell back to sleep. It felt like just moments later when she heard the click of Rex's paws on the floor and knew Jake was there. The weight of his arms shifted her weight towards him.

She managed to open her eyes to see him sitting, arms crossed on the bed and his head down on top of them. Reaching up, she was able to stroke his head as he cried.

"Please don't leave me, Stella. Mom," he said, his voice broken. "Patrick is right. We should have been calling you that all these years. You've been there for me in so many ways. You kept me alive. I don't think I ever told you that, but you did. Knowing you were here, and that I could always count on you, got me through the worst days of my life. I could never possibly thank you enough for what you did for me. And for Charlie."

"You don't need to thank me," she whispered. "I love you."

"And I love you. I'm sorry if I took you for granted," he said. "And I don't mean to make this about me, but if you could stick around, I would really appreciate it."

"What are they saying?" she asked, realizing she didn't even know what was wrong with her.

"Pneumonia," he said. "They have you on some strong antibiotics. They told us they are doing everything, and we just have to wait for them to start working. But I know what the most important thing is when facing death. And it's wanting to live. I know you have that fight in you."

"I do," she said. "I'm just so tired."

"You rest," he said. "I'll stay until they kick me out."

"You stay strong," she said, closing her eyes as he nodded.

As promised, Jake sat by her side until she heard the nurse return for the third time, asking him to leave. They were gentle with him, and she guessed they saw that he was having a hard time. Once he left, she settled into a deeper sleep, knowing he was back with the family that would support him.

***

When she woke again, the sun was bright outside the window. She was trying to remember if it had been as sunny when Jake had been in the room when her eyes landed on the clock on the wall. It said eight, which could only be in the morning based on the light. Had she been asleep for nearly a day?

Her bladder was screaming at her to find a bathroom, so she started to climb out of bed, but stopped when an alarm sounded. The door burst open, and a nurse rushed inside, stopping and putting a hand on her chest when she saw Stella. "Oh, you scared me," she said. "Are you trying to get up?"

"I need the restroom," Stella said, surprised at how hoarse her voice sounded.

"Let me just help you," the nurse said. She quickly unplugged the IV pole and brought it to Stella's side, where she offered her an arm to lean on. "You're going to be weak. We're going to leave the oxygen on, so you don't get dizzy."

They slowly creeped along, Stella leaning on the nurse heavier than she would have thought, before getting into the bathroom. The nurse made sure the oxygen tubing fit under the door before stepping out, reminding her to pull the cord when she was finished. They repeated the process to get Stella back to bed when she was done.

"I think we'll be moving you to a regular room today," the nurse shared. "You seem to be doing much better. You gave your family quite the scare. They haven't left, you know. Sat here all night. At least, your husband and sons."

"They did? Can I see them?"

"We're only allowed to have one visitor in here at a time," the nurse said. "But I'll see what I can do. Just between us girls, everyone came in today hoping to catch a glimpse of Patrick. We are all big fans of his."

"I'm sure he'll be happy to meet everyone," Stella said.

"I'll see if I can get them all back at once," the nurse said. "If not, I'll work on getting you moved quickly so they can all be with you. If we can only do one person, do you have a preference?"

"My husband," Stella said quickly. "Not to deny you all, but I'd like to see him first if they can't all come. But I'll make sure Patrick visits with you all even if it's after I move."

She felt weak and short of breath from just the walk to and from the bathroom. Every part of her body ached, and her chest hurt with each breath she took. But when she realized she was as bald as the day she was born, she gasped and stared at the nurse. "Where is my hair piece?"

"Oh, I'm sorry," the nurse said. "I think it came off before you went in the ambulance. We have some knit caps that a local group donated. Would you like me to get you one?"

"Yes, please," Stella whispered. She fought off tears as she watched the nurse leave. Yes, her whole family had seen her bald. But there were worse things than that, and she needed to cope. She was lucky to be alive, after all. Hair seemed minor in comparison.

Her vanity and ridiculous insecurity had kept her husband at arm's length after her surgery and even had her hiding her bald head from him. Even the day she spent trying on the wigs, she hadn't let anyone see her bald. Being in the hospital was a harsh wake-up call for her to remember what was important. And that was her health, and her family. Not what her body looked like, or her hair.

Chapter 30

"Did we get everything?" Ben asked, looking around the hospital room. It had been a week since Stella went into the hospital, and he was anxious to get her home.

"I think so," she said. She was seated in a wheelchair, waiting to be pushed to the car by Dan.

"Want me to carry that?" Patrick asked, his arms already loaded with the flowers and gifts that had accumulated in the small room.

"You've already got enough," Ben said.

"Plus, you might have to fight off your fans," Dan added.

"I told you it would be easier if you stayed home," Jake muttered. "All those people are here for you."

"It will be fine," Patrick insisted. "You said you parked outside a staff entrance that we can use. No one will even see us. Besides, I don't want to miss this. It's a big day."

"Don't fight, boys," Stella said. "It will be fine."

Ben knew she had taken extra time in the bathroom this morning, worried about the photographers. Her hairpiece was freshly done up by a local hair stylist, and Kendra had brought her a brand-new outfit. Natalie had even stopped by to do her makeup, but had disappeared with Mike before the crowds grew.

"I think we're ready," Ben said. "Let's get you home."

They headed out the door, led by Jake and Rex, who were intimidating enough to make people think twice about rushing Patrick. The nurses lined up at the desk only wanted to hug Stella and wish her luck, having had their fill of the celebrities coming and going during her stay. Over the course of Stella's stay, they had been spoiled with meals, candy, spa treatments, and anything else Patrick and his friends could think to send. The staff had been telling Stella that they wanted her to stay, because they had never been so spoiled. A nurse directed them to a small elevator, which was only used by staff to transport patients.

When they reached the exit where the car was parked, they realized word had spread about their plans. A group of photographers and a news camera were outside the door, along with a group of fans.

Jake stopped and turned back to the family. "I can go move the car, find another exit."

"No, it's fine," Stella said. "I just want to get home, so whatever we need to do, let's do it."

"If I go out and make a statement, you can sneak right out and no one will even notice," Patrick said. "Dan, can you help me? Jake, you help Dad."

Ben took over behind his wife's wheelchair, staying partially hidden behind a wall while his two sons went out to face the cameras. Once everyone was looking in their direction and the hospital security was straining to keep them contained, Jake indicated that they should follow him through the door. Stella held up her hand before they could go through.

"I'd like to walk," she said.

"Are you sure?" Ben asked. "I know you're still weak."

"Benji, I'd rather have pictures of me on your arm than in this chair," she said. "I feel stronger, and if I'm going to send a message to other women who are fighting cancer, I want it to be that. We can battle back from anything."

Jake glanced back inside, looking confused about why they hadn't followed him. Ben shrugged and helped Stella from the chair, tucking her hand into the crook of his elbow. "Ready?"

"As I'll ever be," she said.

They stepped outside, the bright sun blinding Ben briefly. As he blinked to clear his eyes, he saw Jake and Rex standing by the large SUV with the passenger door open for Stella. Patrick and Dan were trying to draw attention in the opposite direction, which would have worked if one photographer hadn't spotted them.

"Is that your mother?" He called out, pointing over to where Ben and Stella were.

Patrick paused, his eyes meeting Ben's, before looking at Stella and nodding. "Yes. That's my mom. And she's going to be healthy and just fine. I appreciate all the prayers and well wishes that have been sent her way over the last week. Not to mention the thousands of cards she received from all over the world. You've made her feel very special. And now we're going to get her home so she can continue to recover."

Ben blinked back tears, still not used to hearing the boys call Stella 'mom'. They had told him of their decision while she was still unconscious, her weak body fighting off the virus that was threatening her. He had cried that day, so happy that his sons had grown into the kind of men who would realize how much that would mean to her.

He helped Stella into the front seat and put the bags he was carrying into the back before climbing in himself. Jake was in the driver's seat, Rex between the two captain's chairs in the backseat. After Patrick gave his final fan the chance for a picture with him, the other two climbed in. Patrick pushed Dan to go into the third row, making his brother groan.

"I just got groped for you. I should at least get to sit in the good seat," Dan griped as he climbed past Ben.

"It would be bad for my image," Patrick said. "Besides, Rex likes me better."

Ben smiled the whole drive home, listening to his boys rib each other. They kept the mood light in the car, making Stella laugh as they teased each other. Over the years, they had spent plenty of time in cars, just the five of them, but it had been a long time since that had happened. Now their family had expanded and grown even more beautiful, and he couldn't be happier. But for this one moment, he soaked in the feeling of peace he had from them being together.

***

The girls had worked their magic at home. Ben had barely been there, other than to sleep and change clothes, so even he was surprised when he walked in. Every surface was spotless, and even the air smelled clear and clean. Kendra and Zoe had cleaned out the kitchen and restocked the refrigerator and freezer while Shea and Emma tackled the rest of the house. What had already been a tidy cottage was now gleaming.

"Are you exhausted?" Kendra asked Stella, a worried expression on her face. "The kids are all next door with Charlie and JJ. We didn't want to overwhelm you, but if you are up for it, we can do a big dinner over there."

"I'd love that," Stella said. "Unless you're too tired, honey?"

Ben grinned at her. "You can keep the focus on you a bit longer," he said. "Don't start taking care of me already. I have big plans to be the best, most helpful husband on the planet now that you're home. If you're up for dinner, I am as well."

"You were already the best husband in the world," Stella said, kissing him softly.

"Hey, now," Dan said. "I think I do a good job."

"Same," Jake said with a laugh.

Patrick shrugged, throwing an arm around Emma. "You all give me something to aspire to, should the right woman come along." When Emma jabbed him in the stomach, he laughed. "I mean, when we decide we're ready to take that step. Because I clearly already have the right person."

"The best husband over the age of fifty," Stella said, making everyone laugh.

"No age jokes," Ben said quickly. "Why don't you all head next door and let Stella rest, and we'll be over in an hour or so."

Ben snoozed in his recliner for an hour while Stella rested in the bedroom, and once ready, they walked across the yard, hand in hand. "If you get tired, just let me know," he said. "We can leave at any point."

"I will," she said. "It will be nice to be with everyone, though."

"Be careful with the kids," he warned her as they got to the door. "I know you love them, but Calle and Charlie are in school and carry a lot of germs."

"I'm on every antibiotic in the world," she said with a soft laugh. "I can't possibly catch anything."

"Still, I'd feel better." When she nodded, he turned the handle, and they walked into the kitchen that had been her domain for all those years. He still expected to see her behind the large island, a mixing bowl and spoon in hand, every time he walked in the door. Kendra and Dan hadn't changed much in the kitchen, and he knew that was to honor how much Stella loved the room.

The adults were all gathered in the kitchen around the table, two bottles of wine open in front of them. The sound of a Disney movie was coming from the living room, where Ben knew the kids would be found. Based on the sounds, both babies were awake and enjoying their noisy toys.

"Wine?" Kendra asked, holding up a bottle. "Or something else?"

"I'd love some tea," Stella said.

Ben accepted a glass of wine as Stella followed Kendra to the cabinet to choose her tea. He pulled out a chair for her when she returned, then sank into the one next to her.

"I'm so glad you're home," Shea said, reaching over to grasp Stella's hand. "You gave us all quite a scare. What's the plan moving forward?"

"I have two chemo appointments left," Stella said. "They pushed them out another week so I can fully recover. After that, it should be smooth sailing."

"Do they need to do the chemo?" Patrick asked, looking concerned. "It just almost killed you."

"I asked the same," Ben said. "They feel it's best to finish what they had planned. But they won't start until she's stronger. And we'll really try to seclude ourselves for those two weeks. No offense to any of you, but phone calls would be better than in-person visits. Just until she's done."

The group all nodded, more subdued than they had been. Stella glanced around and shook her head. "This is my welcome home party," she said. "Not a sad time. We'll be fine for two weeks, I promise. And think of the celebration we can have when I finish."

Charlie and Calle appeared at the kitchen door a moment after Shea and Kendra excused themselves to get the babies ready for bed. "Grandma," Calle cried, running towards her. Charlie followed, giving her a hug after his cousin was pulled from Stella's lap by Dan.

"Hi," Charlie said. He had grown another few inches over the last year that he had been living with his dad and Shea and had been struggling to put muscle on his frame. He still had the appearance of a teenager, but Ben could see the man he would be one day. Charlie crouched down to hug Stella and stayed close to her as he let go. "Did you think about it?"

"I did," Stella replied.

Ben looked between them, the confusion he felt matched by the other adults in the room. "Think about what?"

"I asked what she would like us to call her now," Charlie said. "I've been wanting to change for a long time, since you guys raised me. But I didn't know how to bring it up."

Stella's eyes were bright with unshed tears. "I think either Mimi or Grandma would work," she said. "What do you prefer?"

"Well, I was leaning towards Queenie, after you suggested it," Charlie said, a smile on his face. "Because you're so regal. But Mimi feels a little more natural."

"Mimi instead of Grandma?" Calle asked from Dan's lap. "That's what I call my other one, too!"

"You can call me Grandma if you'd prefer, sweetheart. Whatever you would rather."

"It's easier if you're both Mimi," the little girl replied. "Unless you're in the same room, then it will get confusing. But I'll just point at the one I'm talking to."

"We'll figure it out," Dan said, kissing her on the head. "Go back and finish your movie. We'll eat soon."

She scampered off his lap and tugged at Charlie's hand. "Come on, you promised you would watch the whole thing."

"I'm not singing," Charlie responded as he let her pull him from the room.

"He's so good with her," Stella said.

"You did a good job with him," Jake responded.

"We all did," Ben stated. "It was a team effort."

"But mainly Stel—," Jake cut himself off and blushed. "I mean, mom."

"True," Ben agreed. "She did a good job with all of you. We all know she's the reason you turned out so good."

Kendra and Shea came back downstairs and started serving dinner, Emma jumping to help. Everyone insisted that Stella sit and relax, and although Ben could tell she wanted to help, she did as ordered. Zoe had made the entire meal before heading to the restaurant and had cooked enough for their family, plus most of the town.

The night was perfect. He had his wife home, his entire family under one roof, sharing laughs and enjoying each other. The last week had shown him how important it was to enjoy each moment and show his family how much he loved them. He couldn't predict the future any more than the next person, and knowing it could all be ripped away from him any second made him value it even more.

Chapter 31

Before she knew it, Stella was in the passenger seat, being driven back to the hospital by Ben. This time it was for her scheduled treatment, rather than an emergency, but he still was making it clear he wasn't happy about it. He had been voicing his concerns for days, saying that it was too soon for his liking. She had gently reminded him that she had improved each day and felt confident she was ready.

Finley was waiting for them at the door when they arrived and gave Stella a fast hug before leading them inside. "I'm so glad to see you," Finley said. "I was so worried. You're feeling better?"

"I am," she said. "Thank you for everything you did while I was in the hospital. And for checking on me every day once I got home."

"I would have come by if you needed me," Finley said. She led them down the hallway to the familiar spot where Stella would get her treatment. "But it sounds like you had plenty of help. JJ said he was by every day, and you were never alone. And that Zoe cooked enough to feed you for years."

"And then some," Stella said, laughing. "Our freezer is bursting at the seams."

"I swear, I gain weight now just sitting in my apartment," Finley said. "Zoe is at my door constantly asking me to try things or bringing me dinner. I keep trying to tell her I'm dieting, but she insists I don't need to."

"You don't," Stella cried. "You're perfect."

A throat clearing brought their attention to Dr. Lincoln, who stood in the doorway looking uncomfortable. Finley's face turned bright red when she saw him, and she busied herself fiddling with the equipment in the room rather than look at her colleague. "How are you feeling, Mrs. Burrows?" The doctor asked.

"I'm doing well, thank you," she said. "I appreciate you checking on me as well."

"Not a problem," he said. "Any questions for me before you get started?"

"Yes, did you ever find your way to the Windsor Palace to meet Finley's brother? Have him introduce you around to people?"

Dr. Lincoln looked surprised, then shook his head. "I'm afraid not. But I meant questions about your treatment."

"No, thank you." Stella silenced Ben with a look, knowing he was going to push back on restarting the treatment so soon after her hospitalization.

"Okay, I'll let you get to it," he said, ducking out of the room.

"You have to tell me what's going on," Stella said to Finley the second he disappeared.

"What's that?" The nurse held up a bag of fluid and examined it in the light, clearly avoiding Stella's question.

"Why do you two act like that around each other?"

"If you must know," Finley whispered, glancing out into the hallway before continuing. "We just don't like each other. Never have."

"There must be a reason," Stella insisted.

"I can't think of one," Finley responded. "He's just never been very friendly and is quite cold to me. As I said before, he's a phenomenal doctor and I respect his opinion, so I try to just stay out of his way."

"That's a shame," Stella murmured to herself.

"Not nearly as much as you think," Finley said. "I have plenty of friends, and he doesn't seem interested in a social life around here. We all think this is a quick stop for him on the way to a big-name city somewhere. He talks a lot about the research potentials at bigger hospitals."

"That would be a shame for this hospital to lose him," Stella said.

"I'm sure they'll find another one to replace him," Finley said. "It happens every few years."

"I know that look," Ben said. "Focus on your health, not the doctor's social life or future."

"I wasn't doing anything," Stella argued.

"Keep it that way," Ben insisted. "Let's play cards after Finley gets you hooked up."

***

Once they were home for the evening, enjoying a chicken casserole from the stockpile in the freezer, Stella brought up a topic that had been eating away at her. She had debated for days whether to let it go or confront it head on, and finally decided she needed to clear the air.

"Ben, I wanted to talk to you about something."

"That never sounds good," he replied. "Should I be concerned?"

"No," she said. "I just feel like there's an elephant in the room, and I want to address it."

He frowned, looking at her. "I don't know what you mean."

"Before I got sick," she said. "Or before I had pneumonia, because obviously the cancer is also sick."

"Yes," he said, looking as though he knew what she would say.

"We had some tension between us about Isobel."

"You had kept some secrets from me," he said. He didn't sound angry or defensive, which she appreciated.

"I did," she said. "I was torn between two of my best friends. And then I was weighed down by grief, and by love of you and the boys. It was a lot to handle. I was barely twenty-six and suddenly had three boys under five to help raise. And the man that I'd loved since I was their age who needed me."

"What would have happened if Izzie hadn't died?"

"I probably would have married someone else," she admitted. "Someone who didn't want children, so I didn't have to think every day about what I couldn't give him. Someone I could love just enough to take my mind off you."

"Did you take a back seat to Izzie because of your hysterectomy?" He looked confused as he asked.

"In some ways," she said. "Every time I thought about telling you how I felt, I thought about what I would be denying you. If I had told you, we wouldn't have this amazing family. And I would have ruined Isobel's happiness."

"You sacrificed your own for hers," he said slowly. "And for mine. Because you knew what it meant to me to have children."

"You were born to be a dad," she said. "I knew that. You were so close with your own dad, and I just knew you would be good."

"Lucky you were right," he said. "Do you think that we would have ended up together, even if you hadn't made that promise to Izzie?"

She reached for his hand. "Of course I do. I have always loved you. I struggled for a long time with guilt, thinking that I didn't deserve you, or the boys. That somehow the universe took Izzie away and gave me her life to make up for the fact that I lost so much in the accident."

"But that's crazy."

"Not to me it wasn't," she said. "That's how it felt for a long time. How could I be so happy in this life, knowing it was supposed to be her that was living it?"

"We couldn't control that," he said. "Or change it."

"I know, but it was what kept running through my head. And then you really threw me for a loop when Patrick started school," she said.

"What do you mean?"

"You started asking me if we should have a baby," she reminded him. "Maybe get a girl into the mix. Come out with our relationship and have another one that was ours. I nearly cried myself out of tears over that."

"What? You never let on," he said.

"How could I? You didn't know that I couldn't have your baby, no matter how much I wanted to," she said. "And I knew if I told you, it would crush you. I made excuse after excuse, and insisted on keeping things a secret between us. My one omission made me live a life I didn't love, but I didn't know how to get out of it."

"You could have just told me the truth."

"Hindsight," she said. "I know that now. But at the time, I stood to lose everything. Not just you, but the boys as well."

"And you're sure that's not the driving force behind our relationship?" He looked so unsure of himself suddenly, making her feel terrible.

"I'm positive," she said. "They're grown up now. I would have had a relationship with them regardless of what happened between us. Even back then, if things had fallen apart, I know now that you never would have taken them away from me. Or me from them. But panic does funny things to us."

"I get that," he said. "You've put me through it enough over the last few months."

"Benji!"

"Not of your doing," he said. "You know what I mean. In those moments of worrying that I could lose you, I would have done anything. So, I do understand what you're saying. And for the record, I love you. I have loved you for a long time, and it's only because of who you are. Not because of circumstances, or convenience. But because you are the most amazing woman I know."

"I feel the same way about you. Where do we go from here?" she asked, almost afraid of the answer.

"Forward," he said. "Together. Stronger. We get through this last bit of your health crisis, and then we settle back into enjoying our kids and their families. Being grandparents. And loving each other throughout it all."

"Ugly parts included," she said. "I'm sorry I didn't want you to see me after the surgery, or that I worried so much about you seeing me without hair. I realize now that none of that matters."

"No, it doesn't. I love you in any form, any shape. It's who's inside that I love," he said.

"I feel the same way about you, so I don't know why I let my insecurities run wild like that."

"No more," he replied. "We'll share everything, no matter what. Open honesty from this point forward. If you have anything else to confess, let's hear it now."

"I love you, Ben Burrows. I have all these years, and I will forever."

"I'm glad to hear it, because I happen to love you right back." He stood and offered her a hand. "Are you ready for bed?"

"It's not even eight. We never go to sleep this early," she said, glancing at the clock. "And I have to clean the kitchen."

"I'll clean it in the morning," he said. "And I never said we were going to sleep."

***

The day of her final treatment, Dr. Lincoln gave her permission to bring more than one family member to accompany her. Ben had been steadfast in his determination to see her through all of her chemotherapy, and yet the rest of the family had asked regularly if they could go. On this final day, she would be accompanied by Ben, all three boys and their significant others. Everyone had taken the day off work, and friends had been asked to watch the two youngest children while the other two were in school.

Patrick had wanted to arrange an enormous SUV limousine to bring them all, until Stella had pointed out the attention that would bring him. Instead, all eight of them managed to fit into Kendra's large SUV. The sight of all three men crammed into the third row made everyone laugh, and as expected, they were acting like they did as kids by the time they pulled into the hospital.

"We're going to wait out here," Kendra told Stella when they arrived, indicating the waiting room. "Finley said she would come and get us when you're done."

"We'll walk in with you to drop this stuff off and then come back out," Dan said. All three men were carrying trays of food, prepared by the Palace as a treat to the hospital staff. "Patrick will probably need all of the time to meet everyone back there."

Finley's smiling face appeared in the doorway as they approached. "Hi," she said. "Gangs all here, I see!"

"We brought you all some food," Jake said, holding up his tray. "To thank you all for taking such good care of our mom."

"Oh, that's so nice," Finley said with a smile. "Come in, let me show you where you can put it. Patrick, I hope you're prepared."

"I am," he replied, grinning at her. "I haven't been swarmed in days. I'm missing out."

"I promise they'll all be on their best behavior," Finley said. "But we seem to have way more staff here than usual."

Stella settled into her usual spot and watched as the nurses enthused over the food. Dr. Lincoln stopped and made sure she was ready for the final treatment. Finley insisted on taking a picture with him, Stella, and her boys, managing to get the doctor to smile with some gentle prodding. Before she knew it, Stella was hooked up to her final dose, watching as Patrick charmed the nursing staff. Jake and Dan had retreated to the waiting room, promising to return if Stella needed them.

"I can't believe this is our last day," Ben said. He was at her side, a deck of cards in his hand, glancing around the room. "I feel like this nightmare just started, and it's over."

"That's what happens," she said. "Remember how many times the boys would have bad dreams, and we would tell them to focus on something good? The thought of whatever monster had been chasing them was gone in a flash. We had enough good to focus on all this time once we got our heads on straight."

As they played their card game, nurses and doctors stopped to congratulate her on completing her regiment. Other patients who she had seen over the weeks called over to her, making her realize how lucky she was.

"I look around here," she whispered to Ben. "And see people who are so much sicker than me. I think this was a blessing in disguise."

"Why would you say that?"

"Look at us," she said. "We're better than ever. I feel closer to the boys and their significant others. I value each day, because I've realized we can never predict when our time will come. And we learned what really matters in life."

After Finley unhooked her for the last time, her family surrounded her as she rang the bell, signaling the end of her treatment. Everyone cheered, and Stella let the tears of happiness fall. She was on her way to good health, she had a family that loved her, and that was all she needed.

Chapter 32

"We want to have a party for mom," Patrick stated. Ben was sitting at the Palace bar with his three sons, after a day of playing golf. Stella had completed her final treatment two weeks prior and was feeling strong and healthy. He no longer felt the need to hover over her, and she had virtually kicked him out for the day so she could get things done at the house.

"To celebrate being done with her treatment," Dan added.

"I'll have to ask her if she would want that," Ben replied. "It's still soon, and her hair hasn't grown back. Not to mention, she needs to be careful about germs for a little while longer."

"I know what kind of party she'd like," Jake said.

"What?" Dan asked, smirking as if he already knew the answer.

"A wedding," Jake said, pointing at Patrick. "Her baby getting married. Or even an engagement party."

"Don't push him," Ben said.

"Come on," Dan responded. "What are you waiting for?"

"Unlike you, I don't need to jump into marriage three months after dating someone," Patrick said. "We're young enough to take our time."

"Three months, plus all the years when we were teenagers," Dan said under his breath.

"Whatever," Patrick said. "I have some stuff coming up that I need to be focused on, and then we'll see."

"How romantic," Jake said, elbowing Dan. "I bet Emma loves that."

"That's enough," Ben said. "No one pushed you two. He'll do it on his own time. And if you want to celebrate Stella, your mother, then it should be about her, not Patrick."

"Good point," Patrick said.

"Most things end up being about Patrick anyway," Dan pointed out. "Her last day of treatment he was the center of attention."

"I can't help it that people love me," Patrick responded. "And you brought all the food, and I'd say Rex got as much attention."

"Let's focus," Dan said. "We should be celebrating her, and all that she's overcome the last few months."

"Let's try to keep it small," Ben suggested. "That will keep it from being overwhelming."

"This whole town will want to come out and celebrate her," Dan said. "There's no way to keep it small. Besides, by the time we pull this off, she'll be okay to be around a crowd."

"I had an idea of what we could all do for her," Dan continued. "Let's see what you think."

Ben was touched by the boy's desire to celebrate Stella and was so proud of the men he had raised. Seeing them all come into their own, with relationships and now their own families, had been exciting enough. But now, seeing how considerate they were of Stella, and the lengths they wanted to go to show their love, brought him even more pride.

***

"How are you?" Kendra hugged Ben when he arrived at the restaurant to meet her. Over the last month since Stella had completed her treatment, Ben and Kendra had been dragged into planning the latest town event. The town had added festivals to almost every month of the year after seeing how popular the Harvest Festival had become. Oktoberfest would be held over the long weekend in October, and the Harvest Festival could still kick off the ski season in November. Today's meeting at Town Hall to plan the upcoming Oktoberfest had given Ben the perfect excuse to get out of the house.

"I'm exhausted," Ben admitted. "I didn't realize how hard it would be to keep a secret from Stella. I feel like I'm constantly tripping over my own words. Or starting a question and then trailing off, like I forgot. She's probably ready to drag me off to a neurologist."

"Imagine that she was able to keep a secret for weeks," Kendra said in a teasing tone

"And one much heavier," he agreed. "I don't know how she kept her diagnosis to herself for all that time."

"Luckily, she's on the other side of it now. And that gives us a reason to celebrate."

"I heard the Inn is booked solid for the weekend, with everyone coming for the party," Ben said. "She'll probably catch sight of someone and suspect."

"No," Kendra said. "Everyone is on board with staying clear until Saturday. It helps that you can keep her busy at home until the party."

"As long as I don't put my foot in it," Ben said.

"It will be fine," Kendra said. "We've got everything organized at the restaurant, and everyone knows what their responsibilities are. Shea and I will bring the babies early. Finley and Desmond said it was no problem to set up the portable cribs in their apartment and let the kids hang out there. I heard Charlie is bringing a girl to help him babysit."

"Really? This is the first I'm hearing of it."

"Don't make a big fuss. Jake gave us strict instructions to play it cool," Kendra said.

"Now this is another thing I have to keep to myself," Ben groaned.

"No, she knows we're going to this meeting together," Kendra said. She passed through the door to the new Town Hall building in front of him and then turned back to continue. "You can just say that I heard he might have a girlfriend."

"I might take a vow of silence for the next few days," Ben said. "That would be easier than all these secrets."

Kendra laughed and placed a hand on his arm. "It will be over before you know it. And this will be a beautiful event."

***

Saturday morning, he was up too early, and was such a nervous mess that he spilled his first cup of coffee all over the newspaper. As he cleaned it up, Stella laughed and made him a new one. "You're certainly out of sorts lately," she said.

"You could say that," he mumbled.

"Anything wrong?"

"No," he said. "Just didn't sleep well."

"We can cancel dinner with the kids if you want," Stella suggested. "Do it a different time."

"No," he said quickly. "That would upset them. I'll be fine."

"Why don't you run into town and get a new paper, and maybe you can do my shopping for me while you're there?"

"Sure, he said, happy to have a task that would take him out of the house. He could take his time shopping, and only have a few hours left to kill by the time he got back. If he was lucky.

Even with his slow pace and willingness to talk to everyone he passed, he was still home two hours later. Fortunately, Stella was on the phone, so he slipped back out again to hide in Dan's home office under the guise of helping with the Oktoberfest plans.

Dan and Kendra left late afternoon to bring the kids to the restaurant and get everything set up, which put him back on edge. When he walked back to the cottage, he found Stella freshly showered and dressing for the night out. What she thought was a simple family dinner at the Palace was her surprise party, and he was happy to see that she was wearing a new dress for the occasion.

"Is this too much?" she asked him, twirling in front of a mirror. "Patrick had all these new clothes sent to me as a gift to celebrate my clean bill of health. Kendra was by earlier and said she loved this one, and suggested I wear it tonight. I thought it would be nice to wear, but it's just dinner. I don't want to overdo it."

"I'll wear something nice too," he said. "Maybe we can walk over to the Inn after dinner and have a drink. Make a night out of it."

"That sounds perfect," she said, beaming at him. "You go ahead and shower, I don't want to be late."

He drove them into town and parked near the front door of the Palace, in a spot that had conveniently been left available. As he climbed out and went around to open the door for his wife, he realized his hands were sweating. He had never surprised her like this before, and he hoped she enjoyed it. And that she would see it as a testament to how much her family loved her.

Stella stopped just outside the door to the Palace and placed a hand on his chest. "Thank you for this," she said. She stepped on her toes and kissed him softly. "For all of it."

"What do you mean?" He stared at her in shock and laughed when she winked at him.

Still laughing, he pulled the door open and gestured for her to go in first. Their family was right by the door, all wearing T-shirts with pictures of Stella from over the years. The three boys had all chosen their favorite picture of themselves with her, ranging from infancy to Dan in a tuxedo ready for prom.

Not to be outdone, Kendra had her prom picture with Stella from the same night.

As everyone yelled "surprise", Stella stopped and put her hands over her mouth, as if the shock were overwhelming. Ben watched as their boys stepped forward and engulfed her in hugs, each taking the time to say something private to her. Once they finished, then she took a moment with each of the girls, and then Charlie and Calle, before she was passed around to everyone else in the crowd.

"I can't believe we pulled it off," Patrick said, grinning ear to ear. "And the shirts are a huge hit. Everyone had so much fun picking one out to wear."

Across the restaurant, Ben could see pictures of Stella from over the years. It was a flash through his memory, seeing her face from childhood to a recent picture from the holidays. The room was full of people all waiting their turn for her, and she tugged him along with her, greeting former and current neighbors. He would swear anyone who had ever lived in Windsor Peak was in the room.

In addition to the pictures of Stella that everyone wore, the restaurant was filled with family pictures and memories. Clips from the local newspaper featuring one of the boys, or a picture of Stella and Ben volunteering at a local event. There were photos of Stella on a red carpet with Patrick or one of his co-stars, most of whom were in the room to celebrate her.

A tap on the microphone brought the crowd's attention to the stage, where Jake, Dan and Patrick were standing. Jake and Patrick each had a guitar around their shoulders, and all three had microphones. "Thank you all for coming," Dan said. "We are so happy to be able to celebrate our mom beating cancer and everything it tried to throw at her. As you can all see from the massive turnout we had tonight, she is an amazing person and loved by everyone who knows her. We wanted to kick the night off by dedicating a song to her and my dad and asking them to share a first dance with us."

"Dan will be joining us in the singing," Patrick said, grabbing his brother by the back of his shirt when Dan tried to make a run for it. "Just try to ignore his part, please."

Jake and Patrick started playing the guitars, and singing in their beautiful voices, as Ben led Stella to the dance floor. Dan had taken a step back from the microphone and appeared to be more of a backup singer, but he was willing to take this step out of his comfort zone for Stella. As the lyrics to the song began, he realized it had to be one written specifically for Stella and for their family. This explained all the time Jake and Patrick had spent together over the last few weeks, locked behind closed doors.

"How did you know?" he whispered in her ear as they danced.

"You're not nearly as good a secret keeper as you think," she said with a light laugh. "But it was obvious that you all wanted to surprise me, so I couldn't spoil that. This is a wonderful gift you've given me."

"The boys did almost everything, with the help of their better halves, of course."

"No, I don't mean tonight." When he pulled back and looked at her with a question in his face, she pulled him tighter and spoke into his ear again. "This life. The boys. Our family. All of it. Thank you."

He could barely see through the tears that threatened, but he nodded. "I feel the same. I never would have had the relationship that I have with the three of them if it wasn't for your gentle guidance. Most of the decisions I've made were the right ones, because you've helped me work them out. I owe you everything. You brought happiness back into my life after I thought I lost everything. You taught me what strength is. I'm so incredibly lucky to have you at my side."

"And I'm so lucky to have you," she replied.

"I have a gift for you at home, it was too fragile to bring here," he told her. "But I want to tell you about it. I read about Kintsugi years ago and thought of it when you were sick. It's the Japanese technique of repairing broken vases with gold, so that the cracks make the vase more valuable. I thought it was the perfect representation of our love and life together. What was broken was put back together and made even more beautiful."

"That's the loveliest gift I've ever received," she exclaimed. "And that's exactly what I've been trying to put into words for months now."

"Great minds think alike," he said, grinning at her.

They kissed as the song came to an end, and the three boys jumped off the stage to hug her again. A DJ took their place, putting on dance music, and soon the floor was filled with their family and friends. Stella was smiling, his kids were happy and full of love, and all was right in his world.

Chapter 33

"Can we steal you for a minute?" Shea asked, indicating herself, Kendra, and Emma. Stella nodded and let them lead her to a quiet corner, where a large, wrapped gift was against a wall next to a table.

They all sat, and Kendra pulled the gift closer. After exchanging looks with the other three, she addressed Stella. "We had something made for you, to thank you for all you have done for us. You've been there for me for so many years. I can't remember a time when I couldn't come to you for advice."

"And although we haven't known you for as long," Shea added. "You've become instrumental in my life. I always know I can count on you, and you set such a great example for me for how to parent."

"You welcomed me in when I was lost and alone," Emma said, smiling at her. "I was so afraid to meet you all, and you just took me in your arms and never questioned me."

"On top of all that, you raised the three men that we love," Kendra said.

"And Charlie," Shea added. "My bonus that I got when I married Jake, and I'm so grateful for him every day. You did an amazing job with all four of them."

Kendra pushed the gift closer to Stella and indicated that she should unwrap it. When she did, she gasped in delight. A tree was carved into the wood, with three large branches trickling into smaller ones. At the base of the tree, Ben and Stella's names were carved into a large wooden heart. Isobel's name was carved into the tree just above their names, with angel wings on each side. On each large branch, more heart ornaments bore the names of each of her boys, and their partner, and then their children on the further branches. Even Jenna was represented as Jake's first wife and Charlie's mother. It was exquisitely made, and the most touching gift she had ever received.

"It's so beautiful," she said. "I can't thank you enough."

"The artist is local, so we can add more ornaments over the years," Kendra shared.

"Some sooner than others," Shea said with a wink.

As the other two women gasped and looked at Shea, she nodded. "It's early, but Stella already knew."

They both hugged her, and Kendra glanced across the room. "I better get Dan moving," she said with a laugh. "We were talking about waiting a year, but this might move up our timeline."

"I'm so happy for you," Stella said. "For all of you, and the families you're growing. We love you all so much."

"And we love you back," Emma said. "There is no family quite like this one, and we credit you with that. We all know you're the most important woman in their lives, and we're okay with being a close second."

"I'd say it's more of a tie," Stella said, wiping an eye. "Or you guys might have the edge now. But I'm thrilled to share that spot with all of you. I couldn't have picked better partners for my boys if I had searched the whole world over."

They all hugged her, and Kendra carefully placed the piece of art on a table against the wall to be admired by guests. When they went to rejoin the party, Dan was waiting for them.

"May I have this dance?" he asked Stella, offering his hand.

"I'd be delighted," she said, smiling at him. She recognized the song as the one he had chosen for them to dance to at his wedding and felt even more emotional. They were making this such a special night for her. "Thank you for all of this."

"You deserve it more than anyone I know," he said. "I wouldn't be where I am today without you. I know that for a fact."

"You can't say that," she insisted. "None of us could know our fate if circumstances had changed."

"I know if you hadn't called me out for being a fool with Kendra, I would have probably gone back to New York and left this life behind," he said. "You all came together to make me realize what I had lost and helped me to get it back."

She smiled at him. "And now you have a beautiful family. You'll see one day that your dad and I were just doing what we could to keep everyone alive and happy most days. We got lucky and all three of you came out as good people, which made it easier to guide you the right way."

Dan glanced at something over her head and then down at her. "We have one more surprise for you, and my brothers are getting impatient with me."

"You all have done so much already," Stella said. "I don't need anything else."

"Just this one last thing," he promised, leading her across the busy room to where Jake and Patrick were waiting.

Patrick was holding a small ring-shaped box, while Jake held a longer wrapped one. Dan took an envelope from Jake as they approached and then turned back to her. "We've done a lot of thinking over the last few months," he said. "Especially when you got sick. We realized that we took you for granted for a very long time."

"No, you didn't," she objected.

"We did." All three responded at the same time, making her laugh.

"We never thought to call you mom, or to honor you. Every Mother's Day, we let pass without acknowledging the woman who had raised us. Yes, Isobel gave birth to us, and we will always love her and be grateful for her," Dan said. "But we were blessed with two moms. And we should have realized that a long time ago."

Stella wiped away a tear. "It's not your fault," she said. "Your father and I were so sure that keeping our relationship a secret was the better thing to do. If we had been honest with you all, it would have been easier for everyone."

"We can't change the past," Jake said. "But we wanted to do what we could to honor your role in our lives."

Dan handed her the envelope he held, and she slid out a sheet of papers. It looked like a legal document, and the lights were too dim to read. "What is this?"

"Adoption papers," Dan told her. "I wrote them, and we'd like to all sign them together, with you. This won't be legally binding, but if you tried to leave us, we would use it to chase you down. We're a little old to be adopted, but we thought of a way around that. And we also don't want to forget our first mom, because we do love her and know she watches over all of us. We would like to adopt you as our second mom, if you're willing. And grandmother to our existing and future children. This won't be filed in any court because it's a little unorthodox, but we'll hold you to it."

"I would never leave you. You can count on that. This is so thoughtful," Stella said. "Does your father know about this?"

"He does," Ben said from behind her. "I believe there is a place for me to sign as well."

"Well, who has a pen?" Stella demanded, smiling through the tears of joy.

They all signed and then posed for a picture with the photographer that Patrick had hired for the event. Once they were done, Dan tucked the papers back into the envelope and then into his pocket. "I'll make you a copy and get the originals framed," he promised.

"My turn," Jake said, stepping forward. "As Dan mentioned, we blew it on Mother's Day through the years. We made you this to start to make up for it."

She opened the box that Jake offered her and found a coffee table sized book. The cover was a picture of her with the three boys when they were still babies, and as she flipped through the pages, she saw their lives. All the love shared, the memories made, caught on film. Her, as their mother, in the center of their lives and documented over the years without any of them realizing it. And at the very end, a picture of Stella and Isobel, arms wrapped around each other, grinning at a camera. Stella could remember the day, and knew Ben had been the one taking the picture, and she could only think it was her friend's way of giving them all her blessing. She hadn't seen this picture in years, and seeing their faces together, she knew deep in her heart that Izzie would be happy with how their boys had been raised.

"This is so beautiful," she whispered when she reached the last page. "How did you find all these pictures?"

"We scoured the attic, garage, computers, and begged everyone in town to do the same. Thankfully, most of them were digital, so it was easier than we thought it would be," Jake said. "I loved seeing the pictures of you with Charlie while I was gone. It made me feel like I was making up part of that time, seeing him grow up. And how happy he was, and that was because of you."

"He was an angel," Stella said. "Still is. Far easier than you three to raise."

"In our defense, there is only one of him," Dan said. "We had each other to cause trouble with. The good news is, as these pictures show, we looked good doing it."

"I will treasure this always," Stella said, clutching the book to her chest.

"We made copies for ourselves as well," Jake said. "And it's stored safely with the company that made it, in case anyone ever needs a new copy."

"One final gift," Patrick said, offering her the small box.

She unwrapped it slowly, seeing Kendra, Emma and Shea join them as she did. When she opened the box, a light came on, making the circle of shining stones nearly blind her. A perfect circle pendant was on a necklace, made up of diamonds and other various gemstones. It was breathtaking and looked far fancier than anything else she had ever owned.

"I don't know what to say," she said finally.

"I'll explain," Patrick said. He pointed at the top two stones. "These two are you and dad, the diamond and sapphire. Then it's our birthstones, and these three lovely ladies. Finally, the kids. And we put diamonds in as placeholders for any future kids, so everyone is a little spaced out now. If we ever run out of space, the jeweler assured me he could make more room. But I somehow doubt that we'll have more than eight more kids between the three of us."

"That sounds like a challenge," Jake said, dropping a kiss on the top of Shea's head.

"Challenge accepted," Dan said, grinning at Kendra.

"This is too much," Stella said finally. "You boys can't spend this much on me."

"Trust me when I say this: Patrick can afford it," Dan said with a laugh. "And we let him. It's the least he owes us for putting up with him."

"Hey," Patrick called out, poking Dan before looking at Stella. "No one ever lets me buy them nice things or help out. Please let me do this for you. For our family."

"For the family?" Kendra asked, peering over at Patrick. "You mean from our family."

"No," he said, pulling three more boxes from behind him. "For our family. I had them make the same necklace for you three. And I have two more at home, for Calle and little Izzie. Plus, he can make more as we need them."

"Patrick," Shea said, throwing her arms around him. "This is so nice of you. I love that you included us."

Emma and Kendra joined the group hug, leaving Jake and Dan staring at each other. "We just need to go with it," Jake said in a stage whisper to his older brother. "Pretend it was all our idea."

The whole group laughed, and Stella watched as her boys fixed the necklaces around their partner's necks. Ben helped with hers, and soon the four of them were sparkling in the light. "I don't want to think about the cost of these jewels," Stella whispered to Ben. "I'll be afraid that I'll lose it."

"If you do, Patrick will get you a new one," Ben said. "That boy is good and generous, right down to his toes. He wouldn't want you to worry one second about the cost. And we can have it insured, if that makes you feel better."

"Already done," Patrick called over. "My manager took care of that for us. If anyone loses it, they'll replace it no problem."

"But try not to," Jake said to Shea. "I know how forgetful you get when you're—"

"What?" Dan asked, staring at him.

"Pregnant," Shea said with a laugh. "We told almost everyone by now, might as well share. We're having another baby."

"Did you know?" Dan asked Kendra, who nodded. He shook his head at her. "We need to catch up, I can't let Jake win."

"It's not a competition," Kendra said with a laugh. "But we'll see what we can do."

"And we will eventually," Patrick said, kissing Emma on the cheek. "Once I finish the latest movie, and we have some time to breathe."

"Promises, promises," Emma teased him before kissing him. "Luckily, you're worth waiting for."

As more food came out of the kitchen, the family got separated once more. Everyone wanted to wish Stella well or talk to one of the boys. Zoe stopped on her way back to the kitchen to give her a fierce hug, JJ right behind her to do the same. Shea's sister Holly was there with her boyfriend Liam, who grabbed her as she was heading to the bathroom. Natalie and Mike quickly joined them to share their friends' wishes, and she enjoyed talking to the group for a moment.

When she came out of the bathroom, her sister and brother-in-law were waiting for her along with Ben. "Are you having fun?" Heather asked.

"To put it lightly," Stella said. "This is the most amazing night. Everyone that's here, the gifts I've been given. All this love being showered on me, it's overwhelming."

"You deserve it all," Heather said.

"Natalie and Mike just gave us a ten-day, all expenses paid trip to Ireland," Stella said. "Holly and Liam, not to be outdone, gave us a two-week trip to Hawaii. And that's on top of all the other amazing things my family has given me tonight."

"That's amazing," Andy said. "You deserve it."

"Fortunately for you two, they both planned the trips for another couple to accompany us," Stella said, grinning at them. "I hope you're ready to travel."

"We'll go anywhere," Heather said. "Now that you're healthy and there are no more secrets, we are ready to celebrate all year."

"Do you mind if I steal my wife for one more dance?" Ben asked the other couple. When they shook their heads, he led her to the dance floor and took her in his arms. Heather and Andy settled in next to them on the dance floor, and he saw his sons do the same with their partners.

"Look at all this love around us," Stella said to him. "I am the luckiest woman in the world."

"We're the lucky ones," Ben said. "When I think of all the times that I almost screwed this up, and you were patient enough to put up with me until I got it right, I can't believe it. I don't know what I did to deserve you, and this life, but I'll be grateful for the rest of my days."

"Right back at you," she said, smiling up at him. "We have a wonderful life here, Benji. I'm so glad to be sharing it with you."

"And I'm glad you're healthy and sticking around," he said. "I love you to pieces, Stella Burrows."

"I love you right back," she said. "All of this is a lot to take in, but I'm so happy. I love you all so much."

"You make us who we are. You are the heart of our family. Never forget that. Our lives, our happiness, our home, our bond, it's all because of you."

They kissed softly and swayed to the music, content in their love for each other and their family who surrounded them. Laughter and joy filled the air as Stella took in Ben's words. They warmed her from the inside out, soothed over any rough edges from the last few months. Everything she ever wanted, everyone she ever loved, was here with her now. It was a wonderful life to live, and she was looking forward to enjoying it for many more years with the man who held her in his arms and in his heart.

Acknowledgements

My sister-in-law Danielle planted the idea for this book months ago. I had never considered writing a book on Ben and Stella, because we already had their happy ever after. But Danielle was adamant that readers would want it, so I listened! And I'm so glad that I did, because this story really came from my heart. From exploring how the loss of Isobel impacted everyone, to Stella's health battle, it was an emotional roller coaster, and I hope you all enjoyed it.

My mom is a breast cancer survivor, nearly twenty years now. When Stella sees herself bald for the first time and sees her dad in the mirror, that was a little tribute to my mom. She was so strong during her surgeries and treatments, and I see that same strength in so many women I know who have been through the same battle. It's hitting women younger and younger now, and my friends Tracey and Jackie had to fight it at an age where we wouldn't have thought it possible. They have both been vocal in telling other women to get their mammograms, so do it! You are not too young, and it could save your life.

None of this would be possible without all of you. I still can't believe that people around the world are reading words that I wrote, but I see every day that it's true. Your messages, reviews, comments, emails, and attendance when I do events is beyond valuable to me. You keep me motivated to write, and to believe in what I'm doing. I spend most of the day behind a laptop alone, thinking that I'm crazy to be doing this. You have all made me feel less crazy!

My family is as excited for each new thing that happens in my writing career as I am. My parents not only read all the books and show up at all the events, but they tell everyone they meet about them. I'll admit, I love to see them bragging about me! Jeff and Danielle are also always there and are equally enthusiastic about sharing the books and in supporting me.

I have the world's best nieces and nephews to cheer me on as well. Timmy, Tessa and Emmy light up my life, and their desire to write their own books now still blows me away. To think that something I was afraid of doing for so long now seems possible to them is the best reward! Brendan and Taylor, your love for each other and kindness towards each other is right from the pages of a book. Keep that up! Conor, I'm so proud of you for your hard work at college. I know you'll do great things when you graduate.

Thank you as well to my extended family. My aunt Marilyn is an avid reader, and we have shared so many books over the years. When I got the stamp of approval from her and my cousin Kathy (who told me she was prepared to lie, and was relieved when she didn't have to!), it meant the world to me. On the other side of the family, my cousin Chris's wife Christine has shared the books with her extended family, and it's been so exciting to see them all at signings! It's like getting a new branch to my own family tree, and I love it. I have a lot of aunts, uncles and cousins on both sides, so I won't thank them all individually, but I appreciate all you do to support me! And whoever reads this and yells at me for not saying their name, I'll add you to the next one.

My hockey moms! I'm so grateful to have you in my corner. The friends I have made through my boys hockey teams will remain in my life forever, and I'm so happy about that. There are too many of you to list out here, but you know who you are!

Thank you to all of my friends who cheer me on every day. These books have helped me reconnect with friends from a long time ago and make new friends. Your support and love means so much to me, and I hope that I return it back to you!

And finally, to my family. My husband Tom, and our two boys, Camden and Calum. My boys are growing up way too fast, and I need to find a way to freeze time. I am so proud of both of you for all you have accomplished. Cam is the busiest teenager I know, playing three varsity sports, participating in school activities, and still being a good friend. Calum is the kindest person I know. He goes out of his way to share a smile with someone and looks out for the little guy every time (especially on the ice). He's going into middle school next year, and I am not emotionally prepared for that at all! My husband is the hardest working person I've ever met and would do anything for us as his family. He might not show his emotions easily, but he shows up for us in so many ways and is our biggest fan. I love you all!

Stay in Touch

Be sure to follow me on social media @deniselathamwrites and visit my website to sign up for my newsletter. Then you'll be in the know before the books hit the shelves! www.deniselatham.com

Please continue sharing the books with your friends and family and leave reviews where you purchased the book. I can't tell you how much it helps, and how much I appreciate it!

Windsor Peak Series